Artania: The Pharaohs' Cry

Nana & Papa,

To two of the kindest in-laws a girl could ever ask for. Thank you for all of those supportive years. I am blessed to have been part of your family. Hugs!

Lauri

Artania

The Pharaohs' Cry

Laurie Woodward

Published 2017 by Creativia (www.creativia.org)
ISBN: 978-1974414758
Cover art by Dave Zaboski

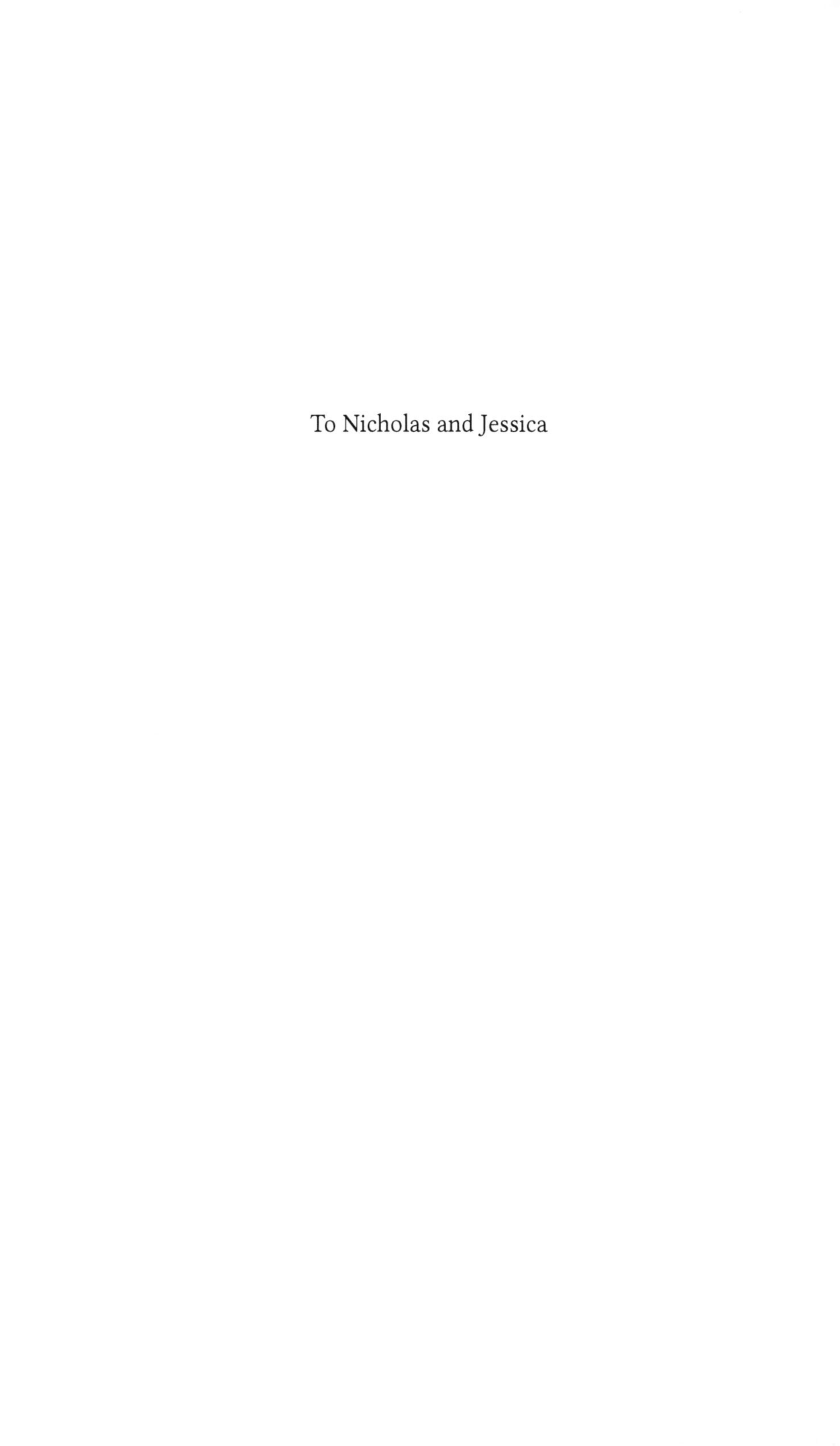

To Nicholas and Jessica

Chapter 1

The air was more antiseptic than usual that spring morning. Coughing on bleach fumes, Bartholomew Borax III rolled out of bed and put on his monogrammed robe. That's when he noticed the strange noise.

He cocked his head. It sounded nothing like the usual sloshing mops or whirring vacuum cleaners. When Bartholomew opened his bedroom door and poked his head into the long hallway, a muffled wail met his ears.

"Hic-hic-hic-hoo. Hic-hic-hic-hoo."

Pulling last night's precious sketch from under his pillow, Bartholomew gazed at it for a moment. There three generations painted side-by-side. Although impossible, it was a dream he'd had many times. *It would have been amazing, Grandfather, Father, and me, all bound in color.*

Last night, he'd finally escaped prying eyes long enough for his hands to race over the page. While his pencil scratched furiously, the impossible took shape, and for a while, he lived in the dream.

Sighing, Bartholomew tucked the sketch in his pocket and patted it flat. With the forbidden art safe from snoops, he tiptoed down the winding staircase to the front parlor.

There at the arched doorway, he froze, unable to believe his eyes. It was normal to see Mother sitting stiffly in the wing-backed chair, platinum blonde hair in a tight bun with the veins pulsing in her forehead. But fat tears rolling down Hygenette Borax's pale cheeks?

No way. He'd seen her disgusted more times than he could count, yet crying? Never. Much too messy.

After eight rhythmic hiccups, she daintily dabbed each eye with a lace handkerchief, gave one long sniff, and rang the little bell on the marble table next to her.

Bartholomew felt a rush wind as Yvette blew past, curtsying three times. Like a white flag, Mother waved her hanky so the maid could drop it in a basket and signal to the butler who always stood at attention in the hall. He strode in with a silver tray containing one neatly folded handkerchief and bowing at the waist, held it out for Mrs. Borax.

"Mother, what is it?" Bartholomew's voice was barely a whisper.

Mother snatched the hanky in her quivering hands. "It's your... grandfather. He has... he has... he has... passed on!" she sobbed, hiccupping again.

"Grandfather Alabaster?" Bartholomew gasped.

"No, silly boy. Grandfather Borax. He... had a... stroke. And we... have... to," hiccup, hiccup, "go soon."

Bartholomew's private tutor, Mr. White, entered and stared sadly at his student, broccoli green eyes popping more like a fish than ever.

"Is it true?" Bartholomew asked. But he didn't need an answer. Mother's pale face told him everything.

"I'm afraid so," Mr. White said.

"Not Grandfather! He was so... so wonderful." He paused remembering.

Bartholomew's grandfather, Bartholomew the First, had been merrier than a hundred Christmases. Every summer, he would visit and tell stories that made the boy laugh until his stomach hurt. Bartholomew loved hearing over and again how he had turned one small factory into one of the largest bleach companies in the world.

"I used my wits and a trick or two," he would say, slapping his knee. "The competition never saw it comin'!"

Next, he'd pat whoever was closest on the back, which was usually Mother. With a wan smile, she'd endure the back slaps then quietly excuse herself. Bartholomew knew she was off to bathe and change; hands on her clean dress would never do. Bartholomew smiled at the memory.

"Tell him the worst of it," Mother said.

"Well, you see..." Mr. White cleared his throat again. "...your grandfather put a strange provision in his will. In order for your mother to... hmm...hmm... inherit the business, you must... hmm... move to his house in California and live there until you are twenty-one."

"If only your father were here, he'd know what to do!"

Bartholomew shrugged uncomfortably, not wanting to imagine how life might have been different if Father were here. If he had survived the accident. That terrible day just weeks before Bartholomew was born when Father had hit his head and drowned in a mud puddle. He'd been jogging on a wooded path, and reports said that he must have tripped right in front of the boulder that knocked him unconscious as he fell face down in the puddle.

Bartholomew heard in whispers how that accident had forever changed something in Mother, turning her from a smiling bride into the germaphobe who kept hand sanitizer on every table and made Bartholomew bathe six times a day.

"And that house is disgusting. So fil-thy!" Mrs. Borax wailed, burying her face in her hanky.

Mr. White walked stiffly forward to pat his hiccupping employer on the back. Bartholomew was surprised that for once, she didn't rush off for a shower.

He nodded solemnly. "May I be excused?"

"Of course, Master Borax. I understand you wanting to be alone."

He felt numb. He'd never get to hear one of Grandfather's stories again. The wild-haired man used to straighten his bent form and wink before starting in on a giggly story. Bartholomew loved Grandfather's elfin face and the way his eyes crinkled in the corners when he was spinning a tale or pranking someone. He often sketched the man and even soap-sculpted a pretty good likeness the summer before.

But on the other hand, the idea of moving intrigued Bartholomew. Homeschooled and lonely, he had long dreamed of escaping Mother's antiseptic mansion. Hygenette loathed travel so much that he had been to Grandfather Borax's house just once when he was six for Grandmother's funeral.

They'd had their own train car designed just for the journey. Of course, Mother first had it stripped to the walls, repainted, and carpeted, along with installing brand new plastic seats, tables, and shining bathroom fixtures. But renovations weren't enough. Next, she ordered their maid army to attack with an enough disinfectant to make a bleach bomb.

The trip may have been the same old take-a-bath-prison, but the Borax mansion in Santa Barbara had been too wonderful.

Real trees and shrubs surrounded the estate, not the plastic ones Bartholomew was used to. And the rooms! All kinds of fantastic things filled them: old photos, knick-knacks, and souvenirs from Grandfather's travels around the world. Every one was a different color, from vibrant orange in the kitchen to humming violet in the downstairs bath. A study with deep wood paneling that hinted at secret passageways held an insect collection, telescope, and star charts. Grandfather's own oil paintings and outrageously designed furniture gave Bartholomew a thousand ways to feed his imagination.

One day after a long game of hide-and-seek, Grandfather took him for a walk. The grounds around the estate were even more magical than the house. With paths to secret gardens, koi ponds, and fountains around him, he felt like one of the adventurers he'd read about. He was Robinson Crusoe stranded on an island, James in a giant peach, or Harry Potter riding a Nimbus 2000.

Plants of all types seemed to bow as Grandfather entered a glass-walled conservatory draped in vines. As soon as they were inside, he grabbed a handful of soil and balled it in his hand.

"Bartholomew, what could you create with this?" he said, holding out the dark globe.

Bartholomew knitted his brow trying to think of the correct answer. Was this a test? "Soil is good for growing things like trees and flowers," he said, trying to sound older than his six years.

"Yes, I know. But what more do you see?" He looked expectantly into the boy's face.

"A brown tennis ball?"

"No. I want you to look further. Use that imagination of yours. Don't tell me what it is. Dream. Like your father used to." He paused and held it closer to Bartholomew's face.

Bartholomew stared at the brown sphere. At first, he saw nothing but a clump of dirt. But as he looked more deeply, shapes appeared. He gazed into the emerging planet.

"There are rivers in the cracks and mountains in the rocks, and there is a little city. I see people, all kinds of them, tall ones and round ones with eyes in weird places." As he spoke, a grin sprouted on his face.

"What wonderful eyes you have," Grandfather said, tousling the boy's hair.

"It's beautiful," Bartholomew whispered.

Grandfather nodded, then turned Bartholomew's face gently toward his. He explained how he and Father had often painted here, their splattered smocks jiggling with every joke.

"This is our special place. Generations of Boraxes have come here to be true. From well before I was born on down to your Father. We have all found inspiration here. Please remember that Bartholomew."

"I will." The boy had bowed his head solemnly and glanced around taking mind photos.

Grandfather would have understood my art.

Bartholomew stopped halfway up the stairs and crumpled.

But I never told him. The marble was cold. He looked for warmth in the crystal chandelier, but it only made him shiver. Bartholomew's vision blurred, making it hard to focus on the lights while wet droplets fell on his robe. Sniffling, Bartholomew brushed his cheeks roughly with the back of his hand.

He wiped his nose on his sleeve. *So what if I get stains? Who cares anyhow? He's gone! My best friend is gone.* Reaching in his pocket, he pulled out his recent sketch. He unfolded it and stared at the dream of them all together.

"Just nonsense!" He crumpled the drawing in his hands and shoved it deep into his pocket. Hugging his knees to his chest, he rocked rocking back and forth.

He sat for hours just like that, listening to his mother's grating complaints below. The day wore on until he finally returned to his room. Standing in front of the waste bin, Bartholomew pulled out his crumpled sketch and slowly tore it into pieces. As each shred of creation fluttered downward, memories flashed. Soon every bit of his glorious drawing was gone.

Just like Grandfather.

Bartholomew rang the silver bell on the desk and waited for the curtsying Yvette to enter his room.

"Filth. Get rid of it," he said with a vacant stare.

Chapter 2

The bronze Thinker knew it was coming. The Deliverer had destroyed art. Who would be lost this day?

Far below in the valley, the war raged on. Scores of sketched and sculpted creations were struggling to preserve this land where art was alive. For centuries, every time a human lifted a paint brush or dipped his hands in clay, a wondrous being like The Thinker had been born. Artania's leader loved how their landscape was a perfect blend of watercolor, collage, and mosaics—a mix of multihued lives.

In Pharaohs' Valley, painted Egyptian warriors and Greek sculptures alike battled Shadow Swine, a hunchbacked army intent on bringing art to an end. Every year, these yellow-eyed, bat-eared creatures attacked in greater numbers as brave Artanians tried to drive them back to their underground lair.

But Artania kept losing.

Shards of light leaped off crossed swords and assaulted his eyes. The Thinker blinked. With an effort, he continued watching as one young hieroglyph squared off with a particularly vicious Shadow Swine.

"Go back to Subterranea where you belong!" the painted stick figure soldier cried.

The pig-nosed monster opposite hissed, spittle spraying through jagged teeth. "Not before I take a few creations with me,"

His hulking body shadowed Hieroglyph, but he didn't flinch. Instead, he raised both fists and glared at his enemy. The Thinker shivered with pride.

Hieroglyph was young and brash. Like many Artanians, he saw through painted eyes. He couldn't help it. He was full of the joy the creators felt in the moment of conception. Instead of paying attention to what was going on around him, he was focusing on the beauty of each blow.

Hieroglyph couldn't see the hole opening behind him as he drew his fist back. But The Thinker could. Crying out a warning, he leaped to his feet, dreading what might come next.

The hulking Shadow Swine lifted a jack-booted leg and kicked. Sputtering, Hieroglyph staggered back, closer to the black pit. Arms outstretched, scant inches from the edge, he started to regain his footing.

The Thinker sighed.

But then the Swiney's tar-like hands reached out and shoved. Dust billowed, and when it cleared, Hieroglyph was gone.

"No!" the Thinker cried, staring helplessly into Pharaohs' Valley.

Sickhert's army was winning. From their underground lair beneath Artania, the hunchbacked monsters lined up immediately under the soil. Then they opened their horrible mouths, and with great slurps swallowed brilliant chunks of the valley's beauty.

Like a fading photo, every bite turned the valley whiter. At the same time, it shrank. If something didn't change soon, the entire land would become the Blank Canvas, a white hole where no art lived.

Apis the Bull brayed. "Retreat! The battle is lost!"

Creations fled both right and left, trying to dodge the ever-growing crevices. Panicked cries filled the air. The Bull led them away to the safety of color but seventeen brethren were gone. Swallowed by the earth, they vanished into the caverns of Subterranea below.

The Thinker hunched over, knowing the horrors that awaited these beautiful paintings, sculptures, and hieroglyphs. A single tear rolled down his bronze cheek as ripples of loss threatened to take him over.

But he had not been chosen as their leader to give way to panic.

Drawing his steely brows together, The Thinker closed his eyes and rested his chin on a clenched fist. After a few moments, he stood.

In a strong voice that friendly winds carried over Pharaohs' Valley, past the Giza Pyramids, and throughout Artania, he recited two lines of the Prophecy.

"Hope *will* lie in the hands of twins. Born near the cusp of the second millennium."

Chapter 3

With a foaming mouth of toothpaste, Alexander Devinci smiled down at Rembrandt. He swished and spat before turning to admire the dog's form. That goofy canine followed him everywhere. Alex loved the way the white stripe between dark eye patches split the dog's face in half like some sort of clown jester and had sketched that lovable head more times than he could count.

"Come on, boy. You can help me with my new painting," Alex said.

Rembrandt was Alex's art buddy. He'd carry brushes, spread drop cloths, and even use his tail to fan paintings dry. He also kept watch over the studio to make sure no one disturbed Alex while he worked. Whenever someone approached the garage door, he'd yip to let Alex know.

The studio Dad built in one corner of the garage was Alex's favorite place. Coffee cans brimmed over with markers and brushes. Shelves were filled with paints and palettes, while sketch pads and easels lay in disarray on the floor. And there was a huge skylight that lit the whole space. Even when Boulder got its fiercest snowstorms, his corner harbored a warm glow. He did have to share it with a minivan, assorted bicycles and weights, and gardening tools. But that was okay because every time he stepped in front of that easel everything else just faded away.

And what creations he made! Mutant heroes with seven arms and wheels for feet. Dolphin-hawks leaping in and out of enormous waves.

And the princely robot with binocular eyes that Alex particularly liked.

"What do you think, boy? Should I make the eyes bigger?"

Rembrandt padded from his sheepskin dog bed and stared at the painting. He wagged his tail once.

"Okay, you're the boss." Alex laughed. "Now grab your end and pull."

As usual, Rembrandt put his end of the drop cloth in his mouth and started to back up. But then in mid-yank, he came to a complete standstill.

"Come on, Rembrandt. Pull," Alex said, tugging on his corner.

Rembrandt's ears perked up as if he'd heard something nearby. He froze, looking around the room, his silver-blue eyes suspicious.

Alex moved beside the dog. "What is it, boy? Someone coming?"

A low growl rumbled from Rembrandt's throat as he turned toward Alex's newest painting.

"What?" Alex asked. "You don't like it?" He lifted a chin at the robot creation.

Rembrandt suddenly relaxed and leaned against Alex's knee. This was a signal Alex knew well. It meant he wanted affection.

"You silly pup," he chuckled, patting the dog's head. "Okay, I'll do it myself. You keep supervising." Alex stretched the fabric and smoothed the wrinkles. Rembrandt stepped onto one corner, crossed his front paws, and settled onto the drop cloth.

Hours later, Alex stood in front of the easel admiring the new painting. Then he added one last dab of Golden Yellow to the sword.

"I think I'll call you Sir Cyan," he said. Feeling a little itch, Alex rubbed his left eye.

Sir Cyan's binocular eyes looked back at him as if they really were alive. Alex leaned in for a closer look. So big and blue, he thought. *I really did capture a cool twinkle there.*

Then it happened. Sir Cyan winked. At the same time, Rembrandt let out a short yip.

Alex gasped and leaped back. "Did you see that, Rembrandt?"

The dog raised one ear and then the other as if to reply, *Beats me.*

Was it just his imagination? Alex rubbed his eye again. Holding his breath, he leaned closer.

And saw the other eye wink.

"Huh?" He jerked back.

"Alex! Dinner!" Mom called through the garage door.

Alex shook his head, snorting at his silliness. But before he went inside, he got an idea. Raising one eyebrow, his mouth curled upward in a grin.

Trying to look casual, Alex strolled toward the door. But two steps later, he stopped and shot a glance over his shoulder. Nothing. Darn! He took two more steps and twirled. Just a painting. He rubbed his eye angrily. At the exit, he held the doorknob and counted to three. Pivoting on one foot, he peeked inside. Sir Cyan was motionless

He fell into a dining chair, head reeling from the vision, wondering if Sir Cyan really wink or it was his imagination. He raised and lowered his fork, staring into space so long that even though he hated the lima beans, he forgot to pass them to the patient Rembrandt waiting under his chair.

When Rembrandt nudged his leg, Alex suppressed a groan. He'd eaten every slimy bean but one. Gross. He quickly slipped the last to his buddy and stroked Rembrandt's fuzzy ears. But now Alex had a bitter taste in his mouth, so he munched on some stir-fried carrots to get rid of it.

"Kiddo." Dad turned to him. "What is that in your eye?"

Alex shrugged.

"You have paint in your eye, silly," Mom said leaning forward. "Here, let me get it." She dabbed the corner of his eye with a napkin.

Now that he thought about it, his eye had been bugging him. He'd been rubbing it for twenty minutes. And he thought he'd seen Sir Cyan wink. Yeah, right. He exchanged a glance with Rembrandt. The dog looked at him as if to say, *Dork*.

"Creation is all well and good," Dad said, giving him one of his mathematical stares. "But Dr. Bock says that children need balance in their lives."

Lima beans were bad enough, but quotes from the Dr. Bock book? Not now, please.

"Oh, I know," Alex said, steering the conversation in another direction. "Nick and I skateboarded this afternoon. Two hours. That's a lot more exercise than Chapter Two says I need."

Dad nodded appreciatively before exchanging a glance with Mom.

Dodged that curb, Alex thought, shooting Rembrandt a triumphant look.

"Alex," Dad cleared his throat. "Your mother and I need to talk to you."

Alex felt an immediate pit in the bottom of his stomach. He reached for Rembrandt under the table.

"You do know that my job depends on whether I get funding?"

"Yeah, so?"

"Well, grants have been hard to come by." Dad paused. "Near impossible."

"Bummer." Figuring this was just going to be another *please turn off lights* talk, Alex's tight shoulders relaxed. "Mom, can you take Nick and me to Surveyor's Hill tomorrow? We're gonna practice fakies."

"Alex, you're not listening. What your father is trying to say is that he is losing his job. He'll need a new one."

"Good luck, Dad," Alex said. He wasn't worried. Dad was a great mathematician. His equations had been written up in all kinds of fancy journals.

"Son, we'll have to move. As soon as you finish the school year."

Alex felt his pulse in his throat. "No way. What about Nick and Bryce and the guys? What about skating Surveyor's Hill?" He swallowed hard. "What about my studio?"

"I know it'll be hard. I'm sorry, hon," Mom said. "But Dad'll make you a new studio in California."

Mom kept talking, but Alex barely heard. This was crazy. Leaving the only home he had ever known? He couldn't believe it, refused to. This ten-year-old was not moving to a strange city. Uh, uh. A long argument followed, and Alex forgot all about that strange wink.

Until much later.

Chapter 4

The Thinker watched and smiled. What neither Alex nor Bartholomew knew was there was a very good reason to safeguard their creations. Each had a life of its own. But none could move until the Chosen Ones were fast asleep.

The Thinker closed and opened his sculpted hand twice, and the starry skies of Boulder came into view. Then as if he were viewing the scene through a camera on a dropping parachute, Alex's street rose to meet him. Zooming in on Alex's house, the Thinker checked to make sure the boy was sleeping before peering into Alex's garage.

The paintings stacked up against the wall shook and rattled as colorful creatures stepped off their canvases and headed for their posts throughout the city. Hawk-dolphins took to the skies, a seven-armed mutant rolled under the door, and snarling painted dogs loped down the dark and empty street.

The Thinker blew into his palm. Warm air passed through the steely crevices until a light breeze whistled up Alex's drive. Papers fluttered throughout the studio, and the robot painting quivered.

"Painted Knight awake and know all," the Thinker whispered.

Sir Cyan's robotic head made a humming noise as he cocked it to one side.

"Ready for duty, sir." Turning right and left, he blinked his binocular eyes. "But I do not see you."

"I am home in Artania, but worry not. My voice will be your guide." The Thinker knew he must teach this knight well to keep the Shadow Swine from frightening another human away from art. He drew his palm closer to his lips. "Time to guard sleeping children. Don't let the creatures of the dark grow. Their powers increase in lightless corners beneath discarded crayons and lost coloring books. Use the light of creation."

"I will be ever watchful." The blue robot saluted stiffly, passed under the garage door, and rolled down the street.

"Beware. The Shadow Swine are wily and unfeeling. They will try to trick you," The Thinker warned.

Three doors down, the Bulop family was already forgetting the joy of creation. While bottles of paint dried and became as hard as a Shadow Swine's heart, they watched television. And now two of these ugly creatures, Stench and Sludge, emerged from their dark portals, sniffed this air, and found a place to grow.

The Thinker shuddered. Humans were denying creativity right and left, and in so doing, bringing more death to the Artanians. Would another child be turned from art this night? The Shadow Swine opened their horrible mouths and swallowed the sadness of the broken paint sets, immediately doubling in size. Their hunched backs swelled while their clawed fingertips lengthened.

"Madison is only six years old," The Thinker said. "Don't let them invade her dreams."

"I will use our light," Sir Cyan said, drawing closer to the house.

Sludge ran a forked tongue over his jagged teeth. "Yes, Madison Bulop. Your dreams are mine."

"We gonna get her, Cap'n?" his pig-nosed comrade asked.

"We will turn her away. Art will be the monster of her nightmares. Come." Leaving a trail of slime behind him, Sludge led the way across the yard. When he reached the place right below little Madison's window, he rubbed his mud-dripping hands together in glee.

The Thinker grimaced. Although the Painted Knights of Light stood guard, this was a dangerous time. He wasn't sure if these heroes could stop the dream-draining Shadow Swine.

The Thinker felt the connection between his world and Earth fading. He knew he could only reach across dimensions for so long before his strength would wane. He'd have to choose his words carefully.

The Thinker watched two Swineys slide up the wall toward Madison's room, but the painted robot was scanning the sidewalk and didn't notice.

"Shadow Swine above," the bronze leader rasped, his voice weakening.

Sir Cyan flew up to a branch opposite Madison's window.

"Use your laser eyes—fire!" Every bit of The Thinker's fading strength went into these words. Now all he could do was watch.

Thankfully, Stench and Sludge hadn't noticed Sir Cyan yet. They were too busy trying to ooze in the cracks around the windowpane.

"Halt or be destroyed!" Cyan commanded.

Now, most of the time a Shadow Swine would slither away from a Painted Knight as fast as he could ooze. But on this night, Stench and Sludge had managed to grow rather large for their kind. So instead of running, they turned to fight. Stench raised his jet-black arms while Sludge curled his clawed hands into fists.

From his perch in the maple tree, Sir Cyan pointed his binocular lenses at the creatures. "I am warning you," he said.

"Go back to your canvas, Creation!" Sludge guffawed with a wave of his hand.

Sir Cyan twisted the lenses to magnify his eyes. They brightened behind the glass and shot beams of light through each lens.

"Noooo!" Stench fell back onto his hunchbacked comrade.

Sludge almost lost his footing but managed to stay upright by grabbing onto Stench. He raised his black cloak over his head for protection.

"Battle, Painted Knight. Rage against them," the Thinker urged, wishing his voice could still reach into that world.

Sir Cyan flapped his wings and rose a few inches off the branch. Narrowing his beams, he locked onto each monster. As he flew in closer, he kept the light trained on the Shadow Swine. Although unable to burn, beams full of enough color could shrink a Shadow Swine.

Keep your distance, Knight, the bronze statue thought.

The Swineys shriveled beneath Sir Cyan's colorful lasers. But Sludge was not so easily defeated. He made a desperate sweep with one arm, knocking the knight off balance. Sir Cyan's rays flickered, and he plummeted toward the ground.

"No!" the Thinker cried.

An instant before crashing, the knight extended his wings and took to the air. Skirting the concrete sidewalk, he skimmed over the lawn and flew toward the Swineys. Cyan kept multiple bursts beamed at the shortening creatures as they dove into the sewer drain.

"You haven't seen the last of us, Paint Pot! We'll get you for this!" Sludge cried slinking down the drainpipe portal.

"You just try it," Sir Cyan said and gave a short wave, "and we'll see what happens." With a satisfied smile, he placed his fists on his hips and resumed his post under the street lamp.

Upstairs, Madison Bulop slept soundly, a soft smile on her heart-shaped lips. She snuggled deeper into the covers as The Thinker sent her a beautiful vision of a rainbow to draw when she woke. The nightmares in the city of Boulder had been quieted, exactly like in Philadelphia where Bartholomew's creations also stood guard. The cosmos was in balance. Almost.

The Thinker closed his palm. That was too close.

The stars were changing, and he feared for the future of his world.

Chapter 5

Alex sat on the curb watching the gutter water run under his bent legs. Occasionally, he tossed in a leaf and watched the tiny boat. It drifted away like he had from the Rocky Mountains and all his friends. He'd left the only home he'd ever known and now was in Santa Barbara. Summer in famous Southern California. Big deal.

He sighed. There was nothing to do, no one to talk to, and for some weird reason, he didn't even feel like painting. He'd already sent a couple of emails off to his buds back in Boulder, but it wasn't the same as hanging out or skating with them. He'd offered to help, but the movers carrying boxes and furniture just grunted at him to get out of the way.

"I'm going for a walk, Mom," Alex called over his shoulder.

"But wouldn't you like to help organize the kitchen? Decide where the glasses go?" Mom's voice had an irritating plea to it.

Alex gave her an incredulous look. Didn't she know he was still mad about moving? Anyhow, organizing glasses? How lame.

"No way. I mean, no thanks. Wanna check out the neighborhood."

"You know your way around?"

"I'm not a baby. I'll figure it out." To keep her from worrying, he used a talent he'd had for years. He struck a pose, stroked his chin, and impersonated Dad. "Dr. Bock says that children need independence at times."

His mother shook her head and smirked. "All right, Mr. Impersonator, but be home for dinner."

"'kay."

He walked up one street and then another, trying to release some of his nervous energy. Before the move, art was the one thing that had always soothed him. So many times, he sat at his easel, Rembrandt's head resting in his lap, and chilled.

But, ever since the move, he felt so different. Empty. No art begged to be made. Now, his mind was as gray as a tomb. What was happening?

Chapter 6

Bartholomew looked around the empty space that would be his bedroom. So far, the only piece of furniture in it was a brand new king-sized bed, still encased in plastic. He stared at the blank walls and tried to imagine sketches filling them. But no ideas came, which was strange. He was usually so full of dreams; he could hardly wait to draw.

Bartholomew yawned. His mother ordered him to his room to read, something he absolutely loved, but the book she chose was as dry as desert sand, and he quickly tired of it. He wanted to get out like the heroes he read about in fantasy, but he couldn't just tell Mother he was going for a walk. It would send her into a panic attack. "What about germs? You'll get dirty. Heaven knows how much filth is out there."

"This is too much," Bartholomew said to himself. "I cannot take it anymore. I have to escape, if only for a while." He went downstairs and found his mother sitting on the crème-colored settee looking through a recent catalogue of super cleansers.

"I believe that we should be using Saniscrub instead of Powerclean." she muttered, never glancing up from the page. "It destroys ninety percent more germs."

Bartholomew cleared his throat.

She didn't seem to hear. Instead, she pursed her lips as if thinking of something particularly filthy.

"Umm, Mother?"

"What is it, Bartholomew? Can't you see I'm busy?" She pointed to the catalog.

"I'm sorry. I just wanted to tell you, well, umm, you see…"

"Speak up, child!"

"I'm tired."

"And why is this significant to me?"

"I, uh, plan to take a nap and do not wish to be disturbed."

"Fine, fine. I'll let the servants know. Now shoo." Mrs. Borax waved her son away.

Bartholomew's heart pounded as he ducked out the backdoor. He'd never snuck out before. But darn it, he was getting tired of his mother's control. Just because she had nightmares about cleaning bubbles didn't mean he should be trapped in one. He was almost eleven after all—not a baby anymore.

As soon as he closed the gate, he set off at a trot down the street, then a run. Oh, how glorious it was to be free! No one to tell him to stay clean. No one to order him to write rows of perfectly boring numbers or long division problems.

He felt like Clark Kent stripped down to his superman suit, ready to leap tall buildings in a single bound. Street after street passed by in a blur. He rounded a corner, picking up speed when suddenly, *crash!* He bumped into a boy.

A lightning flash of color lit up his mind.

For a moment, both time and space were suspended. In that instant, the blank canvas once occupying his head was filled with wondrous creations. Brightly painted faces smiled and waved. Brilliant blue doves fluttered overhead. A fluorescent rainbow arced through the sky. But as soon as he fell back, the vision disappeared, and his mind was as white as the concrete beneath him.

"What the heck?" the other boy gasped.

"Am I well?" Bartholomew glanced down to see if his clothes were soiled. He leaped up, brushing the dust from his pants and arms, checking every inch of his body for dirt. Oh no! His hands were scraped, and the dirty sores were oozing blood. Bartholomew began to shake. He'd never been so dirty. What would his mother say?

"Ah, you're okay." The curly-headed boy jumped to his feet.

"I'm a mess!"

"It's just dirt," he said glancing up and down Bartholomew. "Besides, you look pretty clean to me."

"But I'm bleeding!" Bartholomew gasped, his lower lip trembling. He wasn't in pain. He was only scared of what his mother would do if she discovered he'd lied to her. She'd probably lock him in the colorless room forever.

And he'd almost talked her into letting him go to school. Oh, to be around other kids and get away from fingernail-obsessed Mr. White. He just had to get cleaned up before Mother found out.

"What? That's nothing. You should've seen me when I crashed my skateboard on Surveyor's Hill. I still have the scar, see?" The brown-eyed boy pulled up his tee shirt to show the long white scar extending across his chest.

Bartholomew barely noticed. "I must get clean before Mother sees this." He reached into his pocket, pulled out a small bottle of hand sanitizer, and squirted a bit into his palms before pacing back and forth nervously.

"Okay, okay, you don't have to be a baby about it. Come home with me, all right?" He gave Bartholomew a disgusted look.

Bartholomew nodded in relief. He rubbed the stinging gel into his skin and said a prayer of thanks to the sky.

"Well, are you coming or not? Jeesh!"

Bartholomew trailed along like a puppy following a new master. The dark-haired boy in front of him walked so confidently. No, this boy didn't walk; he strutted. His street-surfer shoes hit the pavement with such deliberateness that Bartholomew thought the concrete would break beneath him.

Not like me. I trip over my own feet. Probably from thinking about nonsense, like Mother always says.

He looked up from the sidewalk and blinked in surprise. They'd stopped in front of a single-story house that looked exactly like all the others on the street, except this one had cardboard boxes piled high in the open garage. When the kid opened the front door, Bartholomew wiped his feet on the smiley-face welcome mat and followed him inside.

"You can clean up in the kitchen." The boy jerked his head toward the back.

"The kitchen?" Bartholomew gasped.

"Yeah, you know a room with a stove and a sink?" He rolled his eyes.

A lady in faded jeans and a loose t-shirt was sitting at the kitchen table opening a box labeled "Dishes." Bartholomew could tell right away she was this kid's mom. She had the same dark curls and twinkling brown eyes.

She was nothing like Hygenette Borax. Instead of long, perfectly manicured nails on paper white hands, this woman's were smudged with ink, with fingernails so short and jagged it looked as if she were too busy to care for them. At her feet lay a drooling gray and black dog with rough fur. Patting the animal on its head, she stood and brushed the hair out of her face with the back of her hand. "Back so soon?" She smiled at the boys.

"Yeah, well, this kid needs to wash his hands."

Her eyebrows raised in a question.

"We had an unfortunate accident," Bartholomew began.

"He wasn't watching where he was going and crashed right into me."

"Who is this kid?" the boy's mom asked.

"He's… is… hey, I don't know your name."

"Forgive me. In all the excitement, I neglected to introduce myself properly." Bartholomew clicked his heels together and bowed. "I am Bartholomew Borax the Third. How do you do?" He extended his hand but hastily pulled it back again when he saw how dirty and scratched it still was.

"Nice to meet you, too. I'm Cyndi Devinci. I guess you met my munchkin, Alexander?"

Bartholomew nodded.

Cyndi Devinci turned to her son. "Say hello, Alex."

Alex glared at her. You'd think she'd just asked him to shovel manure.

"Be polite, Alex," Mrs. Devinci repeated the order.

"Nice to meet you," Alex mumbled.

"Charmed, I'm sure," Bartholomew replied automatically.

Mrs. Devinci turned and smiled at Bartholomew, but he thought it was a little forced. "By the way, would you by chance be part of *the* Borax family? The ones in all the commercials? The famous bleach manufacturers?"

Bartholomew nodded, then pleadingly held up his hands.

"Oh, I see. That explains it," Mrs. Devinci said before turning to her son. "Alex, the soap is under the sink, and there are towels over there." She pointed to an open box. "I've got some clothes to unpack in the bedroom. Nice to meet you, Bartholomew Borax the Third."

"The pleasure is all mine, ma'am," Bartholomew replied with a short bow.

"Hey, Rembrandt. How you doing, boy?" Alex said ruffling the dog's furry neck. Over here, Bartholomew Three." Alex motioned with his head. But under his breath, he muttered, "A richie, huh? No wonder you're such a sissy."

Bartholomew spoke quickly, trying to hide the red creeping up in his cheeks. "It's 'the Third.' You see, my grandfather was the first, my father the second, and I am the third. I suppose if I ever have a son, he'll be 'the Fourth.' "

"I get it." Alex shoved a towel and a bar of soap at Bartholomew.

Then it happened again. Time and space stopped. As soon as his hand grazed Alex's, the same dreamscape of color shot into Bartholomew's mind.

Alex jumped back. "What the heck—"

"—was that?" Bartholomew gasped, finishing the thought.

"You saw it, too?"

Bartholomew nodded.

"What did you do?" Alex lifted one eyebrow suspiciously.

Me? It's probably you...or this place, Bartholomew thought as scrubbed his hands while keeping one eye on Alex. He wondered if this place hosted some sort of disease like his mother warned him about. Were dangerous fumes lurking?

He looked at the kitchen sink. It was yellow and chipped. Empty Chinese food containers were piled menacingly near his hands like giant flies ready to spread disease. He turned the water up and rubbed at the spots on his shirt and slacks. *Wash it all away. Get clean. Scrub. Get clean. Scrub.*

"Is this how you rich kids get your kicks?" Alex crossed his arms and glared. "Messing with people's minds?"

"What? It is you who play with me," Bartholomew said, slowly drying his hands on the faded dishtowel.

"I know. You probably have some sort of richie kit you use to hypnotize kids. Where is it? In your pocket?" Alex walked around Bartholomew, scrutinizing his clothes.

"I believe it is you who have bewitched me. Perhaps you gave me a brain disease," Bartholomew retorted.

"Ha! You weren't exactly right in the head when you picked out that outfit, Mr. Three." Alex pointed at Bartholomew. "What are you supposed to be? A doctor? A mad scientist? An escapee from the looney bin?"

From under his button-down collar straight up to his face, Bartholomew felt the heat. Blinking repeatedly, he jerked right and left, sweeping the room with his gaze. There were messes everywhere. Half-opened boxes and scrunched up balls of newspaper were strewn about. A smell like old cheese wafted from the Chinese to-go boxes. Then there was that scruffy animal slobbering all over the floor, leaving little drool puddles on the linoleum. It all closed in on him, crawling over his skin and making his stomach turn.

"Well... well, at least my house isn't a-a-garbage dump!" he sputtered with a shudder of disgust.

"Get out!" Alex shook his fist at Bartholomew. "Now!"

"Gladly." Bartholomew threw the towel into the sink, shoved open the door, and stomped outside. "And, by the way, thank you so much for your hospitality!" he called over his shoulder.

Bartholomew stormed down the street nostrils flaring.

Chapter 7

The Thinker watched Alexander fume with a slight smile on his bronze lips. The boys were different, yes, but if their art remained true, they could overcome any dissimilarities.

"What an idiot that richie was," Alex muttered. "Dump. Yeah, right. All houses are messy when people move." The young Deliverer shook his head and the Thinker knew why. An insult wouldn't bother one as confident as he. It was the vision that shook his psyche.

"Focus, young one," The Thinker said into the image in his palm. "Let that moment inspire."

Alex spent long moments staring at the easel in his new room and then applied just a splash of color. He stood back and hesitated.

"Recall the beauty of Artania," The Thinker said curling and uncurling his brass fingers to help Alex remember the vision. "Create."

"That vision was trippy, though. A glowing mountain was over here and a tinge of ocher there. A rainbow encircled it all," Alex said as his brush dipped into the paint faster and faster.

His mother came to the doorway.

"Hungry?" she asked.

Alex ignored her, never once ceasing in his work.

"Alex?" She took a step into the room.

"I'm painting."

"I thought you might want a snack."

She held out a plate of apple crisp bars. The curly-topped youth had often gobbled these treats greedily. "Don't stop now, Deliverer. We need you," The Thinker whispered.

Alex glanced at the crispy dessert but shook his head.

"All right. But if you get hungry, they'll be in the kitchen."

"'kay," Alex said with a quick wave. His hands sped faster as he painted, stirring colors wildly from one end of the canvas to the other.

The fantasy took shape. A mountain range covered in what looked like ice cream had purple streams roping down hillsides, a valley carpeted in flowers, and a rainbow encircling it all.

The Deliverer worked late into the night, and The Thinker sighed. Santa Barbara would be safe this night.

Finally, at half-past midnight, the boy's father came in. "Time to stop, kiddo. Even if it is summer vacation, you still need your sleep."

"Just a little more?"

"No, sir. Off to bed."

Tucked under the covers, Alex happily stared at his new painting until his lids grew heavy. As he was drifting off to sleep, the rainbow flickered. Blinking twice Alex continued to stare until the colors massaged his fluttering eyes closed.

Of course, the painting really was moving. This time, the Thinker could not let the Painted Knights of Light wait until Alex was completely asleep to assume their posts throughout the city. The stars had changed. and there was disharmony in the universe.

Shadow Swine were on the move and growing stronger with each step.

It was a time of great danger for the world. If allowed to continue, the Shadow Swine Army might gain control, and anti-art life could spread like dark storm clouds.

The rainbow grew, filling Alex's room with color. It shot beyond the window and cast a net of light over the sleeping town of Santa Barbara. The foothills shone translucently, while the waves reached foamy fingers toward this protective arc. If Alex's mother were to come in right then, she'd see nothing, but if the boy were to awake, his mouth would drop open in wonder.

Two blocks from Bartholomew's mansion, Stench and Sludge opened a portal and crept through, ready to begin their dream draining. They slimed over the streets until they found a potter's wheel rusting in the corner of a yard. Chuckling, they slithered onto the broken machine, immediately growing by a third. But it was power these evil monsters desired, not size, and for this, they needed a child.

However, The Thinker was ready.

Searching for prey, Sludge raised his piggish nostrils in the air. He grinned at Stench, his muddy lips rippling with each rattly breath.

"Whose dreams will lose their color this night?"

His eyes scanning the streets, Sludge led his comrade through the wealthy neighborhood of mansions and estates. He sniffed each home as he drew ever and ever closer to the Borax estate. Something was there that could give him all the power he desired.

The Thinker shook his head. The very air of the Borax manor was filled with suppression odor, a cage-like smell that drew Shadow Swine ever closer. He heard Captain Sludge's greedy mutterings. "The scent is strong here. Ahhh. I could turn many in this place and Lord Sickhert would be most pleased. Come, Stench. Let us find it. Find it now." Sludge stopped at the gates of the Borax estate and took a deep breath.

This place would be challenging to protect. The Thinker feared that with Mrs. Borax squelching art in every action, it wouldn't take much to turn this entire household from all creativity.

Sludge and Stench snaked their way past the iron gate and up the drive before oozing under the massive front door. Chuckling, Sludge smeared past unpacked boxes and up the stairs towards the bedrooms, Stench right behind.

Even though the oppressive scent was strong, the person responsible for it was sleeping in a nice, clean hotel miles away. Mrs. Borax wouldn't know a creative thought if it hit her on the head with a hammer. Even hours after she had left, her antiseptic suppression hung in the air, and any Shadow Swine worth his slime could easily catch a whiff of it.

Only a few servants and Bartholomew lay sleeping in the bedrooms above. Bartholomew had begged his mother to let him stay in the house that night. The Thinker knew the boy would be confused by the day's events and need time alone to think.

"What happened? Am I sick?" Bartholomew had asked the air as felt his forehead for fever.

Then he'd gone to the back of the walk-in closet and turned over his red designer suitcase. He unzipped the bag and gingerly lifted one corner of the lining to expose the secret compartment he'd sewn inside. There, wrapped in tissue paper, was the soap carving he'd done of his Grandfather Borax the summer before. The Thinker was proud of how Bartholomew managed to save it for an entire year by hiding it in this secret place.

Carefully, Bartholomew folded back the paper and looked into the tiny face. "I miss you."

The sculpture looked up at him with eyes that drooped in both corners. Bits of soap flaked off during the trip, altering some of the features. Bartholomew massaged the cheeks with the tips of his fingers, trying to mold the face back into shape. It stared back blankly, missing that twinkle the elder Borax always had.

"I had the oddest experience today. I met a boy, just my age. When I bumped into him, I saw…colors. Then later in his kitchen, I saw a world. Oh, it was so beautiful. You would have loved it. Alex said he saw something, too. Was that magic?"

The Thinker wished he could pass through and tell the boy all, but he had no such power.

The boy stroked his grandfather's soap face with the back of his hand. He sighed, set the statue on the nightstand, and crawled into bed. He rolled over and closed his eyes. He tossed and turned and finally drifted off into a fitful slumber.

* * *

xxx Sludge reached the boy's closed bedroom door in time to see Bartholomew's dream of playing tag with his dead father begin.

"Ahh! A child sleeping. He thinks these visions are things of beauty, but I have other plans." Sludge leaned a slimy face against the door frame, stroking it with his claw-tipped fingers. Then he licked his bulbous lips. "Stench, come. The child awaits."

Captain Sludge was the best dream drainer in Subterranea, besides Lord Sickhert, of course. His record was twenty-three nightmares in a single trip. He was revered as a celebrity, and Sludge relished this role. He loved how everyone bowed when he marched along the River of Lies in the capital city. Even though he was six inches shorter than the average Shadow Swine, they all were afraid of him.

He planned to keep it that way.

He shrank into oozing slime and snaked under the bedroom door, reforming at the foot of Bartholomew's bed. Sludge exchanged an evil glance with Stench and began to blow. Curling wisps of smoke rose from his cavernous mouth, creeping through the cracks of his shark-like teeth. Dark clouds floated over the bed and poured into Bartholomew's right ear.

The boy was still trapped in sleep fantasy when he gasped and sat upright. Sludge reached into the vision to twist the stupid dream. Now, the children playing tag with the father morphed into distorted soldiers clutching paint-filled bladders. They surrounded the elder Borax, linked arms, and screeched, rising in the air to launch their painted globules. One after another hit the man in the face as dream-Bartholomew watched in horror.

From his post at Bartholomew's bedside, Sludge smiled at his skillful twisting. Knowing that even in a dream, Bartholomew would try to rush and help his father, Sludge made sure to trap the boy's dream legs knee deep in cement.

"No! Father!" the dream child cried as his father was splattered with blotches of bleeding color.

Bartholomew's hallucinatory shrieks fed Sludge's appetite for fear. The Shadow Swine captain gave a short laugh before twisting the dream even more. The man sputtered and choked, drowning in paint exactly like he drowned so beautifully in mud eleven years before.

The dream Bartholomew swung his arms wildly, but Sludge kept the morphed soldiers just out of reach. He sucked in more of the boy's terror and grew. This would be his *magnum opus*, his *tour de force*, his masterwork.

Sludge blew another puff of locust-like air to release his final ball of paint. This one exploded on the father's head. Oily raindrops dripped down until the colors coalesced into a waxy coating. The man's face loosened at the edges like a multi-colored mask slowly being removed.

Now Sludge would form words to turn the child away from art. He moved his slimy lips and the puppet image spoke: "Bartholomew. Help!"

In the dream, Sludge finally released the boy's legs from the cement and made a bucket and sponge appear at his feet.

"Get it off," Puppet-father said with Sludge's voice.

But Bartholomew still didn't act. Instead, the dream child merely gaped at the bucket.

Sludge clicked his claws together, and the old man's face began to dissolve. When the captain of the Shadow Swine moved his dull red lips, the dream father spoke again.

"I'm drowning! Again!"

"I'll save you, Father," Bartholomew sobbed in his sleep.

Now the boy reached down and grabbed the sponge. He dipped it in the water, and washed his father's face. The melting slowed.

Sludge felt it. With each pass of the sponge, a bit of the boy's desire to create disappeared. When he washed the paint from the sad eyes, the boy hardened to sculpting. Bartholomew's heart turned from sketching as he swabbed the man's head. When he rinsed the glow from his father's skin, Sludge tried to turn the boy away from all art.

"Release my family!" a voice boomed.

Sludge jerked around to see the soap sculpture on the nightstand glaring. It raised both arms and two silvery beams shot past his head.

Easily ducking the assault, the captain sniggered. "This one is mine. Back off, Creation."

"You will not turn this boy." The twerp raised his arms higher, and the room hummed with light.

"No! The child is ours. Art is already his nightmare." Sludge opened his mouth wider, letting more smoke escape.

"His dreams drain." Stench stepped toward the small sculpture, clawed hands reaching through the light.

The little statue smiled.

"Power of Pigment, come forth!" the soapy miniature cried.

A rainbow torpedoed into the room, exploding into strands of light that twisted and twined into a red, orange, green, and blue net.

"No!" Sludge screeched. He covered his mouth with a clawed hand, clamping it shut. He knew that ingesting such beautiful color would mean his demise.

The rainbow looped round Sludge. He backed up, trying to escape, but was trapped like a fly in a multicolored spider's web. The colorful net tightened, lifted him, and hauled him out the window. Then like a stone being released from a slingshot, he was catapulted through the sky, arcing towards those ugly bits of starry light.

He sneered at them as he fell. Descending. Plunging. Pitching. Plummeting. Sludge flailed his arms wildly and covered his eyes. The ground rose to meet him.

He hit with a great splash. There was a horrible smell all around. Flapping his arms, Sludge felt something soft. He pulled it closer and glanced down. A gob of toilet paper!

"Uggh!" he cried, flinging the foul wad away. Now Sludge realized that he had landed smack dab in the middle of a sewage treatment pond.

Gross, even to a Swiney.

Suddenly, a yelping Stench splashed down nearby. When he bobbed to the surface. long strings of toilet paper hung from either side of his face. One curled into his left nostril and rolled in and out with each breath.

No swimmer, Stench struggled to stay afloat but only got more tangled in toilet paper.

"Sir, I no can escape," he gurgled.

"Idiot," Sludge growled.

Shaking his head angrily, he raised both hands and clapped. The sewage thickened as they faded, but immediately before they disappeared, Sludge noticed the control room's gauges going crazy.

Leaving the baffled sanitation engineers to argue about how the heck liquid sewage had hardened to a solid gel in a matter of seconds.

Chapter 8

The next few weeks passed by as slowly as one of his mother's cleaning inspections. With Mr. White on vacation, Bartholomew had lots of time to sneak into the closet and sketch or hide out in the bathroom and sculpt. So why didn't he? Every day he waited for inspiration to come, but strangely, it never did. What was it about Santa Barbara that made his mind so empty?

Then on his birthday, he woke with art in his eyes. He bounded out of bed and leaped to the window. Twilight still hung over Santa Barbara, but the foothills glowed with the rising sun. He had to capture it.

Bartholomew quietly slid back one of the wooden screens separating his room into two sections. This half of his suite had a fireplace with brick so brilliantly white you'd think it had never been used. Ignoring both the cold hearth and the leather loveseat in front of it, he headed straight for his writing desk, yanked open the drawer, and felt around for the latch to his secret compartment. He pulled out five pencils and laid them in a neat row.

Glancing at the scene in his window, he ran a finger over each. He chose one with a flattened tip and rolled the others into the corner. Eyes narrowed, he surveyed the sunrise, composing the drawing in his mind. Like a photographer studying the quality of the light, he sketched the outline of his window onto paper before adding dark hills and fingers of clouds.

The crescent moon should go in the corner. Don't forget those two stars. One for Father and one for me. Hurry, before they're gone, he thought, quickening his pace.

Dawn exploded before him. He switched to a fine point for the rising sun, tracing the rays as they grew longer in the sky. His gaze darted from window to drawing and back again. Faster he went, scratching furiously over the paper. Oak trees. Lupines. Shadows on the golden poppies. His pencil was a seismograph needle recording a super quake.

Catching his breath, he held the sketch up. Just a touch more on the clouds.

A distant door snapped closed, and heels clicked across the foyer. Mother!

He shoved the pencils back into the drawer and slammed it shut. Grabbing his drawing, he leaped into bed and hid it beneath the covers.

Mother opened the door. "Bartholomew?" she called. "Where are you? It's June twenty-first." She stepped past the center divider. "Oh, there you are in bed."

Pretending to be asleep, Bartholomew yawned and rolled over. Good acting if he did say so. It was just one of the many masks he put on for her benefit. He wondered how she'd react if he ever showed his true face.

"Are you still asleep? It's already six thirty."

Even though they were tucked deeply under the covers, Bartholomew's hands turned to ice. He ran one over the sketch. Did she know? Would she rip the room apart and find them all?

Hygenette crossed the floor and gave him a quick shake.

"What, huh?" Bartholomew mumbled, wondering if he were over-acting.

"Your hairdresser will be here at eight, and I want you bathed before then. You *must* look like a proper Borax today."

Bartholomew groaned.

"Oh, and happy birthday, dear."

"Umm, thank you, Mother." He ventured a peek into those pale blue eyes. No suspicion. Maybe even a little affection. It was his birthday, after all.

When the door was closed firmly behind her, he got out of bed. Before bathing, he made sure to hide his drawing beneath the mattress and tuck his pencils back in the secret compartment.

"You could have been caught, dummy!" he muttered, shaking his head. "Then she'd probably ban pencils, too."

Trudging into the adjoining bathroom, he took a moment to glare at his reflection in the mirrored wall before he stepped into the glass-enclosed shower. He looked so stupid standing there. He'd like to erase dumb face he saw and start all over.

"You dolt! Be more careful." He turned the chrome shower handles on full blast and thrust his head under the spout.

Bartholomew rubbed soap onto the washcloth and scrubbed his face. If he could scour hard enough, maybe he could erase all these dumb mistakes. Scrape off tripping into Alex. Wash away forgetting what day it was. Dig the wax from his ears so he would hear Mother approaching.

He turned the hot water up and forced himself to face the scalding spray.

"Stupid!" he muttered. Cursing all the while, he made rough circles on his cheeks, forehead, and chin.

When he finally got out of the shower and looked in the mirror, he was shocked to see how raw and red his cheeks were. He put hands to his hot face and groaned at his reflection.

"Great, now you'll have a nice red face at the party. Some birthday."

Chapter 9

The Thinker closed his sculpted fist, and the flickering images of Bartholomew faded. "Poor child. If only he could see the shadows as I can."

He looked out over the valley. It was bleached white, part of Sickhert's realm now. The Shadow Swine were gaining ground. Another pyramid had fallen, taking a score of Egyptian creations with it.

"Why do they continue to die?" he asked the stone statue opposite him. "Alex and Bartholomew are the Chosen Ones. I am sure of it."

"I wish I knew," the bearded man replied.

"Their move to Santa Barbara has altered the stars, making creation a rare occurrence. The boys used to create daily, but now they are blocked by the sky's energy."

"Then we must unblock it." The marble statue leaned forward. "The only question is how?"

The Thinker put his fist to his forehead.

"Art has come to call when their minds hold the same thought or when their skin is close, transferring electrons."

"Not enough. We must change that."

"Yes, but I don't have the strength," The Thinker replied.

"Is not today the longest day of the year, a solstice of light? We might be able to tap into its energy."

"I believe so, Olympian King. Why, yes!" The Thinker suddenly clapped a hand on his companion's shoulder. "With sunrays at their strongest, the Power of Pigment is visible. But I need one who is strong. One with the power of the gods.

"I, myself, will go."

"You are sure?" The Thinker asked. "It may be dangerous."

"Bah." The bearded man raised an eyebrow. Then to illustrate his point, he shimmered and morphed from statue to oil-painting. "I'll give them a glimpse that will inspire. Their thoughts will ride waves like surfers atop tsunamis."

Although the bearded one spoke truth, The Thinker couldn't help but think how unbearable it would be to lose one so great. Trying to ignore the knots of worry, he brought his bronze fingertips together to trigger electric sparks. As he rounded them into an open shape, mini lightning bolts flashed from hand to hand.

"May the Power of Pigment sustain you," The Thinker said. He pressed his fingers together, and with a loud pop, his companion disappeared.

Chapter 10

His burning face helped to remind Bartholomew of how close he'd come. He had to be careful. Mother had talked about letting him go to school, and he didn't want to do anything to mess that up. He tried to act interested while she ticked off party instructions.

"Keep your hands clean with the antiseptic wipes on the table. Smile. Applaud like a gentleman after each act...."

Blah, blah, blah. It would be just like his tenth birthday, his ninth, and his eighth. Yawn...yawn... yawn... sit up straight. Chew slowly with your mouth closed. Wipe your mouth forty-five times with your napkin. Use the outside fork when eating salad, for Heaven's sake!

The one intriguing thing was the location. At the Yacht Club, he could at least look at the ocean, even if he wasn't allowed swim and play in it. And other kids would be there. He figured they'd all be little ones; it seemed all of Mother's colleagues had small children. But he was so lonely that he'd welcome the company of anyone, even some preppy kids half his age.

In his crème-colored coat and chokingly tight tie, Bartholomew felt more like a condemned man wearing a hangman's noose than a birthday boy. He placed a bookmark in his paperback, tucked the book inside his suit pocket, and entered the room stiffly. Trying to remember to nod his head to thank the elite crowd for their polite applause, he followed his waving mother past the groups of people seated on bleach bottle-shaped chairs. Bartholomew searched the room for anyone he might play with later. Just as he suspected. Babies. All of them.

Mother led him to seats at the head of the long table facing the audience, and gloved waiters pushed their chairs in jail-door tight. She smoothed her dress, ready to begin her yearly speech. Bartholomew suppressed a groan. Here it comes. The long lecture on the greatness of bleach.

She stood, clinking the side of her crystal goblet with a spoon and waited for the crowd to quiet.

"Ladies and gentlemen. Children." Mrs. Borax's tightly wound bun didn't move a millimeter as she nodded at the people in the room. "Thank you all for joining us. It is with great pride that we celebrate my son's birthday. Thus, getting one year closer to taking his rightful place in the Borax Empire."

Bartholomew tried not to look incredulous. This was a celebration? It sounded more like a radio commercial. Not for the first time, he wondered what sort of speeches Father gave when he was alive. He liked to imagine they were funny and somehow made everyone feel welcome.

"And I'm sure he won't mind the presents, either." Her mouth twitched into a grin about as sincere as a fox smiling at chickens.

Bartholomew glanced at the table piled high with brightly colored gifts. Big deal. He'd never get to open any of them. Mother wouldn't have it. Heaven knows the kind of germs these people might have. No, they'd end up where all his presents did. In the homeless shelter's donation bin. Oh, well. At least some poor kids would get to enjoy them.

"But enough about children. Look at the white of your tablecloth. Brilliant, isn't it? Imagine how it would look if we Boraxes weren't around." She gave her finger a quick shake. "Gray, dull, stained." Mother shuddered. "I'll stop there since I don't want to ruin your meal."

A few chuckles and guffaws filled the room. Mother cocked her head to one side with a confused look, and Bartholomew realized she didn't understand why they were laughing.

"But you won't have to worry about that in your homes. Oh, no. Each of you has a gift bag containing five samples of the newest scents of Borax's Famous Bleach. These odors are outstanding, if I do say so." Mother rubbed the back of her hand against her suit jacket as if polishing her fingernails. She raised her eyebrows amid scattered chuckles. When giggles subsided, she said, "Plus a coupon redeemable for a six-month supply of whichever amazing cleanser you choose." She sat to enthusiastic applause.

Bartholomew looked past the happy crowd. Now he really was trapped. Outside, sparkling blue waters beckoned him closer, but inside were Mother's pale hands pointing out every time he strayed a single millimeter from the rules.

"Bartholomew, you are forgetting to wave," Mrs. Borax hissed under her breath, pinching his arm beneath the table.

Bartholomew jerked and raised his hand. Next, Mother put her index finger atop the napkin on her lap and pointed from behind the tablecloth. Bartholomew followed her direction, giving each guest a stilted wave. He knew these people weren't here for him—he just met most of them today—but he also knew the importance his mother placed on good manners. She nodded her approval at him and captured his gaze.

"Do as I do," she rasped through clenched teeth, demonstrating how to arrange a proper face.

Copying her, he pasted on a plastic smile and did his best to keep it there. Yes, this was quite the celebration.

But by the time operatic diva sang "Happy Birthday" to him in Italian, of which he didn't understand a word, Bartholomew's cheeks were so sore from fake smiling he thought they'd crack. Then there was still the multi-tiered cake to contend with. Trying to remember everything his mother told him about being a gentleman, he sat straight, bent forward from the waist, and pursed his lips. It took him three breaths before the candles went out. He didn't want to blow too hard. His mother warned him that under no circumstances was any spittle to escape his mouth like on his 6th birthday when he sneezed all over the designer cake, embarrassing her terribly.

After thirty more minutes of opera, Bartholomew couldn't take it anymore. The sea was calling to him. He wanted to walk on the beach and feel the spray on his face. But of course, Mother would never allow it. Sand scratching your nicely polished shoes? Dirty seawater getting under your finely buffed nails? Heaven forbid.

With the excuse of a needing to use the restroom, he stole away, hoping no one would see him on the pier. Outside, Bartholomew loosened his tie, took a deep breath, and let the ocean air fill his lungs. No chemical smell here. A light breeze lifted his gelled helmet of hair and tickled his scalp. Strolling along until he found a section of wooden railing without seagull splatters, he leaned over to watch the Pacific heave and sigh below him. His gaze followed the waves to the shore where he spotted another birthday party. He couldn't quite make out the faces, but they all seemed so happy.

When the group sang a raucous "Happy Birthday," the boy leaned toward the cake. Then back. Forward again.

"Hurry up, kiddo. We want to eat this cake while you're still eleven," the man next to the kid quipped.

Bartholomew smiled.

With a single sweeping puff, the boy blew out all the candles, then cut the cake and passed pieces to his guests. *Look at them eating any which way,* Bartholomew thought. *I'll bet they don't worry about using the right fork or getting crumbs on their clothes.*

When the party wound down, and the guests waved goodbye, the other birthday boy went to sit by the water. Bartholomew watched him for a moment, and then his gaze followed the lapping waves out to sea.

Its beauty instantly hypnotized him. Undulating blue crests slapped at the pier pilings. Sailboats bobbed in the distance as scattered white-caps rose on the horizon. He watched a pelican fly overhead and dive into the sea. It popped back up like a balloon.

He wished he could be like that bird. Then he'd fly to a place with no soap, and art would be his wings.

A large wave rose beneath the pelican and kept getting bigger until Bartholomew thought it would swallow the bird. He was about to shout a warning when it flew off.

The wall of water kept growing until it was over ten feet high. Bartholomew's heart raced. It was headed straight for the pier.

Right at him.

That was crazy enough, but next, a curly head with a leafy crown rose from the foam. Bartholomew gaped as a bearded face and strong shoulders appeared in the swells.

Didn't anyone else notice? Bartholomew glanced around. People walked by as if nothing were happening. He rubbed his eyes and looked again. Still there. Was he the only one who could see it?

An emerald shield formed in one hand of the giant who smiled, tossed it onto a passing wave, and leaped aboard. When the swell crested, the giant paddled furiously and stood up as he shot toward shore.

"Surfing mirages? Impossible," Bartholomew muttered. He pulled out his hand sanitizer and rubbed a bit into his palms.

When the giant passed and gave Bartholomew two thumbs-up, the boy stumbled back. He almost returned in full scurry to the party, but some strange fascination held him.

The bearded man rode wave after wave. It was all so weird, but the oddest thing was there were no other surfers anywhere. The rest of the bay was completely calm. Bartholomew dashed to the other side of the pier to make sure. Gentle waves rolled to shore there.

Taking a deep breath, Bartholomew forced himself to walk back. The giant surfer was sitting astride the shield, his muscular legs dangling in the water.

"What are you waiting for?" Bartholomew asked.

The giant didn't reply because just then, a huge wave surged, and he sprang onto the board. As the enormous swell sprayed foamy streams beneath him, his long beard and hair trailed behind like a smoky flag.

"Go!" Bartholomew urged.

The bearded surfer leaned forward until his palms were flat on the shield. He straightened his arms into a handstand, held it for three seconds, and did a triple somersault into the air.

Shyly, Bartholomew waved at the acrobat. The giant balanced atop his board, stood at attention, and tipped his leafy crown in salute. With a grin, he grew. His body stretched until he was as tall as a five-story building with arms as long as the pier. The giant reached one hand to Bartholomew, beckoning him to take it. The other extended toward the shore.

Glancing over his shoulder to make sure no one was watching, Bartholomew laid a tentative hand on the giant's enormous index finger. The giant closed his thumb over Bartholomew's hand and shook it.

It wasn't cold at all. Instead, it was like sipping hot chocolate on a cold winter's night. The creature's grasp warmed him right down to his bones. Bartholomew cleared his throat.

"Hello there, Mr. Giant. How are—" He blinked.

Where'd he go? One second he was there; the next he was gone. That strong face, surfboard shield, and comforting hand simply disappeared into thin air. He scanned the beach. The same people played in the surf. He looked out to sea. Sailboats, buoys, and seagulls but no giant. Even the waves returned to normal size.

Then he saw Mother's glowering face heading towards him. He looked at his watch. 2:45. Oh, no! He'd been gone an hour.

"Young man," she scolded her face a knot of anger. "You may find sneaking away and keeping our guests waiting amusing, but I, for one, do not."

"I just wanted to look at the ocean. I'm sorry."

"Out here in filth?" Mother pointed at the seagull on the pier. "You do know what happened to your father? I don't want to lose you in the muck, too." Mother's usually pale face was now so white the veins showed through. "Come back inside where you are safe."

With a wistful glance over his shoulder, Bartholomew trudged to the party. He put his plastic smile back on and kept it there for the rest of the afternoon. But his thoughts were in the bay with the friendly giant. A new friend. He dreamed of exactly how he'd outline the body when he realized how inspired he felt again. A smile curled the corners of his mouth as he imagined a new creation.

Bartholomew glanced around at the room. Not one kid was near his age. He was so tired of being alone. Well, he could at least read for a while, which was kind of like having a friend. Resting one elbow on the table, Bartholomew started to sneak his book out of his jacket pocket.

Mother pinched him. "Sit up like a proper Borax."

He obeyed, but when she wasn't looking, he shook his head, thinking, *I just have to go to school.*

Chapter 11

The Thinker nodded. Using the bearded one worked. The cosmic interference had been overcome, and the boys could create once again.

Alexander Devinci found himself drawn to the water that day. The foam tickled his bare feet as the great wave appeared, his jaw dropping with the Ancient One's surfing antics.

Even when the bearded surfer extended a hand, Alex showed no fear. The sign was a good one. He thrust his arm out easily to the outstretched hand in front of him and shook it as if it were any human's.

The Thinker was glad when he saw the giant's warmth fill each boy with peace. They had both been so confused recently.

Although the giant surfer disappeared when Alex's mother placed her hand on his shoulder, The Thinker knew the vision remained. As Alex reached up and stroked Mrs. Devinci's fingers, the change was written all over his face.

The Deliverers would find joy in paint and pencil once again and so much more. Paper and crayons. Clay and canvas. More Knights of Painted Light would be there to guard dreams. The bronze statue sighed. The prophecy would be fulfilled. Yes, there still was hope for Artania.

Chapter 12

The moment with the giant inspired. Alex just had to paint that mythical-looking man, and this time it would be big, bigger than any project he'd ever done. So he asked Dad if he could have only one more thing for his new garage studio. Money was tight, but Dad had a friend at the university who was a painter. She sold him a large piece of canvas she didn't need for a good price.

When Dad brought home the large rectangular board, Alex couldn't believe it. It was covered in one hundred percent Belgian linen! The kind so strong it resists tears even when it is re-stretched. He immediately saw the giant's face in the fabric. He wouldn't need a single practice sketch.

"Thanks, Dad." Alex nodded but didn't hug his father. One present didn't make up for having to move across country.

They carefully carried the four-by-six feet of canvas out to the garage and leaned it against the wall. When his father bent down to adjust his corner Alex noticed how Dad's light brown hair was getting a little thin on top. Alex grinned and exchanged a glance with Rembrandt.

"Hey, Dad, I think you're missing something."

Mr. Devinci stood. "What?"

"Half your hair!" Alex slapped his knee and guffawed while Rembrandt wagged his tail.

"Some thanks I get." Dad shook his head as a slow grin filled his face. "I take a break from work and rush to Karen's to pick this up. Why? So I can be insulted by a pint-sized painter."

"Yep."

"Well, then, I expect to see something amazing, kiddo. You know what Dr. Bock says?"

"Oh, you will. Really amazing," Alex interrupted, trying to avoid another *Guide to Being the Perfect Parent* lecture.

Dad ruffled Rembrandt's ears and smiled before heading back to the university.

Shivering with excitement, Alex flew to the cabinet on the east wall, grabbed an armful of brushes, and handed them to Rembrandt. The Australian Shepherd gathered the bundle in his mouth and padded to the drop cloth. After depositing them, he settled into his sheepskin bed with a snuffling sigh.

"Good boy," Alex said as he dashed back to the cabinet and scanned the tubes of paint on the shelf. Scooping up a dozen in his t-shirt, he carried them to the easel and laid them side-by-side on the little paint-splattered table. He ran his finger over the row until he found Translucent Turquoise and Zinc White. He squirted some of each onto his wooden palette and stirred carefully until he had the perfect color for the shield.

His gaze swept over the canvas, paintbrush at the ready. Palette resting on his forearm, he paced back and forth. He saw the giant surfing, sailboats bobbing in the bay with the pier off to the right.

He laid down the first brushstroke just as Mom came in holding a plate of blueberry muffins. With a shaky smile, she offered Alex one. He started to reach for it. Then a vision of hanging with his buddies back in Boulder tugged at his memory. He shook his head and turned away.

"I just baked them."

"Sorry. Just not hungry." It wasn't a lie. Remembering his friends took away his appetite.

"I know, but a growing boy needs his strength."

"I'll get one later. Okay? Can I get back to work now?"

Mom nodded silently and walked out.

That night, Alex began painting and kept on until the rest of the summer swam by like a dolphin leaping in and out of the bay. Every morning he rose early and headed straight for the garage. When his grumbling stomach grew too loud, he'd dart into the kitchen to gulp down a quick breakfast. No time for testing Mom's recipes now.

After eating, he was right back at it, until his hands were so cramped they felt like claws. Only then would he take a break. He'd have loved to keep going, but his Dr. Bock quoting Dad would take away his paints if he didn't get daily exercise, so he made sure to skateboard down to the boardwalk. Once there, he'd scan the horizon for the giant, but the smiling creature never returned.

He did find a cool skate park between the boardwalk and the beach. Skirted by palm trees and always busy, it was the perfect place to make some new friends. There was a group of about twenty kids who skated daily. Some were still shrimps, only around six or seven with their moms sitting nearby in case they got hurt. Others were in high school and completely ignored Alex.

But there were three kids just his age who he liked as soon as they skated up in triangular formation. Their elbow and kneepads were worn from so many falls, and even though they each had different colored hair, blond, brown, and red, they all had the same sun-bleached streaks.

"Hey." Alex jerked his head up greeting the blond boy. "That's a pretty cool board. Where'd you get it?"

The kid with the gelled spikes stopped on his way through the gate and eyed Alex before replying. "My mom took me to L.A. Check it out. Sugar-maple deck."

"Awesome. I read in *Skater* those are pretty tough," Alex said.

"Yeah. Dude, you ride?"

Alex nodded.

"What's your name?"

"Alex."

"I'm Zach Van Gromin and over there's Gwen Obranovich and Jose Hamlin." He pointed at the boy with a long dark ponytail standing next to a skinny girl wearing a baseball cap backward. Zach waved Gwen and Jose to come. After they made their introductions, all three watched Alex kick off.

"Okay, Alex. Let's see what you got," the red-headed Gwen said leaning up against a palm tree.

Alex skated around to get a feel for the concrete of this skate park. It was a lot like the one back home in Boulder. Hills, curves, valleys like a huge, empty swimming pool. Then he crouched to try at trick he'd been working on before they moved. Quickly he straightened his arms and legs for the ollie, but his board was going too fast. He fell on his side.

The trio of street surfers laughed. Zach rolled in his direction, Gwen and Jose right behind. They ground to halts in front of him. Zach put out his hand to help Alex up.

"I'm good, thanks." Alex shook his head.

"Not a wimp." Gwen nodded in appreciation, her red pigtails bobbing up and down.

And then he had friends.

For the rest of the summer, they tried more tricks. Gwen was the most daring. She pushed herself to go faster and higher. Alex watched her, analyzing where she put her feet, how she bent her knees on a turn, and the bounce of her skinny legs when she did jumps. So different from Jose who went more for graceful moves where his body and the board became one. Or Zach, who was Mr. Entertainment, waiting for an audience to gather before doing his signature move, a handstand followed by a jump.

Since most of these tricks were new to him, Alex wiped out a lot at first, but he never complained. Gwen wouldn't ever let him hear the end of it. Instead, he would pause a minute and visualize what he'd done wrong. He imagined how he should position his body, which way to lean, and how much to bend his legs. Then he'd tried again. Soon he was doing three-sixties, jumps, and ollies along with the rest of them.

In the evenings, he'd repeat his morning performance, eating as fast as he could before returning to the garage and Rembrandt to paint. Even if his mother invited him to play a hand of rummy or sit and talk on one of the ever more frequent nights when Dad was working late, he declined. He had to create.

One July evening, she asked three times, "Are you sure you don't want to play Scrabble tonight?"

Alex just shook his head. He was too wrapped up in his art to notice the look of loneliness on her face. If he'd been paying attention, he would have seen the forced smile, slight sniffle, and moist eyes.

As he exited the door into the garage, he thought he heard a sob escape Mom's throat. He glanced in her direction, but by then she had put back on her motherly mask, saying, "I must be getting a cold."

Then she turned away.

Chapter 13

Bartholomew yearned to create a sketch or a sculpture to honor the giant. It was all he thought about, but it wasn't allowed. So, he had to be surreptitious, sneaky, and covert. While Mother was busy barking orders at the maids, he crept into the kitchen and opened a cabinet door. Here he found one of the extra cutlery sets. After making sure the coast was clear, he opened the case and glanced at the knives. He selected a larger one for the rougher cuts, a serrated one for the hair, and a small knife for the fine details. Wrapping them in a cloth napkin, he slipped the bundle inside of his sports jacket.

"She'll think they were lost in the move," he said to himself, carefully closing the cabinet door.

As he was heading back up the winding staircase, a voice stopped him dead in his tracks. "Bartholomew, come here."

He looked down to see his mother at the foot of the stairs, her thin white arms crossed over a satin gown. Could she see the outline of the knives in his pocket? Bartholomew swallowed hard, straightened his jacket, and turned to her. "Yes, Mother?"

"I cannot stand all of this remodel filth." She wrinkled her small nose that could sniff out dirt better than a vacuum. "It is unacceptable. So many—" She paused and shuddered. "—messes my nightmares are returning. Thus, I have doubled the cleaning schedule."

Hygenette Borax complained of filth nightmares for as long as Bartholomew could remember. Every time she had one of her bad dreams, she reacted with the same cleaning frenzy.

"Yes, Mother." He took a step.

"I am not finished." She widened her pale blue eyes meaningfully before continuing. "Mr. White has all of the appropriate changes in his calendar. Be sure to go over it with him. But I warn you. Closet Day is now both Tuesday and Saturday. Germs are seeping in through the walls. Make sure your room is ready."

Bartholomew nodded and turned to go.

"And Bartholomew..."

He didn't turn for fear of what she'd say.

"Do bathe. Your face is covered in disgusting perspiration droplets."

He heaved a silent sigh. Gladly! The bathroom was the one place he had privacy. He jogged up the stairs, double-checked the lock, and turned on the faucet to muffle any sculpting sounds. With a quiet smile, he unwrapped the new bar of soap. One good thing about having a mother obsessed with cleanliness was she kept dozens and dozens of them in the linen closet.

His fingers tingled as he set the knives in a neat row on the bath mat. He chose the longest one and leaned over the tub to make that first glorious cut. Then a second. A bit off the top. Long soap shavings fell like autumn leaves into the swirling water. He remembered how the giant's flowing hair had trailed behind him in the breeze, his strong arms and the laurel crown.

Slowly, his vision took shape. Bartholomew picked up a smaller knife and started in on the finer details. He chiseled out the face and trimmed the beard to get the curls just right. Then he smoothed the entire surface with the corner of a dry washcloth until it shone like polished marble.

He placed the finished product on the counter and stood back to admire his work. "You look like an ancient Greek or something."

Almost expecting the sculpture to reply, he leaned in and stared into the tiny face.

A sudden knock made him jump.

That clipped British voice called through the door. "Seventeen minutes, Chappy. Make haste."

"Yes sir, Mr. White." Bartholomew unplugged the tub in case his tutor listened, splashed some water on his face and gave his fingernails a quick scrub. Inside the linen closet, he shoved some towels aside and gently placed the sculpture and knives behind them. He made a mental note to move everything before Closet Day as he smoothed it all back in place.

"See ya soon!" he whispered as he closed the cabinet door. "I'm off to another day's dull lessons with Mr. White.

* * *

Hours later, Bartholomew finally escaped. Could the man have gone on any longer about dependent clauses? Bartholomew got it the first time, and the only reason he made one mistake was he'd been thinking about the giant. He didn't need to spend three hours in an antiseptic room writing and diagramming two hundred sentences.

He needed fresh air. Not the kind hanging over their fumigated patio where all of the sweet-smelling fruit trees had been ripped out, the herb garden bulldozed over, and the fishpond filled in. Everything there was now plastic, Formica, and specially designed astro-turf. Even the plants were artificial.

Parts of the estate were still as lush and green as always. Grandfather Borax's will made sure of it. The acre around the glass conservatory could not be changed. No flower, shrub, or tree could be removed unless it was diseased, and the old gardener, Sam, was who got to decide. When the lawyer told her she couldn't raze the corner acre, too, Mother fumed. "But those nasty weeds are breeding grounds for disease and vermin! Do you want my son to be infected?"

"We have no choice, Mrs. Borax. If you could only see reason," the chubby man in the too tight suit said.

"*If* nothing. How will I keep my child clean?"

The lawyer shrugged, and eleven new rules were added to the list. Eleven different ways to forbid Bartholomew from entering the wooded acre. All typed neatly and placed in the "Cleanliness is Safety" binder.

When he got to the edge of the patio, Bartholomew stole a backward glance at the house. "Please let Mother stay at the hairdresser's," he whispered as he slipped through the gate.

Praying none of the servants had seen him, Bartholomew squirted a dollop of sanitizer from the bottle in his pocket for luck and rubbed it into his hands before ducking into the underbrush. He tiptoed past ferns, miner's lettuce, and valley oaks. Bartholomew breathed in the sweet smell of bark and earth as he remembered walking here hand-in-hand with Grandfather.

He parted a wall of weeping willow branches and gasped. He had forgotten how magical this place was. An enormous glass house with a sunburst-shaped gable over white-framed double doors perched at the top of a little hill. Flagstone walkways curved up to the entry where friendly vines waved him in. The low rose-colored wall supporting the structure contained stones so smooth that when Bartholomew ran a hand over them, he felt like he was touching Grandfather's freshly-shaven face.

Bartholomew turned the door handle, took a tentative step inside, and whistled long and low. Color was everywhere. Vibrantly painted ceramic pots. Flowers of every hue. Inspirational plaques. Next to the door, a clown-shaped shrub peppered with cloth polka dots and a wig of yarn welcomed him.

"Hello," Bartholomew said, running his hand over the rainbow hair sprouting from its head.

Then he saw the bubbling angel fountain and recalled Grandfather's words. "This is my special place. Please remember. . . ."

"I remember," Bartholomew said, holding his hands to his chest. He slowly turned round and round. "I will care for it, Grandfather."

Bartholomew knew what his vow meant. It wouldn't be easy. All his lies would have to be carefully thought out.

"I won't get caught, either." He knew if Mother so much as found him near a filthy plant, she would destroy every single one of them. Even if keeping them alive was required by Grandfather's will.

"Aww, a sick fern." Bartholomew bent down. "Do you need water?" He rubbed one brown leaf between his fingers. It was plastic! Why would Grandfather put a dead-looking plastic fern in here?

He turned the brown leaf over. Glued on the underside was a small sign: *Pull, Bartholomew.* Shrugging, he gave it a yank.

A sound like a key turning a lock clicked under him. He looked down. Nothing unusual. He was just about to tug the leaf again when the ground disappeared, and his feet hung in space.

"Hel-l-p!" he cried.

Arms flailing wildly, he slid below into the darkness. Whooshing, skidding, bumping trying to claw at the emptiness.

Then, umph-thud, and he was at the bottom, feet splayed out. Spluttering, he sat there, his back against something hard. He started to reach behind to figure out what it was, when he heard a noise. His eyes widened.

He looked up to see a trap door rigged with wires. It was making a mouse-like sound as it swung back and forth. As he adjusted to the dim light, he realized he was sitting on a long plastic chute leading to the conservatory above.

This huge underground room of cement block walls seemed to go on forever. Bartholomew knew this was just an optical illusion, but it was still creepy. The floor was tiled in polished adobe squares, and there was a spiral staircase about 30 feet away, which led to a hatch in the wood paneled ceiling. Why didn't Grandfather ever mention this place?

Biting his lip, Bartholomew took a tentative step onto what felt like a squeaky toy.

"Welcome Bartholomew!" A booming voice filled the room.

"Grandfather?"

"You are hearing a recording, dear boy…one made just for you. I know you have a thousand questions, and all will be answered in due time. If you will walk forward, we can begin."

Tripping on his shoelace, Bartholomew fell backwards and triggered the squeaky toy's blaring message.

"Welcome–"

With a groan, he bent down and tied his shoes in a double knot. Shaking his head, he reminded himself to be more careful.

"Switch on the lights to your right."

Bartholomew groped to his left but found only air.

"Your other right, boy. You always did have trouble with directions. Hee hee!"

This time Bartholomew found the switch and turned it on. What he saw in the basement made his jaw drop. All around him were art supplies. Not just a few crayons. Oh, no! There were shelves from floor to ceiling with bags of clay, potter's wheels, and sculpting knives. Large canvases were stacked in one corner with an assortment of paintbrushes, paints, and pencils above them. A huge gas-fired kiln sat in one corner. A library of instructional books, videos, and DVDs waited near the trap door. And so much more. It was a dream come true.

On one wall, hung a television and DVD player with a sign: *Turn on. Push play.* He obliged and sat in the La-Z-Boy chair opposite to see what greater mysteries this place had in store. As the screen flickered, an image of his grandfather took shape.

He was standing in front of the bookshelves. He looked as he always had with hair a little wild like Einstein, an old-fashioned waistcoat hanging loosely from his shoulders, and his mischievous grin showing perfect teeth in a wrinkled face. "If you are watching this, then I am dead, and your mother has followed the instructions in my will."

Bartholomew nodded sadly.

"As you can see, I have carefully hidden this fortress from all but the most adventurous. I knew Hygenette would never set foot in here, but I was banking on you maybe bending her rules a bit."

Grandfather's eyes twinkled.

"I've been watching you, boy. Ever since you were a little feller, I've noticed a faraway look. I thought you might have inherited the gift. I wasn't sure until two summers ago. Remember when I came to visit?"

"Yes," Bartholomew whispered.

"While you and your mother were out one day shopping for one of those fine outfits she so painstakingly chooses for you, I decided to have a look around your room. I hope you don't mind, but I thought it odd a boy your age would spend so much time in the bath. Even with a mother like Hygenette. I found your hidden lion sculpture. Oh, Barty, it was wonderful."

Tears welled up in Bartholomew's eyes. Someone to share his joy! Never in his wildest dreams did he think he'd meet someone who could understand. Why did it have to be now after he was gone?

"I kept looking around. I had to know how far you'd come, and if you were one of us. I found your sketches behind the picture frames. I must say how very clever to put them where your mother couldn't find them. It was when I knew. You were exactly like your father and me. You had to create or feel your soul shrivel. We were lucky and could do so in the open, but after you were born, your mother turned away from it all. I suppose the accident had a lot to do with her reaction. It's when I changed my will and made this fortress for you."

Grandfather paused and turned the camera toward the art supplies behind him.

"Here you can make all you want and more," he said with a sweeping motion of his arm. "You will find doorways to places in your mind you never knew existed. I left enough supplies to last you years. I even included a shower and washer and dryer so you can return to Hygenette 'unsullied.'" Grandfather made quotation marks with his aged hands at the last word. "The power is tied into the pool house, cleverly, if I do say so. Your mother need never know about this place."

Grandfather paused and stepped closer to the camera. His face became very serious.

"I do want to warn you, though. Dangerous forces lurk out there. Those seeking to change people like us. You will need to be on your guard and keep creating because when these forces aren't successful…" Grandfather trailed off and got a very sad look on his face. "People close to you can get hurt. Badly."

Bartholomew thought of Father's drowning. Was it possible it hadn't been an accident? He chewed on his lower lip.

"So go on. What are you waiting for? Get to work, boy." The TV image of Grandfather waved and disappeared.

Bartholomew stared into the screen, and a tear rolled down his cheek. He didn't wipe it away.

"Thank you," he whispered. Bartholomew mused until the screen faded to blue and static crackled from the speakers. He blinked, and a smile crept up at the corners of his mouth.

Free to create anything? Sketches I can hang on the walls and smile at? Sculptures of clay I can talk to? Grandfather was right. What was he waiting for? There was work to do.

And he knew just where to begin.

* * *

Bartholomew skipped into the house, smiling brightly at everyone he saw. When he passed Mrs. Borax in the hall, he called out, "Good afternoon, Mother!"

"What are you smiling about?"

"I guess I'm just happy."

"Well, stop it."

"Yes, ma'am."

"In business, there should be no nonsense. How are you ever going to take over if you go around with such a silly look on your face?"

"Sorry, Mother." Bartholomew frowned solemnly. Until he walked past her. Then his grin spread as wide as the arms of the giant on his magical birthday. Even hearing "nonsense" couldn't mar this perfect moment.

Day after day, Bartholomew snuck into his underground workshop to work on his sculpture. He always began the same way. First, he'd wiggle his fingers to warm them up. Then he'd stretched out his arms and picture the giant. Finally, he did his clay dance. Like the *Nutcracker* ballet he'd seen last Christmas, he performed pirouettes over the eyes, waltzes through the hair of his new friend, and leaps over clothing folds.

Sometimes he even thought he heard the applause of an audience roaring in his ears. Then he'd give a celebratory wave to his imaginary fans, giggling to himself all the while. When his giant was complete, Bartholomew bowed deeply before it. "Welcome to my studio, dear friend."

Carefully following the directions his grandfather left him, he fired the sculpture in the kiln. Then he applied the glaze and baked it again. What came out made his jaw drop. Not only did it look exactly like the giant he had seen on his birthday, but it also seemed alive. Bartholomew was sure if he turned his back, it would tap him on the shoulder and ask him to play. But of course, sculptures don't move. That's impossible.

Just as Bartholomew had bowed at the feet of his finished giant sculpture, he was bowing to the orders of ever-frenzied Hygenette Borax. It was time to get ready for school.

School. A real school. Maybe he'd join the swim team and make lots of friends. He'd been training with a swim coach since he was five and was now pretty good. Thankfully, there was one sport even a cleaning obsessed woman like Hygenette could approve of.

Bartholomew could barely contain his excitement. For years, he dreamed of this, but only now did his mother think he was ready to face a foul world.

Mother was reluctant at first.

"I mean really, all of those filthy little children with their nasty noses and dirty fingernails. How can I send my nice clean baby out into that?"

Bartholomew promised to wash his hands with his own soap and carry an arsenal of towels, cleaning wipes, and anti-bacterial lotions in case he were to touch any other children. (He thought the emergency kit idea was close to genius, knowing how much his mother loved cleaning supplies.) In the end, his mother relented, but not until after she'd inspected the local schools. She planned to send him to a private one at first, but when she saw their neighborhood school, she decided it would do. It was moderately clean, for a house of sniveling little germ makers, that is.

"Come, Bartholomew. Time to shop for more slacks. What if the other seventy-three pair become sullied by those disgusting children?" Mother asked, waving Bartholomew into the stretch limousine.

Mrs. Borax designed this limo herself. The headrests had been removed and replaced with rolls of examining room paper. Every seat was covered, so whenever Bartholomew rode in it, he felt like he was at the doctor's office ready to get another vaccination against the latest disease. If he moved even the slightest inch, the paper would crackle, making Mother scold, "Be still, Bartholomew, like a proper Borax!"

There were three built-in hand sanitizers: one on the front dash for the chauffeur, and two behind the front seats. A scented air purifier hummed from the floor. Of course, this wasn't enough for a woman like Hygenette Borax. She had to be able to bathe, so behind the second privacy screen, a bubbling bathtub was always ready.

Bartholomew smilingly went along with the hours of shopping, the constant disinfectant wiping on each department door handle, and the midday stop to bathe. It didn't bother him one bit. Even the idea of Mr. White returning from his holiday to prep him for sixth grade didn't give Bartholomew the usual knot in the pit of his stomach.

It was school he was going to, and he knew it would be just great.

Chapter 14

Fighting the urge to read just one more chapter in *The Olympians*, Bartholomew sat up straight in his seat, paying strict attention to every word passing Mrs. Rodriguez's lips.

"There will be respect and responsibility in this class. We have a tradition of high standards at Montecito Elementary, and as sixth-graders, I expect you to set an example for all the younger children."

Bartholomew nodded at his dark-haired teacher. *I like her face. It reminds me of* La Pietà *by Michelangelo Mr. White showed me last year.*

A grin crept up at the corners of his mouth as he stole a glance at the other children. Maybe if he were very well-behaved, they would notice and want to befriend him. Perhaps there was a kid like from the *Ivan the Inspector* series who would ask Bartholomew to solve a mysterious case. Or another, like in the science fiction short he'd read, who was looking for an inventing partner. Maybe he could design robots with the long-haired boy in the front. He wondered which kid would ask him to come over and do homework. He smoothed the crème-colored sleeves of his sports coat. Maybe all of them!

He glanced around again. His heart sank and the smile disappeared. Oh, no!

The boy he'd bumped into last summer, Alex, was sitting two rows away, exchanging nods with a few of the kids. He scanned the room and, to Bartholomew's horror, Alex's eyes met his.

The single look made Bartholomew feel naked. He gulped and turned back before breaking out in a cold sweat. His palms felt like ice. He rubbed them over his neatly pressed slacks, leaving two long skid marks of perspiration.

"Look, a kid wearing a tie. What a freak." A huge boy right behind Bartholomew said under his breath.

When Bartholomew turned, the gigantic kid with spiked hair was sneering.

Until that moment, Bartholomew had no idea how different it was for a kid to wear a suit and tie to school. In the books he read, many children wore uniforms. At his birthday party, the boys dressed like him. He glanced down at his shining black shoes. comparing them to the tapping and wiggling feet around the room. He was the only one wearing dress shoes! Even the girls wore tennies.

Bartholomew tried to find something else to think about so he wouldn't turn red. He looked around at inspirational posters of cartoon characters reading, a shining globe, and baskets of flash cards. When he saw an entire art center, he gulped. Wallpaper-covered coffee cans filled with paint brushes, markers, and scissors, stacks of construction paper sketch pads, and a pile of glorious colorful clay all welcomed him in.

He always knew his family was different but hadn't realized how different until that moment. Why had his mother forbade art? Did she revel in torturing him? He became so lost in this puzzle he didn't notice the teacher calling him. "Bartholomew? Bartholomew? Bartholomew!"

"Yes, ma'am?" he mumbled as if waking from a dream.

The huge boy sniggered again, and there were scattered giggles from the back of the room. Bartholomew's face grew hot. Mrs. Rodriguez held up her hand for silence. "Tell us your name and your favorite animal."

"Me?"

"Yes, you." She gave him a patient smile.

"My name is Bartholomew Borax III. And my favorite animal, well, it's a difficult question, ma'am."

"Yes, but which one do you like best? If you could be one, which would it be?"

Bartholomew thought for a moment. Would he fly? Or swim? Or run like a cheetah? Only then, he couldn't sculpt. Which animal was a sculptor?

The class waited in silence. Seconds passed, but still Bartholomew couldn't come up with anything. One red-haired girl snickered, showing a mouthful of bright green braces. If he hadn't been so nervous, Bartholomew would have made a mental note to draw them later. The teacher raised her eyebrows expectantly as kids shifted in their seats.

"An African termite!" he finally blurted.

The entire class burst into laughter. Even the kind-faced teacher grinned. Bartholomew hung his head, trying to hide the crimson creeping up in his cheeks. It only made things worse.

"Look, he's even hunched over like a bug!" the spike haired boy jeered, sticking two fingers on either side of his head like antenna. A round of laughter crawled into Bartholomew's ears.

Mrs. Rodriguez's smile vanished. She placed her hands on her hips and said, "Ty Bragg, pull your card! You have lost recess."

Ty pushed back his chair angrily and glared at Bartholomew as he trudged to the detention cards. His eyes burned into Bartholomew's already hot face. *So not only am I a joke, but now somebody is in trouble because of me.*

He wished he could be anywhere else. Even sitting at the dinner table with his mother who cried filth at the slightest crumb was better than this.

The rest of the morning dragged by so slowly that he thought he was in some kind of time warp. Every time he got the courage to steal a glance at one of the other kids, he was met with one of two things: a scowl or indifference. Some kids looked like they'd be really nice. One boy with a long brown ponytail had such a depth to his eyes it made

Bartholomew sure he'd be interesting to talk to. But the boy never looked his way.

At recess, Bartholomew decided to make himself invisible. *If they don't see me, they can't laugh at me*, he thought as he hid behind a tree and watched Alex, Jose, Zach, and the redheaded Gwen dash out to the field. The four bantered and joked as they kicked the soccer ball toward some fifth graders for a game.

At lunch, he ate at the fourth grade table, taking some small comfort in the fact they didn't make faces at him. Then he hid in the stall of the bathroom until some tattletale cried, "There's a boy fooling around in the bathroom!" to the hall monitor.

"Hey, you, kid, get out of there," a boy who looked like he was big enough to drive shouted.

Bartholomew tripped out the door, more snickers echoing in his ears. Afterward, he just stood in the shadows of an empty wall, picking at a small string beginning to unravel on his dress shirt. He knew when he got home his mother would throw it out. No frayed edges in her son's wardrobe. But he didn't care. He kept tugging and pulling on it until he bored a nickel sized hole near his waist.

The afternoon was more of the same. When the dismissal bell finally rang, he tried to pack up slowly so he could be the last in line to leave the room. The huge Ty kid seemed to own that spot. "What do you think you're doing, bug-boy?"

"Lining up." Bartholomew stared at his shoes, afraid to look this kid in the face. Ty towered over him and probably outweighed him by a good thirty pounds.

"Well, line up somewhere else. This is our spot." He jerked a thumb toward Conrad, his thick-necked friend who nodded stupidly at every word.

"I apologize." Bartholomew stood in front of the two gargantuans, but the change didn't make things better. One of them pushed him so hard he bumped right into Alex.

"Hey, watch it," Alex said.

"It wasn't my fault."

Alex rolled his eyes and turned away.

Ty shoved him again, once more launching him onto Alex's back.

"I said, watch it!"

"It's not me. It's them." Bartholomew pointed his chin at Ty and Conrad. To Bartholomew's amazement, Alex didn't cower or move away from these bullies. Instead, he stepped right up to them.

"You guys cool it," Alex growled under his breath. "Or I'll make sure you have no recess until Christmas."

"Yeah?" Ty grunted curling his hand into a fist. Conrad awkwardly copied him.

"Just try me." Never taking his eyes off them, he took a step toward Mrs. Rodriguez.

For long moments, Ty and Alex's eyes were locked in a visual tug-of-war. Just when Bartholomew was sure Ty was about to punch Alex in the face, the gargantuan looked away. "Aww, that wimp's not worth it."

Bartholomew heaved a sigh of relief.

"Thanks." He extended his hand to Alex.

Alex didn't take it. Instead, he shook his head. "Just stay away from me."

Bartholomew looked down and trudged forward. *Wouldn't even accept my hand.* When he saw the white limousine idling in the parking lot, he forgot about the no running rules and tore loose from the line like a sheet in a hurricane.

He jerked the door handle open and collapsed on the paper-covered seat. A loud rip filled the car. Bartholomew looked down. He'd split the seat cover.

"Bad day, chappy?" Mr. White asked, raising his perfectly waxed eyebrows.

Bartholomew didn't reply. He crossed his arms and slouched down as far as

he could.

Chapter 15

While skating home with Jose and Gwen, Alex thought about the figure slumped against the wall watching their soccer game earlier in the day. The rich boy stood there every day for two weeks now. Straightening his stupid white tie he always wore with a hangdog look on his face or rubbing in more hand sanitizer. Part of Alex felt sorry for Bartholomew, and Alex even thought of asking the guy to play. For about four seconds, maybe. Then he remembered the strange vision he'd had when they grazed hands. The memory sent a chill up his spine. He shook his head. Better stay away from the kid. He's creepy.

Gwen ground her board on the curb, then came to a stop. "Gotta go. My dad's waiting."

"See ya," Alex called, watching her do a 360 before kicking off toward her house. He turned to Jose, whose long brown hair came loose from its ponytail. "Want to head to the park? We could practice fakies."

"I have yoga class. Maybe Saturday."

"Okay. Later."

Jose's exit was less flashy than Gwen's. Alex admired how he carved a long arc in the street as if he were doing a figure eight, before effortlessly jumping the curb to head east.

Alex didn't really want to go home, but Zach was gone, too, off to get his hair cut again. It seemed like he was at the barber's every other week. With Mr. Fashion gone, there was no one to skate with. As he pushed off, Alex sighed, imagining Mom begging to play Scrabble or some boring game as soon as he got home. But if it's what she wanted to do, maybe he would play. It was probably about time for him to start being nice to her.

Twenty minutes later, a half-finished glass of milk and chocolate chip cookie crumbs sat between Alex and his mother.

"And then during the soccer game, this jerk named Ty tried to kick another boy and pretend he was just chasing the ball, so I sat on the ball until he stopped. Man, I hate kids like him," Alex said, his mouth full of cookies.

"You've always stood up for the underdog, sweetheart."

Alex shrugged. "Mom, the rich kid, Bartholomew Three, is in my class. He is so weird. He wears a white suit every day like some mad scientist or something."

"That poor boy is only different, hon."

"Poor? *Not.* He gets picked up by a limo every day."

"One can have all the money in the world and still be poor. He seemed lonely when he was here."

"I know you would have wanted me to talk to him, but Mom, there's something wrong with him. It's like there's a spell on him or something."

She smiled and reached across the table. Alex didn't place his hand in hers. She pulled it away and looked at him.

"You don't have to be buddies, but I would like you to try to imagine how it must be for him. Not everyone makes friends as easily as you. I don't."

"You had friends back in Colorado."

"Yes, I did. Thanks for reminding me of that."

Alex gave her a half smile and picked up his dish. He took a step toward the sink. Then he froze. Mom was clutching at her blouse, her jaw open wide. She sputtered and gasped, seeming to fight for breath.

"Mom! Mom! What's wrong?"

Her hands shot to her throat. No sound came out. She mouthed his name.

The dish slipped from his hand and shattered into a thousand pieces. He wanted to go to her but couldn't move. He was trapped as if at the end of a long tunnel.

Mom again reached her hand for his as she desperately sucked for air. Then her head slumped.

"No!" Alex cried. He leaped over the table and grabbed her by the shoulders. He shook her. Once, twice. "Mom, Mom." Her eyes fluttered but stayed shut.

A knot gripped his gut. What to do? What to do? His desperate gaze darted around the kitchen where chocolate chip sweetness still hung in the air. This was the kitchen where she served those crazy tribal recipes and where she'd baked and decorated his paintbrush-topped birthday cake. He couldn't lose her. His vision blurred as he rushed to the phone.

"Nine one one? Help! My mom won't wake up. Come quick," Alex sobbed. "Please!" Leaving the phone dangling, Alex darted back to her side. He wrapped his wiry arms around her and repeated her name again and again. Trembling, he pressed his cheek to hers.

"It'll be all right, Mom. You'll see. It's gonna be okay. Everything's gonna be okay. Come on, Mom. Don't go away." The smell of her lavender shampoo filled his nostrils. "Be all right. Please be okay."

When the fireman tapped his shoulder, Alex gaped at him. Who was this monster in his home? He clung to Mom's blouse. Willing his body to protect her. Refusing to let go.

"No!" he screamed as two policemen pried his arms loose.

One button came off in the struggle. A single brown circle. Almost the same hazel color as her eyes.

Later, in the waiting room of the hospital, Alex sat on cold plastic and took the button from his pocket. It seemed like an accusing eye staring at him. He remembered how lonely she'd seemed all summer. She asked him to play cards or taste recipes so many times, but Alex had been too busy painting. He recalled one night when he thought she'd been crying. *It's my fault. I shouldn't have left you so much.*

He thought and laid a hand on his father's shoulder. At first Dad's bloodshot eyes stared without recognition. Then he opened his mouth.

"In situations like this, Dr. Bock says... says..." Dad couldn't even quote the book. With a choking sob, he grabbed Alex's wrist and pulled him into his lap. He rocked back and forth, cradling Alex as if he were a baby. "It'll be all right. You'll see. These doctors know what they are doing."

Alex buried his face in his father's neck. Long wracking sobs filled his body.

From now on, it'll be different. I swear no more running off to the garage. I promise I'll stop painting if you'll just open your eyes.

It was a promise he fully intended to keep.

* * *

From far away in his lair in Subterranea, Captain Sludge sensed Alex's pain. He would use it to his advantage. Now was the time to invade this boy's dreams. He would use his nightmare weapons. The creations would stop, and victory would be his. The Knights of Painted Light would fade into forgetfulness. He gathered his troops and outlined his plan.

The soldiers crossed over and waited for nightfall.

Chapter 16

Bartholomew glanced around the classroom fearfully, knowing at any moment he might do something to cause the ridicule he learned was part of school. If he raised his hand with the right answer, Ty would hiss, "Suck-up." But if he weren't paying attention when the teacher called upon him, the whole class sniggered.

The faces seeming friendly the first day? Zach's forest green eyes could have shared the secret of the conservatory. But no, Zach was too cool with his designer clothes and haircut. Jose's peaceful voice may have shared thoughts on the latest dragon book by Arthur Mystwrite, but Jose never glanced his way. Bartholomew didn't even want to think about making friends with Alex. He was too tough. Anyhow, he hadn't been in class for a few days.

Just then, Alex walked into the classroom. He looked different. His cocky grin had been replaced by a sad scowl. He was thinner, and his eyes were bloodshot. Had he been sick?

"I'm so sorry to hear about your mother," Mrs. Rodriguez said as she took the hall pass from Alex. "Is she better?"

"A little." Alex shifted his weight from one foot to the other. "We still don't know exactly what's wrong."

Mrs. Rodriguez patted Alex's shoulder.

Mrs. Devinci sick? She was so nice. *I hope it's nothing serious,* Bartholomew thought, but when he stole a glance, he instantly knew the answer. Alex's pale face told him everything. He didn't like this kid but still, his mom. He wished he could do something to make the other boy feel better.

Bartholomew's eyes glazed over as he imagined how it must have been. It'd feel like cold icicles piercing your chest and staying stuck there. Worse than when Grandfather died. His mind wandered so much he didn't notice his hand moving. He glanced down. Where did the pencil come from? To his surprise, he had sketched a portrait of Mrs. Devinci. She looked just like he'd remembered; head full of dark curls, soft brown eyes crinkling in the corners, and a loving smile filling her face.

Should he give it to Alex? Or would it just make him angrier? Bartholomew was trying to decide what to do when Mrs. Rodriguez passed by his desk, stopped, and crossed her arms. "Bartholomew! What is the assignment?"

He sat upright and tried to cover the picture with his hand.

"Umm, sentence corrections?"

"Is this a sentence?" she asked, pointing at his portrait.

"No, ma'am. It's a picture."

"Is it art time?"

"No. Language."

"Then why are you drawing instead of writing?"

He shrugged. "Sometimes a picture just wants to become."

Mrs. Rodriguez picked up the paper as if to crumple it but paused when she saw the picture. Her face softened and she whistled.

"This is beautiful, Bartholomew. I've never seen any student draw like this. Class, look at what Bartholomew drew. It seems we have quite the artist here." She held up the sketch and showed it to the class.

Scattered voices called out compliments. Redheaded Gwen nodded and gave him a thumbs up. Zach asked him if he could draw some Anime characters, and Jose gave him a Buddha smile.

Bartholomew didn't dare look in Alex's direction. He'd already seen an example of Alex's temper and had no idea how he'd react. Nervously, he peeked over his notebook to find Alex's unblinking eyes staring into his. He quickly looked away. Still, he couldn't help but steal another glance across the room.

Alex returned his gaze with a curt nod of acknowledgement. He mouthed, "Recess."

Bartholomew's heart soared! Could this really be a friend?

Time slows when you are a kid waiting for recess. The ticking seconds crept like a sloth with a broken leg. Bartholomew must have looked at the clock fifty times, but eternal minutes still remained.

Finally! The bell! He folded his hands politely, hoping Mrs. Rodriguez would dismiss his row first. Oh, stupid Ty! He's always fooling around. Now our row will be the last out the door. By then it'll be too late. Alex will be on the soccer field. *I'll be left alone. Again.*

With slumped shoulders, he filed out. Last. Great. Bartholomew scanned the halls and blacktop. No Alex. He wasn't on the soccer field or on the swings. *Maybe I just imagined it. Maybe he wasn't even looking at me. I'm never going to make any friends here.* Bartholomew took up his usual post on the wall, trying to blend in with the paint. With a sigh, he leaned back.

"How did you do that?" a voice asked.

Bartholomew looked around. No one was there.

"What?"

"I said, how did you do that? Did you have a photo or something?"

"Who's there?"

Alex stepped out of the shadows, emerging from his hiding place around the corner. He walked to Bartholomew, fists clenched his at his sides. He got up on tiptoes and looked down through narrowed hazel eyes. His strong jaw was clenched, and his curly hair quivered like an angry raincloud ready to release a storm. "Are you trying to mess with my mind?" Alex asked.

"No. I wouldn't."

"Then why?"

Bartholomew shrugged. How can you explain the gift of inspiration? "Sometimes," he said, "things just come. I don't know why."

"I don't believe you. How could you draw my mom so good? It was too perfect. You must have copied a picture. Did you steal one from my house?"

"I didn't. I swear."

"But it was her. With her eyes."

Bartholomew didn't answer.

"Why her? Why not someone else?"

"I don't know!"

"You stole! I know it." Alex cried, grabbing Bartholomew by the collar.

"No, really! Her face just appeared in my mind."

"Liar!" he said shoving Bartholomew against the wall.

It happened again. Time stopped. All around him was a riot of color. Orange and purple lightning bolts split the air. Then far off in the distance, he saw faces but unlike any he'd ever seen, except in dreams. As he stared at this brilliant land, a cheer arose from the crowd, filling his ears with the cacophony of hope.

Alex jerked away, and the dream vanished. Bartholomew stood there, panting. His body shaking, he raised a hand to his face to make sure he was awake and took two steps back from Alex, who opened his mouth. "What was—"

"—that?" Bartholomew completed the question. He grinned. This wasn't a spell or sickness. They had discovered something new, a place beyond. "Did you see the sky?" Bartholomew asked. "If only I could paint it."

"Yeah, and those mountains. Oh, the color."

"Those faces were awfully strange," Bartholomew said.

"Yeah, totally weird. But it's like they were cheering for us. You think?"

Bartholomew nodded. Then he remembered a dream he'd had weeks before. A beautiful world he could hold in his hands. Father showed it to him. Odd he hadn't remembered until just then. He longed to share his secret with Alex, but he couldn't. Not yet. "What do you think all this means?" Bartholomew asked.

"Heck if I know," Alex replied. "But I think it has something to do with being mad or upset or something."

"Perhaps strong emotions bring out our extrasensory perception."

"Extra-what?" Alex tilted his head to one side.

"ESP. You must have read about it. Many scientists believe an entire part of our brains is untapped, except in a special few who have the ability to read minds and step outside of time."

"Kind of like super powers, huh?"

Bartholomew nodded. Then a smile crept into the corner of his mouth. He shot a playful glance at Alex, then ran for the swings.

"There's only one left, and I'm getting it!" he called over his shoulder.

"Not if I get there first!" Alex cried giving chase.

They arrived at the same time, and each grabbed a chain. Glaring at each other like a couple of puppies ready to wrestle, they feigned leaps for the seat.

Then Alex pointed at the sky with his mouth agape. Bartholomew turned, and Alex jumped on the seat, laughing.

"Hey! Foul play!"

"Made you look!" Alex teased, pumping higher and higher.

* * *

The Thinker watched their friendship begin as many friendships do with false starts and feints, goofy looks and games. Alex showed Bartholomew how to relax more on the playground, and Bartholomew helped Alex with English. Both boys dreamed of art projects, but only Bartholomew continued working. Alex simply couldn't paint. Not with his mother so sick. But still neither shared their creations with the other. Old habits of protecting them die hard. If only they had opened those doors, the journey into his world might have been easier.

Chapter 17

Alex glared at the ugly curtain hanging over Mom's hospital bed. He hated this place. The medicinal smell of alcohol and sickness filled his nostrils. He covered his nose, but he couldn't shut out the sounds of the moaning lady on the other side of the room.

Mom looked so small behind the metal railings. He stroked her dark hair, his hand wandering over her short curls like a boat lost in the fog. He spent many hours just like this one, always wishing he were anywhere but here.

He kept thinking about her attack. *Heart attack was what the doctors said.* But she was too young. Those weren't supposed to happen until you were old, with gray hair and wrinkles.

The monitors beeped faster, and Mom's eyes fluttered. Alex pasted his smile back on. No sad faces for Mom.

"Alex?" With a weak yawn, she glanced up. "Honey? Are you here again?" Her voice didn't have any of the joyful song Alex was used to. It was dry and hoarse like a little kid who'd been crying for hours. She squeezed Alex's hand. "You're spending too much time here. It's not good for a boy your age. Dr. Bock says—"

"It's all right," he reassured her. "I don't mind." He shrugged and held out a cup of water for her.

Mom took a long sip from the bent straw. "Sweetheart, you don't look good. You have dark circles under your eyes."

"I'm fine."

She raised her eyebrows. "What about your art?"

"I'm just not into it right now."

"Not into art? You?" Mom propped herself up on one elbow. "Alex, listen. You were born to draw. I've known that since you were a baby. It's part of who you are."

He would have liked to tell her all about it. How he had come to dread sleep. How he paced for hours, avoiding his hateful bed. Yet he didn't. He would deal with nightmares on his own.

He looked at her but kept quiet. She couldn't know every night he stayed awake as long as he could, walking back and forth until he fell into bed, exhausted—hoping if he was tired enough, he wouldn't dream. It didn't work.

As soon as sleep grabbed him, the nightmares clutched his mind, and every happy painting he'd ever made morphed into life-support machines where bellows rose and fell, a heart monitor beeped, and an I.V. dripped precious fluid into Mom's wrist.

Then the horrors began. The I.V. stopped feeding her veins, and Mom's face paled. Holes would appear all over the ventilators thinning her whistling breath. The surreal heart monitor blips slowed until finally, every machine shut off, and there was silence.

He always woke in a cold sweat. Hating art and what it could do to Mom.

"You will not stop painting on my account. Do you hear me?"

Alex nodded miserably. How could he tell his mother he'd taken all his paintings and shoved them into a box in the garage? How he couldn't bear to look at them? That they frightened him? Alex stared at the heart monitor beeping steadily next to Mom's bed. The doctors said she had a weak heart. He couldn't upset her.

"That's my boy. Now you run along and go have some fun. It's Saturday, for heaven's sakes."

Careful to avoid the I.V. line attached to her arm, Alex gently hugged her. He took two steps toward the door but stopped and glanced over his shoulder. Mom looked so thin and pale. The boy reached deep into his pocket for the brown button he'd been keeping since his mother had her heart attack. It wasn't there!

He'd been rubbing its smooth wood between his fingers constantly these last two weeks. To Alex, it was a good luck charm to heal Mom, and he felt like losing it foretold a terrible future.

"It's okay, Alex. If all those tests go well, I'll be coming home tomorrow. Now shoo!" She waved him from the room.

Hands deep in his pockets, Alex wandered the Santa Barbara streets. All around him were happy sights and sounds. Tourists laughed as they yucked it up for photos. Families bicycled on paths near the beach. Runners nodded at him as they jogged beneath swaying palm trees. He didn't smile back. If any of them knew how he'd treated his mom, they wouldn't smile.

He just kept going. For hours he drifted, feeling like a helium balloon caught in cross currents. He floated up and down the pier. Near the skate park, he saw Gwen and Zach practicing. They tried waving him over, but he shook his head.

He went up the hills near the mission and botanical gardens with no idea of where he'd been or where he was headed. By late afternoon, he was surprised to find himself in Bartholomew's neighborhood. Why not? He was there anyhow.

Although they'd exchanged addresses, Alex had never been to Bartholomew's house. He knew the Boraxes were wealthy, but he didn't realize how rich until he turned onto their street. Most of the houses looked like palaces with lawns as big as the one at school.

Alex found it—621 Summer Drive—and shook his head. This was not the entry to a house. No way. This was a king's fortress. Two tall pillars with glass lantern tops flanked a curved white gate while security cameras peered down from either side.

Alex peeked through the wrought iron bars. No wonder Bartholomew was so uptight. This place looked like a prison. After pacing a couple of times, he clenched his jaw and pushed the intercom button.

"Yes, whom may I say is calling?" the voice from the speaker intoned.

"It's Alexander Devinci. I go to school with the rich—I mean, Bartholomew the Third. Ahem. Can he come out?"

"One moment, please."

Tapping his foot, Alex ran his eyes over the estate. What a place. The entry itself was amazing. Two huge stone lions sat back on their haunches a few feet inside the gate. They were so realistic he was sure at any minute, they'd stand up and order him to scram.

"You may enter, Master Alexander," the voice on the intercom ordered.

The gates yawned open as if the waiting boy bored them. Alex took a few tentative steps. He examined one of the bushes and bent down for closer look. It was fake! He waded through a few more. They were all plastic and planted in brown Styrofoam. No way! Curious, he tramped farther in and finally found real shrubs and soil.

Bartholomew jogged down the hill to meet him.

"Hello, there! To what may I attribute the honor?"

Alex looked at him quizzically.

"What? Oh, why am I here? I was cruising around the neighborhood. I don't know." He waded through the ferns, hopped over the bushes, and faced Bartholomew.

"It's a pleasure!" Bartholomew shifted from one foot to the other. Both boys stood awkwardly for several moments, not saying a word.

"So you gonna show me around or what?" Alex said finally, breaking the ice.

"Oh, do forgive me. It's just we get visitors so infrequently." Beckoning Alex to follow him, he turned and led the way up the drive.

Alex trailed along, thinking. This is unreal. Nobody lives like this. It's like being in a movie. The grounds were perfectly manicured with paths meandering off into the underbrush. An oyster-shell white driveway swept up the hill. Even the apartment over the garage was as big as his whole house.

And the mansion! The front doors arched high like a castle drawbridge. Alex was imagining knights shooting arrows at him from above when he tripped and bumped into a tall, thin woman.

"Who is this little, umm… urchin?" the lady in the long white gown asked through tight lips.

"Mother, this is Alexander Devinci. He attends Montecito Elementary with me. Alex, this is my mother, Mrs. Hygenette Borax."

Mrs. Borax wrinkled her nose and looked Alex up and down as if she were examining some disgusting piece of garbage. She smoothed her satin dress. "How do you do, young man? To what do we owe the, hmm, ah, pleasure?" she asked, obviously feeling no pleasure at all.

"I wanted to see if Bartholomew could hang out."

"Yes, well, I suppose children do that around here, don't they? Not as though Bartholomew has ever been like other children. He is particular in his habits, like his mother." She turned toward her son with a reptilian glare of warning. "You do remember, do you not, Bartholomew?"

He nodded and held up his hands for inspection. She gave him a half smile until her gaze fell upon something on the floor.

"Filth!" A screech rose in her throat. "I see filth!" Covering her mouth in horror, she snatched a gold bell from the sideboard and shook it furiously. It sounded like fire trucks clanging triple alarms in one of Alex's dad's old black and white movies.

Out of nowhere, three maids appeared and curtsied. Mrs. Borax pointed at the floor.

Alex looked down. Right behind him were two muddy footprints. Oh, no! He must have stepped in some wet soil, and it stuck to his shoe. He started to apologize, but before the words could escape his mouth, the maids surrounded him and attacked. Prickly broom bristles dug into his shoulders. Chemical wipes tugged at his face. A dust cloth tickled his knees mercilessly. He felt like a comic strip cartoon ducking from a giant eraser.

"I didn't mean—" A towel snapped his shoe.

"Better." Mrs. Borax cut him off. With a smug smile, she ordered the tallest maid to follow along behind the boys. "Do make sure any filth is carted away." Alex wondered if she meant him as she turned on her heels and retreated to another room.

"Sorry," Alex said, feeling sheepish.

Bartholomew shrugged and headed up the winding stairs. Alex ran his hand over the wooden banister as they ascended. Boy, would he like to slide down this beauty! Though he guessed if a couple of footprints caused a team of maids to descend upon him, a slide down the banister might call out the army.

After he'd dismissed the tall maid, Bartholomew checked the hallway, shut the playroom door, and leaned against it.

"Whew! Now we can talk. I hope Mother didn't upset you."

"Aw, it's all right. My mom hates it when I track dirt in, too. We just don't have a maid squad like you."

"How is she, by the way?"

"Mom? She's better. She might even get to come home tomorrow." Then Alex noticed something. B-3 never mentioned a father. "I never asked, but where's your dad?"

Bartholomew's face fell, and he looked down at his shoes. "He died before I was born.

Death? Alex's clenched and unclenched his fists. If a super-rich man could die young, so could… *Why am I here?* he wondered, thinking he should be spending the afternoon with his mom. He stared at the door.

"Did you hear what Mrs. Rodriguez said?" Bartholomew changed the subject.

"About what?"

"The budget. We're so low in funds the school is talking about getting rid of art programs. All of them. Music. Drama. Art." Bartholomew waved his arms in the goofy way of his.

"Ah." Alex shrugged, trying not to think of what he'd given up after Mom's heart attack.

"I do suppose for someone like yourself who has sports to occupy his time, a decision like this doesn't matter much. But for me...for me...art is..."

Alex paused for several seconds before replying. "I like art, too."

"But it's more for me. It's as if I'm transported to...oh, I'm boring you."

"No, you're not," Alex said, leaning close. "You are transported to another world like the one we saw the other day. It's a glorious place. So many colors. It's like being home. And when you hold your paintbrush in front of an empty canvas, it's a perfect pool calling to you. Come on in...the water's fine. And you dive into the canvas, swimming in the colors until you think you are about to drown."

"But you don't," Bartholomew continued for Alex. "Instead, you grow gills and learn to breathe in the color. You are a magical fish, gliding from reef to reef."

Alex stared at Bartholomew as if seeing him for the first time. No father. Living a lonely life. Still, this super-clean kid reminded him of what it felt like to be painting with Rembrandt.

Alex looked away. *Not anymore.* Bartholomew waved a hand in his face as if he had something really exciting to share. "Hey, I want to show you something. It's a real secret. You have to promise not to tell anyone. Okay?"

Bartholomew's puppy-like excitement drew Alex in as he chattered on about a secret studio beneath the conservatory. It sounded cool, but the only way they'd ever be able to go there would be if Alex pretended to leave and Bartholomew hid in the bathroom. Otherwise, they'd be bothered every few minutes by some maid checking to make sure everything was clean enough.

Just then, as if on cue, there was a soft knock at the door. Bartholomew jerked his thumb toward it and raised his eyebrows knowingly. "Come in," he said before the door opened.

"Time for inspection, Master Borax. It has been fifteen minutes," the woman in a black and white maid's uniform said.

Groaning, Bartholomew motioned for Alex to get up from the white couch. The maid, a French lady named Yvette, fluffed the cushions, swept the room, and ran a feather duster over the bookcase. She stared Alex up and down, and he wondered if she might dust him off, too. He held up both hands as if he were facing a robber. and Yvette left with a curtsey.

"See?" Bartholomew said after she'd exited.

"Okay, I'll go along with the plan. Just tell me what to do."

Chapter 18

"Goodbye! Thank you for having me," Alex called from the front door.

"Farewell, and do come again," Mrs. Borax crooned, not bothering to get up as he passed.

Alex was sure she didn't mean it at all. Her voice was as sweet as Snow White's stepmother offering a poisonous apple.

Trying to remember Bartholomew's directions, Alex made his way around to the back of the house. When he saw the wide patio, he stopped dead in his tracks. What was there to hide behind? The only plants close to the house were little plastic ones. Man, even the dirt was clean.

Taking a deep breath, Alex clenched his fists and made a mad dash for the nearest fake tree. He didn't dare look back, sure he'd jinx it if he did. His legs flew over the patio, barely touching the silver tiles. When he reached the edge, he vaulted over a deck chair, around plastic fichus, and through the imitation hedge. He ducked behind a tall palm made of steel.

Whew! He pressed himself against the tree and swiped his brow with the back of his hand. Now, which way to go? Oh, yeah, follow the brick path. By keeping to the ever-thicker underbrush, he could map out the next few hiding places and make his way downhill where some real plants brushed against his jeans. Nervous sweat trickled into his eyes and stung his cheeks. Outside the conservatory door, he shot a quick glance over his shoulder before darting inside.

"Bartholomew?" No answer. He reached into his pocket for the brown button he kept for good luck, but it still wasn't there. God, he hoped he hadn't lost it.

Where was the rich kid? Alex turned around, searching. Flowers, pots, a cool fountain. There was even a shrub shaped like a clown. But no Bartholomew.

"Hey, stop fooling around!" he rasped.

"Hello."

Alex nearly jumped out of his Vans.

"Where did you come from?"

"Over there." Bartholomew jerked his head at the angel fountain. "I've learned to be very quiet. Come on." He motioned with one hand and strolled to a dead-looking fern.

Alex shrugged and followed, thinking Bartholomew could have shown him something nicer than some brown plant. But by now he was getting used to B-3's strange ways.

"Ready?" Bartholomew asked with new twinkle in his eye.

"For what?"

"You'll see." Mr. Clean covered his mouth and giggled.

Alex was about to tell him to cut it out when suddenly the floor disappeared. As his feet slid out from under him, he shook both fists in the air.

"Bartholomeeeew!" He whooshed downward and landed with a thud.

"Look out below!"

Alex scrambled out of the way, hoping not to trip over anything in the dim light.

With a bump and a happy squeal, Bartholomew slid down the chute and hopped to his feet.

"You didn't tell me you were going to—" Alex's mouth dropped open as the lights came on. What a place! It was like a giant art store. Bartholomew was obviously proud of it. He scampered from one side to the other, pointing out chalks, clay, paints, and canvases. He held up a handful of brushes and fanned them out like some goofy dancer before waving at the wall of books and DVDs.

"Welcome to my studio."

"Awesome," Alex said and gave a long, low whistle.

"Want to give the potter's wheel a try?"

"Nah. I'm okay looking around." Something draped in a sheet caught his eye. "Hey, what's under there?" he asked, jerking his chin towards the tall lump under a drop cloth in the corner.

"Just something I did over the summer."

"Can I see?"

"Okay." Like an X-game champ receiving a trophy, Bartholomew strutted towards it. "It's the largest thing I've tried so far. For some reason, I just had to make him big." He yanked the cloth off.

Alex's smile froze. A cold sweat broke out all over his body. For a brief moment, he couldn't catch his breath. Then an angry growl rose in his throat.

"He at was my dream! How did you get inside my dream?"

"Uh-uh. It was mine. I saw him on my birthday."

Alex's eyes narrowed. "When is your birthday?"

"June twenty-first, the summer solstice and the longest day of the year. Why?"

"It's my birthday, too. What did you do for it? Were you at the beach?"

"Yacht Club, actually."

"I had a party on the beach…and I saw this thing." Alex nodded at the sculpture.

"Perhaps he really was there, and we both saw him."

"I don't know. My mom didn't. There were lots of other people around."

"No one on the pier seemed to notice anything, either. Then, why could we?"

"Maybe it's the ESP thing you were talking about." Alex shook his head sadly. "Maybe it's a message telling me not to paint anymore."

"You can't stop. If you love it as much as I do, you have to create." Bartholomew squeezed his shoulder.

The room went blurry, and Alex saw the stormy skies of a cartoon world. The ground quaked while creatures implored with painted hands.

"Stop putting stuff in my head!" Alex pushed Bartholomew away and leaped back.

"It isn't me, I tell you."

"Yes, it is you. You, you, you… freak!" As soon as he said it, Alex was sorry. With bright red cheeks and I'm-trying-not-to-cry blinks, Bartholomew looked like he'd been slapped. Alex wondered why he couldn't keep his mouth shut. Why did he keep hurting people? "I gotta go. Mom's coming home tomorrow, and I need to help my dad get the house ready." He glanced around. "Is there a quicker way out of here?"

Bartholomew opened his mouth but said nothing. With a sigh, he pointed at the spiral staircase.

Alex turned away. "Bye, Bartholomew." He hurried across the room but stopped at the stairs. "Sorry," he blurted before rushing full speed up the stairway. He ran across the grounds, not caring whether the Boraxes saw him or not. He just wanted to get home and help, to do something right for once.

* * *

Nighttime brought little rest for Alexander Devinci. Shadow Swine invaded his dreams and try as they might, the Knights of Painted Light could not defeat them. The powers of darkness were growing stronger as art was being squelched in the world of men.

The Thinker watched and shook his head.

In the Land of Antiquities, his people began to cry. "No! The Deliverers are our only hope."

A smiling hieroglyph walked side-by-side with his wife. Then she gasped and called his name. As she faded before his eyes, he reached out for her, but it was too late. As she disappeared into thin air, his kohl-painted eyes filled with tears. They rolled down his papyrus face, leaving black smears in their wake.

The Thinker shivered as more people slipped from view. Some of the Terracottas melted into the soil. Where once a goddess had stood, only a mound of clay remained. The sky turned dark. Fountains ceased trickling. A pyramid slid below the sand. They were returning to the Time Before, the time of the Blank Canvas.

And there was nothing he could do about it but wait.

Chapter 19

"Remember that you must take notes on at least two art pieces from each room," Mrs. Rodriguez reminded them from the front of the classroom.

Several kids groaned. This was supposed to be a fun field trip, not a time to do stupid reports! Bartholomew suppressed a smile when Alex turned to him and curled one goofy lip upward.

"I know. You all work hard every day. But Principal Stricklin wouldn't even let us go until I proved how it would improve our test scores."

Bartholomew's head shot up with these words. He elbowed Alex, reminding him of an argument they'd had many times over the past two weeks. Bartholomew was sure the school was going to take away art, but Alex didn't believe it.

She gave them a warning look. "Please remember that you are sixth graders. Raise your hand if you want to speak. Do not touch any of the art. Stay with your group. I want everyone on his and her best behavior. Got it?"

"Yes, Mrs. Rodriguez," the class mumbled.

All these warnings could not still the excitement around Bartholomew. Kids shuffled in their seats, peeked inside sack lunches, and waved at each other from across the room. There was so much electricity in the air he could have run his computer on it.

This was his first field trip, and he had no idea how to act or what to do. So he just observed the other children and did what they did. If they groaned, he groaned. If they made faces at the truck drivers on the road, so did he. But when he almost asked Heather for a mirror to fix his hair like the gaggle of girls behind him, he stopped when he noticed none of the other boys were fixing their hair. In fact, about half of them looked like they hadn't even combed their hair this morning. *Must be a girl thing*, he thought.

When they gathered on the stone steps of the Museum of Art, Bartholomew spent a moment taking it all in. Even though the building was white, a color he had seen plenty of in his life, the three arched doorways seemed to welcome him in.

Everyone was chattering. He was nowhere near anti-bacterial wipes. Alex was at his side. Bartholomew put his hand over his mouth to suppress a giggle. *I'm on a field trip with my friend!*

Alex raised his eyebrows and gave him the control-yourself look.

Trying to put a more serious face on, Bartholomew focused on the stucco exterior. He stood with what he thought was a cool pose when the wall swelled before his eyes. His mouth fell open. Then the etched lettering shrank and quivered like an old messed up video.

He turned to Alex, but he was several feet away chatting with Zach. Bartholomew shook his head. His vision cleared, and everything returned to normal.

The class filed into the museum in groups of five. Alex and Bartholomew were with Zack, Gwen, and Jose. Alex said they were cool, but Bartholomew found Gwen annoying. She was always challenging boys to arm wrestle. He guessed she wanted to prove she was as strong as them or something. Zach ignored him. But he liked Jose. Jose actually talked to him, even if it was only to ask him to draw cartoon characters for his binder.

A few kids ooed at the mosaic tiled fountain at the entrance. Even Gwen was impressed by the tall Greek urn in the center of the pool.

"Hey, I wonder if ol' Stricklin would fit in that?" she quipped with a mischievous grin.

Mrs. Rodriguez gave her the teacher stare, which said you better talk respectfully about the principal, or you're going to sit in the bus. Gwen looked away, her red face matching her hair. The other kids snickered at her obvious embarrassment.

Bartholomew noticed a Roman sculpture across the room. Mrs. Rodriguez followed his gaze.

"Oh, I see you've found Hermes, one of the Greek gods. Do you remember which god he was?"

Bartholomew shrugged.

"Hermes was the son of Zeus and the patron of liars, gamblers, and thieves," she said. "Now we don't have anyone in our class who would need this god, do we?" She glanced around at the smiling children with a teasing look on her face. "He also watched over travelers and was the god of commerce. Can anyone tell me what commerce is?"

"It's the buying and selling of things. The economy," Heather called out before Mrs. Rodriguez could choose a student.

"Good job, Heather."

Alex rolled his eyes, and Bartholomew nodded. Heather was always blurting answers, and Mrs. Rodriguez allowed it because she was usually right.

Most of the groups went into other rooms with their docents, while Bartholomew's stayed in the sculpture court with their guide, the gray-haired Mrs. Bueler. Bartholomew walked close to the sculpture and smiled.

"Hi. So you can help me lie, cheat, and gamble, huh?"

Hermes winked at him.

"What? Did you see—?"

He stopped mid-sentence. The rest of his group was across the room, listening to Mrs. Bueler. He took a step toward them, then changed his mind. Steeling himself, he went closer to the marble god and tiptoed round it. He scrutinized every square inch, but it was as still as before. He tried to tell himself it was just a statue, but the hairs prickling the back of his neck didn't agree. He scurried to Mrs. Bueler.

"And here we have a fine example of Greco-Roman sculpture," the docent explained as Bartholomew sidled beside her for safety. She smiled politely at him but was obviously annoyed by how close he was standing. She put her clipboard between them slowly nudging Bartholomew away. "Now, please follow me to the Antiquities."

Ignoring the hint with the clipboard, Bartholomew went around to her other side, sticking to her shoulder like paint to canvas. He tried not to look at Hermes as they passed, but he couldn't help it. He had to know.

The statue winked again, and this time it puffed its cheeks! Bartholomew grabbed the docent's jacket, his mouth opening and closing repeatedly.

"Excuse me, young man." Mrs. Bueler brushed him off her shoulder as if he were an irritating fly.

He hurried to Alex who was standing in front of a foot-high limestone carving, his mouth agape. Bartholomew followed his friend's gaze.

"What?" Bartholomew stopped dead in his tracks and gasped. The statue of an Egyptian prince was waving his staff at them! "You see?"

Alex gave a stiff nod as he backed away. The sound of tinkling music made them both turn. A waist-high bronze sculpture of a Hindu girl was singing a tinny song. She kicked up her bare feet while her ankle bracelets kept time like miniature tambourines.

Bartholomew didn't dare blink. He clung to Alex. The music grew louder like a thousand cymbals crashing together. Their clanging echoed throughout the museum.

"What's going on?"

Alex didn't reply. He just stood there, nostrils flaring with controlled breaths.

"Dudes? Hello," Gwen called from across the room, ignoring the cacophony of music. Why didn't she react to all the noise?

"Come along, boys." The docent tapped her clipboard with her long pink fingernails.

"Doesn't anyone else hear it?" Bartholomew asked. He pulled out the hand sanitizer from his pants pocket and squirted a generous dollop in his palm before rubbing it into his hands.

"I'm going to find out." Alex's voice was barely audible amid the clamor. Holding up a finger, he scuttled to Jose and whispered something in his ear. Jose just shook his pony-tailed head and gave him an are-you-crazy look. When Alex returned to Bartholomew's side, the look on his face told all.

"It's not possible," Bartholomew said.

Suddenly it all stopped. The room was as quiet as before. Well, as quiet as a museum can be with a class of sixth graders wandering around. Bartholomew heaved a sigh of relief.

"Boys," Mrs. Bueler called. "*I said,* come along." She tapped louder on her clipboard.

They jogged to catch up with rest of the group who were waiting with crossed arms and dirty looks.

"Dudes, you are way too into this," Zach said.

Gwen nodded. "Yeah, it's just a museum."

Ignoring them, Bartholomew stared straight ahead. As they entered the next room, he thought, *The paintings here won't move. Will they?* Alex opened his journal and took notes. Bartholomew followed his lead, thankful to have something to take his mind off this strangeness. He jotted down the names, dates, and artists from the labels next to the paintings.

"Alex? What else should I write? I want a good grade."

"I don't know. Just put anything. Say if it's an oil or a watercolor," Alex replied, scribbling more.

Bartholomew felt something brush his right cheek. An arrow fletched with tiny feathers flew over him and landed smack dab in the center of his journal. Immediately writing appeared.

Go to the basement. Find the door.

Pass through it. Or our world will be no more.

"What the heck?" Bartholomew reached to touch the arrow, but as soon as he did, it disappeared along with the written message.

Chapter 20

Alex grabbed Bartholomew's journal and held it up to his face. He looked at it sideways, diagonally, and upside down. No hint of the freaky writing remained.

"Are we going nuts?" Alex asked, shoving it back into Mr. Clean's stiff arms. He turned away and tightened his backpack straps.

The mix of European busts and sculptures in the next room seemed normal at first. Then the marble head of a beautiful woman with her hair done up in fancy bun puckered up her white lips and blew Bartholomew a kiss. He blushed, smiled shyly, and gave a quick wave.

"I'm trying to keep it under control. Could you work with me here?" Alex muttered under his breath.

Bartholomew apologized and wrote notes again.

"And here we have an example of additive sculpture." Mrs. Bueler pointed to a bronze miniature of a girl holding a swan.

The sculpture was completely unmoving at first. Of course, it didn't stay still. With a giggle, the girl twirled around and released the now real swan into the air. It flew over Alex, hovered above his head, and dropped a fluttering trail of feathers which gathered into letter shapes. The word B-A-S-E-M-E-N-T floated in front of his face.

Alex leaped back. As the image faded, he glanced around to see if anyone else was freaking out. Bartholomew was frozen in one spot, mouth hanging open, but no one else reacted at all. Alex pulled Bartholomew aside.

"What the heck is going on?" Alex squeezed his journal so tightly his knuckles ached.

"I don't know." Bartholomew shook his head.

"Hallucination?"

"It is possible."

"What should we do? This is freaking me out."

"Perhaps we should tell someone," Bartholomew suggested.

"What would we say? 'Umm, excuse me, but these statues are coming to life and bothering me. Could you please put them in time-out?' "

"I suppose no one would believe us." Bartholomew thrust his hands in his pockets but not before Alex saw how shaky they were.

Alex clenched his jaw. He would stay in control. The sound of music made him jerk. On the display table behind him, a trio of stone heads was humming in three-part harmony.

"Hmmm," they trilled.

"A-one and a-two and a—" the middle one counted off. Then the statues sang to the tune of "Three Blind Mice": "We three busts. We three busts. See how we sing. See how we sing. You must run for the elevator. And find the path to the secret door. It lies among the ancient stores. Say we three busts."

The song grew louder and louder. Each head took a turn.

"—path to the—" the middle bust warbled.

"SECRET DOOR! SECRET DOOR!" the third head belted out.

They repeated this line over and over, like a scratched CD skipping. "Find the path to the secret door... find the path to the secret door..."

The walls trembled and shook. The sculptures blew smoke rings, and the letters B-A-S-E-M-E-N-T formed in the air. Bartholomew was as close to Alex as he could be without actually touching him, but Alex didn't push him away. He was too busy trying to keep his cool in this crazy room.

With trembling hands, Bartholomew pulled out his bottle of hand sanitizer and reapplied some gel. He took out one of the handkerchiefs from his coat pocket, wiped his neck, and flapped at the smoky word. "Help me, Alex."

"Yeah, like that's gonna work. I'll get out my hanky and make it all go away," Alex said through clenched teeth. "Come on. Let's get out of here."

They darted into the Photo Gallery, where the rest of their unsuspecting group stood waiting. Alex noticed Gwen sniffled and wrinkled her nose as if she got a whiff of something. Jose sneezed. Zach stood a few feet away, turning this way and that in front of a piece of glass. Alex couldn't tell if he was checking the spikes in his hair or reacting to something in the air.

Bartholomew lifted his head and sniffed.

"Do you smell it?" he whispered to Alex.

"It smells like smoke!"

The room darkened. A thick cloud curled its way across the ceiling. Alex sputtered and coughed.

Bartholomew covered his mouth with his handkerchief and sprinted to the docent. "I think there's a fire in here, Mrs. Bueler! I smell smoke."

"What?" Mrs. Bueler raised her hooked nose. "I don't smell anything."

"Look." He pointed at the ceiling. The docent glanced up briefly, then sighed.

"Young man, I'm getting very annoyed with you. There is nothing there. Now stop playing games."

Alex dashed to them. "He's not joking. Don't you smell it?" He waved at Gwen. "You smell it, right?"

Gwen just shook her head at Alex as if he were crazy and whispered something into Jose's ear.

"Are you are talking about the photo?" Mrs. Bueler asked, pointing at one of the Weegee photographs of a burning building.

Alex turned in the direction of her finger. To him it wasn't a simple picture. He could smell the burning building, hear the sirens and sobbing people, and taste the acrid smoke on the back of his throat.

The photo grew larger until the entire wall was engulfed in flames. Life-sized heads emerged from the windows. Desperate cries filled the air.

It was like Mom and the ambulance all over again. Alex shoved his hand deep in his pocket and felt for the brown button he always carried. It still wasn't there.

Sparks flew across the room. Flowers, furniture, a century plant all began to burn. He backed away.

"Fire!" a scream escaped Alex's throat. "Save them!"

The people around him just stared as if he were crazy. No one moved. He had to do something.

The flames leaped to the ceiling, red tongues licking the walls as the room became a furnace. Alex's lungs were on fire. Long beads of sweat poured down his face.

Then he saw it. A fire alarm. He rushed to it and yanked the red lever down.

Whoop! Whoop! Whoop! the alarm screamed.

"Everybody run for your lives!" Bartholomew cried.

Zach, Jose, and Gwen sprinted for the exit.

"You kids come back here!" Mrs. Bueler cried, chasing after them.

But Alex couldn't let them die. He got between her and his friends.

"Get everyone out! Now!" he shrieked.

Bartholomew ran in circles shouting, "Fire! Fire! Call nine-one-one!"

People appeared from all sides—docents, tourists, and the rest of their class. Some ran for the exits, shouting. A couple of angry guards rushed toward the boys, their fists raised in anger. Mrs. Rodriguez put a hand up just in time to keep one guard from throttling a shaking Alex. She grabbed the boys by their arms and marched them straight to the front desk while a guard switched off the alarm.

"What in the world is going on?" she demanded.

"Fire. Those people," Alex said, his lower lip beginning to tremble.

Mrs. Rodriguez's face softened. She may have been a strict teacher, but Alex hoped she'd understand he was being honest.

"Alex, I know you've been through a tough time lately, and some of those images are disturbing, but why did you boys pull the alarm like that?"

"Those people in there are dying. We have to save them. Now," Alex said. Why wouldn't anyone listen?

"There is no fire in here. The alarms would have gone off before you pulled it if there were."

"Maybe they don't sense everything." Alex crossed his arms and hugged his chest tightly.

Mrs. Rodriguez sighed.

Alex was about to argue when a smoky coil floated past. It snaked its way along the tile floor like a great python, then thinned into a single strand before disappearing out the front door. Alex inhaled deeply. The air was clear.

"It was real. I swear."

"Okay, fine." Their teacher shook her head. "You boys seem pretty upset. I think the photography was too intense for you. Go on to the Children's Gallery on the lower level." She pointed to the elevator. "I'm sending someone to check on you in a few minutes."

Alex and Bartholomew hung their heads.

"Yes, Mrs. Rodriguez," they mumbled in unison.

Trying to ignore the snickers of their classmates and the glares of the security guards, Alex shuffled toward the elevator, Bartholomew right behind.

Crash! Clang! Something fell in the other room. The gathered crowd rushed into the West Wing to see what it was.

Bartholomew stayed glued to his spot in the center of the room and gave Alex an imploring look. Alex glanced back at the West Wing deciding to stay.

"Just chill. I'm not abandoning you," Alex said as he turned and walked toward the elevator. A finger tapped him on the back. Without looking back, he said, "Stop fooling around. I said I'd stay with you."

Another tap. A hand on his shoulder.

He spun around. And froze.

It wasn't Bartholomew. No. He was still across the room brushing the dust off his slacks. This hand wasn't even human. It was made of marble, and Alex was in its grasp!

He jerked away, but the Hermes sculpture released its grip and smiled down at him. "I have created a diversion, but time is short so listen carefully. You, too, twin of birth." He beckoned Bartholomew to come closer.

Alex was surprised when B-3 stepped right up. Maybe he wasn't such a wimp after all.

"Stay back," Alex said, holding his friend at arm's length from the talking statue.

"Fear not, young one. I am a friend," the statue said.

"How do I know?"

"You don't, but look at me. What do you see?

Alex clenched his jaw and peered into the statue's face.

"You look all right. For a crazy dream."

Hermes smiled. "We are all made of dreams."

"We are?" Bartholomew stood straighter and smiled.

"Of course. This key is to the basement." The marble god held out his hand. "Insert it in the elevator slot and proceed to the storage room. There you will find the doorway. When it opens, pass through. You are our only hope."

"What hope? What doorway?" Alex stepped back and thrust his hands in his pockets.

"All of your questions will be answered in time. Now, go quickly before they return."

Alex shoved his hands in deeper and found Mom's lost button. Had it been there all this time? He'd searched high and low riffling through every drawer and pocket for weeks now, and it was in his Dickies all along?

"Maybe all these weird things will stop if we do," Alex mused thinking that the button was some sort of a sign.

Bartholomew shook his head.

"It could be the only way to stop all of this," Alex argued.

As if making a sudden decision, B-3 narrowed his light blue eyes, snatched the key from Hermes, and pressed the elevator button. When the doors opened, he stepped inside and said, "Just for a while."

Alex nodded and got in beside him. Bartholomew inserted the key into the slot marked, "Basement," and the two boys descended to their destiny.

Chapter 21

Bartholomew shivered. It was cool down here and eerily quiet. Alex hadn't moved, but his eyes were alert and fists clenched, like he was ready for a fight.

What did Hermes mean when he said he and Alex were their only hope? And the note saying a world being no more? This seemed less and less like a good idea. Bartholomew pulled out his hand sanitizer and squirted a dollop, finding some comfort in the alcohol smell.

"Where to?" Alex asked, breaking the silence.

As if in answer to his question, a large blue jewel appeared and bobbed up and down in front of him. The polyhedron was about the size of his fist and had more sides than Bartholomew could count. Lighting up, it bounced off to the right.

Bartholomew turned to Alex. "We follow it?"

His friend shrugged.

Guiding them through a labyrinth of hallways, the blue light stopped in front of a steel door and flashed off and on.

"I think it wants us to go in here," Alex said.

"It could be a trap," Bartholomew said chewing on his lower lip.

The jewel circled the doorknob faster and faster. Echoing voices streamed from up the hall.

"Someone's coming!" Grabbing Bartholomew by the collar, Alex yanked open the door and dragged his companion inside.

Bartholomew stared at the slit of light on the floor, not daring to move. Or breathe. Two shadows snaked by and stopped right in front of them.

He heard a woman sigh loudly. "How many times do I have to tell people to close doors around here?"

Bartholomew covered his mouth. Oh, no! They had left the door ajar.

One shadow came nearer. Bartholomew closed his eyes.

One second. Two. A loud click echoed.

Bartholomew waited for the inevitable discovery and the march back to Mrs. Rodriguez. What was Mother going to do when the police delivered him to her doorstep?

"You can open your eyes now, B-three," Alex said as clattering heels receded into the distance. He stepped away and wiped his ear. "And stop breathing in my ear! It's gross."

"I apologize. It was just so…"

"Close?"

"Too close if you ask me. Maybe we should just forget this." Bartholomew looked at his watch. "It's already been ten minutes."

"Come on, Bartholomew. You can do it."

"We might miss—"

The jewel flashed in his face, stopping Bartholomew in mid-sentence. Circling in front of the door, it flashed brighter with each pass.

"It looks this was only a place to hide," Alex said. "Not where we're going."

"Were the dust bunnies is that?" Bartholomew fought the urge to grab Alex's arm. Now was not the time to have a fantasy landscape flashing before his eyes.

Ignoring the question, Alex stuck his head out into the hall.

"Let's go. The coast is clear." He tiptoed after the bobbing light, not waiting to see if Bartholomew would follow.

Trembling, Bartholomew jogged to catch up, reaching Alex at a door labeled *Storage*. Here, the blue light shrank to almost nothing and shot through the keyhole. *This is beyond crazy*, Bartholomew thought as Alex gave him a curt nod and stepped inside.

Bartholomew peered through the doorway. The room was a jumble of crates and paintings. Rows of metal shelves were covered with an assortment of boxes.

Several of the lids quivered and slid back. Sculptures of dolphins, swans, and angels peeked out with shy curiosity. Bartholomew thought they looked like rabbits poking their heads out of burrows. He smiled and gave them a small wave, sending the frightened creatures back into their boxes.

When Alex walked to a large oil painting leaning against one wall, Bartholomew tentatively followed. There was something off about this painted doorway making his heart pound.

Then the jewel appeared again directly in front of him, and he almost fell over. Bartholomew's jaw dropped as the rough-hewn doors creaked open, and a rainbow shot from inside, landing at their feet. The polyhedron flashed three times, glided over the rainbow, and disappeared in a pinpoint of blue light.

Bartholomew knew what they were supposed to do but was shaking so badly he looked to bold Alex for support. "Ready?" Alex asked, lips pursed.

"No. I think we should go back."

"Come on." Alex took a step forward.

Bartholomew hung behind. "I can't. You go ahead."

"But all the answers are in there." He pointed inside the painting. "I've had a sign. This is going to help Mom. I know it." Alex held up a small brown button and waved it slowly in front of Bartholomew's face.

"What if we can't come out again?"

"Look at me." Alex turned to face Bartholomew and stared him square in the eye. Bartholomew saw the dark circles. The too-tight mouth. Even the dim light couldn't soften the knot of worry in Alex's face. "I don't know what's going on, but there is a reason we've been brought here, and I believe it has something to do with my mom.

Remember that video of your grandfather you showed me? He said people close to you were in danger and could get hurt."

"Father's drowning," Bartholomew said with a gasp. Once again, he wondered if it really had been an accident. How many people drown in mud puddles anyhow?

"It could be related to all this. Now, I'll go on without you if I have to, but I think we are supposed to go together."

"This is insane."

Alex shook his head. "The answers are in there." He tilted his head toward the rainbow. "We have to find them. For both of our families." Alex took a step closer and waited.

Chapter 22

Alex raised his eyebrows. Why wouldn't Bartholomew listen? This was meant to happen. He felt it right down in his bones and finding Mom's button confirmed it.

"I don't know." Bartholomew glanced at his watch.

"Even if someone doesn't find us right away, they'll look around for a while before telling Mrs. Rodriguez."

"Well, if you think so…"

The rainbow grew brighter. Feeling absolutely calm, Alex took off his backpack and shoved it behind a box. He clutched Mom's button with one hand and reached into the colored bands with the other.

"No, Alex."

"It's okay. It's warm, like steam off a bathtub." Another step. There was a tug at his feet. He moved forward, pulled past the painted doors.

Alex turned. Bartholomew was still inside the storage room, his mouth hanging open but not for long. With a shaky grin, he leaped and was instantly at Alex's side. "Hey! It's toasty."

Alex nodded. A low humming began. The rainbow wrapped around their ankles like ropey ripples on a pond. Everything around them shook as humming grew louder and louder. "What's happening?" he shouted, his voice lost in the ever-growing din. With a lurch, the painted roller coaster climbed. Alex extended his arms to keep his balance. When he noticed Bartholomew struggling to do the same, Alex grabbed his friend's coattail. "I got you, dude!"

Another jolt and they shot forward, picking up speed like gliding ghosts. Colors flashed by as Alex's hair whipped around his face and stung his cheeks.

Then everything stopped. The rainbow was as still as sand. Sighing with relief, Alex released Bartholomew.

A large hole opened beneath him, and Alex plummeted downward. Air howled around him. He fell through empty space his arms and legs flailing wildly.

He heard Bartholomew's cry from above. "Hel-l-p!"

Then it was over. The rainbow dangled at their feet. The mist disappeared, and Alex was standing on solid ground. He patted his body to make sure he was all right before glancing around. "Bartholomew?" he called.

His friend was a few feet away, pointing. "Look," he croaked.

Alex couldn't believe it. The rainbow arced toward a crescent moon made of aluminum foil. Below it, lavender painted mountains wore hats of cotton ball clouds. The sky was a sculpture! This was not Earth. This was art.

Alex knelt and ran a hand over the grass. "It looks like paint, but it feels like real grass. Bartholomew, we're inside a collage!"

Bartholomew turned around and round, gaping. "I don't believe it. A world made of art?"

Construction paper trees swayed in the early morning breeze. A flock of origami geese honked overhead while crayon-colored rabbits and mice scurried about. Alex kicked a play-dough pebble and was surprised to hear it clatter like any regular rock.

Bartholomew grabbed his arm, and they exchanged a glance. "Holy dust bunnies. You know what this is?"

"Yeah, the weird visions we were seeing," Alex said. "This is so—"

Alex's words were cut short by a muddy arm twisting from the soil. The ground opened and out rose the most horrible thing Alex had ever seen. Its features were twisted as if someone had stomped on it at birth. It had a pig nose and a hunched back rippling beneath a dark cloak. Brown slime covered it from head to jack-booted toe. But it was its yellow eyes causing Alex to shiver.

"Go back," the creature rasped.

Alex put a protective arm in front of Bartholomew.

"Leave, or you will forever dream nightmares of *my* making."

"D-dream?" Bartholomew stuttered as he clung to Alex's t-shirt.

"Stupid humans. You who dream of saving your father from drowning." The muddy thing pointed a clawed hand at Bartholomew, then turned to Alex. "And what have you seen in your dreams of late? A hospital? Your mother?" The creature sniggered, its piggish nostrils flaring.

"You shut up about my mother," Alex said through clenched teeth.

"You know nothing, Deliverer. Our powers are great. We invade all dreams. Even those of a Chosen One's mother."

Alex curled his hands into fists. "Stay away from her, or I'll, I'll—"

"What? Paint for me? Your canvas is as dry as the sands of Egypt." The muddy creature spat through jagged shark teeth. "Now leave... or suffer my wrath. As sure as my name is Captain Sludge, I will haunt your dreams forever."

When the monster drew closer, Alex shielded B-3 with his body. His pal grabbed a corner of his t-shirt and whispered to be careful. Alex nodded.

Then the sky brightened, and the distant sound of hoof beats filled the air. Sludge glanced up and shook his fist. "Not him!" Grabbing Alex by the collar, Sludge leaned in, his hot breath like rotten eggs. "Mark my words, the nightmares you've had will be nothing in comparison to those coming unless you do as I say." He shoved Alex back before shrinking beneath the soil without a trace.

Alex could barely breathe. How did the creature know about his dreams? "Let's go home. I don't want that thing near my mom."

"Or mine. Do you think it was telling the truth?"

"I didn't say anything before, but I've had gnarly nightmares lately."

"You have?"

"About Mom. She was so..." Alex shook his head unable to finish the sentence.

"I've had a few myself. Come to think of it, Mother has complained of nightmares for years."

This slow realization horrified Alex. "Dream invaders?"

"It can't be." Bartholomew shuddered.

Alex twisted his face and growled in Captain Sludge's voice. "I will haunt your dreams forever."

"You sounded just like it. How?" Bartholomew's eyes widened.

Alex shrugged. "Let's get out of here, okay?"

They turned, but the rainbow was gone.

Alex looked up, hoping to see it dangling above them. Instead, a golden chariot pulled by a team of white stallions appeared from behind a cloud. The horses' manes looked like they were on fire as they strained wildly against the reins. Then they turned downward.

Right at B-3.

"Look out!" Shoving Bartholomew to the ground, Alex shielded him with his body. He splayed out his arms waiting for the inevitable crush of pounding hooves. One moment passed. Two. No impact. All he heard was a soft thud.

"Whoa, babies," a man's voice said.

Venturing a glance, Alex found the chariot parked next to them, its stallions snorting and huffing as their flaming manes softened to a golden hue.

A weird man stood inside the chariot. If you could call him a man. He was more like a 3-D painting. He was young, around twenty, Alex guessed and built like a surfer. Good-looking dude. Not as if Alex usually noticed other guys, but this one could have been a model.

Suddenly the painted man shimmered. First his head and then on down, he turned all watery like paint brushes under a faucet. Alex almost reached out to help him, but something emerged from the glittering liquid. Not emerged, exactly, but he morphed until the entirely chiseled from marble.

"Whoa," Alex said standing back.

The sculpture stepped down from the chariot and walked toward them, his arms outstretched. "Welcome to Artania."

"Artania?" asked Alex.

"The place to which you have come. Surely the Deliverers would know."

"Deliver pizza? Newspapers?" Alex looked to Bartholomew.

"Sorry," Bartholomew mumbled. "Hermes didn't tell us to bring anything."

The sculpture tilted his marble head to the side. "Not the ordinary kind of Deliverer. I forget my manners. I am Apollo, son of Zeus and Leto, King of Minstrels, Prince of Oracles, and Bearer of Light."

"I'm Alex, 6th grade kid, but could you explain what in Zeus's name we're doing here?"

With these words, a lightning bolt cracked, and Bartholomew dug fingernails into Alex's arm. Again.

"My father doesn't like his name taken in vain." Apollo turned his face skyward and called through cupped hands, "We apologize, Father!"

Alex clamped his mouth shut. He wasn't gonna say anything else. No way. Let Bartholomew do the talking. He was the manners king. Alex just wanted to go home and make sure Mom was okay.

"Sir, I believe my friend was trying to say we do not understand why we're here." Bartholomew paused and extended his hand. "I'm Bartholomew, by the way. Bartholomew Borax the Third."

Apollo took the offered hand and held it between both of his. "Your presence fills my heart with gladness. We have waited so long for the Celestial Twins to grow. There is much to say, but this is not the place. We must keep moving, for the ground has ears. Come."

"I can't." Alex shook his head. "I have to go home."

"But you just arrived."

"My mom—" He pressed his lips together and looked down at Bartholomew's watch. "Hey, it stopped." He tapped on the glass.

"Yes, it did." Apollo smiled knowingly. "Fear not, young Deliverers. When you passed through the doorway, the sands of time stopped in your world. As long as you are here, it remains suspended."

"You mean our friends are frozen, like statues?" Bartholomew asked, eyes wide.

"Let us say their time and ours differ. I do not understand everything. Only the Thinker is all-knowing." He reached put a hand on Alex's back. "But my father can answer many questions."

Alex felt his back warm as if he were in front of a fireplace. Heat traveled through his body and washed away the knots of worry. He forgot all about Captain Sludge and his warning. Sick guilt faded to the back of his mind, and for the first time in months, he felt calm.

"How?" He searched Apollo's face.

"I am also the god of medicine." Apollo patted Alex before stepping back into the golden chariot and beckoning the boys to join him. When they each took a place near him, he snapped the reins.

"To Olympus! Yah!" he cried.

The stallions trotted a few feet and with a jolt, took flight. Their manes grew brighter as they ascended. Bartholomew stumbled and grasped hold of the scalloped railing while Alex held out an arm to steady his friend. Clattering gallops filled the air as they rose above the freaky landscape.

While Alex darted from one side to the other pointing out everything he saw, Bartholomew held onto the rail tightly. Didn't Mr. Clean feel better like Alex had? One glance answered his question. Bartholomew kept swallowing and clutching his stomach as if nervous bile built up in his throat.

They rose higher until they were in a white sea. Bartholomew reached out to touch a fluffy cumulus cloud beside him but drew his hand back when strands of cotton wrapped round his fingertips.

Alex copied him. "Hey, it's like cotton balls." Nudging B-3, he held out a handful. "Feel it."

Bartholomew crossed his arms and shook his head.

Chapter 23

Turning the reins northward, Apollo pointed at the mountain peak jutting from the clouds. "Olympus. Our capital. This is where your tasks will begin."

Barely hearing, Bartholomew blinked at the Greek temple straight ahead. Tall marble columns held up the rectangular building where an assortment of Greek gods carved in the roof chattered excitedly. As the chariot approached them, they pointed at Bartholomew who felt his face flush in embarrassment.

Fighting the urge to duck behind the railing, Bartholomew stole a peek at the Athena sculpture. As soon as he looked her way, the goddess of wisdom touched her breastplate and tipped her helmet. Next to her, Poseidon raised his triton in salute, his crown of pearls catching the sunlight.

Greek gods waving at him? Wow! Bartholomew tingled with a tinge of fear.

"The Parthenon," Apollo said, yanking the reins to the right as the chariot glided downward. "Home."

Bartholomew felt like a phoenix floating to its nest. This was truly magic. Forgetting his fear, he covered his mouth and giggled.

When they landed in front of the temple, Apollo stroked each horse in turn and ordered them to their stable. With a sweep of his arm and a reassuring smile, he turned to the boys. "Come. It is time to meet Father."

Bartholomew followed Apollo into the shadows of the massive building, but when he saw the forest of Doric columns supporting the structure, he had to stop and admire them. *After all, one doesn't get to see Greek architecture up close every day,* he thought, running a hand over a fluted pillar as smooth as fresh clay.

"Isn't this amazi—" But the others had already gone inside, stopping him mid-sentence. Stumbling forward to catch up, he reached a glaring Alex's side just as Apollo began to speak.

The handsome god crossed one hand over his chest and bowed deeply to the statue on the throne with foamy ringlets and a long gray beard curling round his lap.

"Father, I have brought the Deliverers, as you asked."

"I bid thee welcome to Olympus, watchtower of the Antiquities."

Bartholomew grabbed Alex's arm, almost falling over, then squinted to be sure. A crown of olive leaves framed the head, and a chiton robe draped his knees. Yes, right there in from of him sat the same giant he'd seen surfing on his birthday.

"Giant? Is that you?" Bartholomew asked, tugging on Alex. But his friend kept staring straight ahead, jaw clenched.

The winged women etched into his throne fanned him with their feathers as he spoke. "Yes, it is I who traversed the waves as you celebrated your day of birth. I was one of the few strong enough to pass through the doorway."

"You mean the painting back there?" Bartholomew asked.

"There are many doorways, young one. Please, be seated." Zeus indicated a place behind them. In a flash two wooden stools appeared.

"Holy dust bunnies," Bartholomew gasped before bobbing up and down on the stool next to Alex.

"Cool it." Alex whispered behind one hand.

Bartholomew gave him a quick nod and tried to focus on the gods.

Apollo took his place next to Zeus. His wooden throne was decorated like his father's with moving female sphinxes who also used their wings as fans.

Zeus's voice sounded resonant and noble as he spoke. "I am sure you have many questions, young ones."

What an understatement, Bartholomew thought as he surveyed the marble god. Such a wonderful carving. Every line so smooth. From the long curling hair to each sandaled toe. He'd love to be able to sculpt as well. "I don't get it. You look like a statue. I thought the gods were people."

"I am statue and god. I am art and man."

Bartholomew exchanged a glance with Alex and shrugged.

"Umm, still confused," Alex said. "Why are you greeting us instead of this Thinker guy?"

"Our leader has a thousand tasks he must attend to. You will meet him when the time is right." Zeus's skin shimmered and darkened as he morphed from marble to clay. In less than a second, he took on a new form.

"You look just like Bartholomew's sculpture!" Alex gasped.

"I have been reborn a thousand times in the hands of man. I have many forms. Clay, marble, paint, basalt."

"Reborn? Forms? Hands of man?" Bartholomew asked. What was Zeus talking about?

"I shall tell you a story of creation." Zeus took a long breath, and his rich voice deepened. "Long ago, before there was all you now see, there was a planet called Earth. It was perfect for life, and it did spring from this perfect place. Intelligent life. Life with the ability to reach out to the infinite for inspiration.

"The first humans did little but survive. All their devices were to ensure their survival. Out of mud they created pots. Out of sticks and stones, weapons.

"Many generations later, twin boys, a pair much like yourselves, brought a flaming torch into a cave. In the flickering shadows, they imagined the same image. The taller boy reached into the ashes of a cold fire pit and sketched on one wall while his brother drew on the other. When their drawings met, a perfect circle was created."

Zeus raised an arm in the air and the outline of a cave with a large round pictograph in its center appeared in front of them.

"Oh, I see. The cave. The twins. The painting," Bartholomew said dreamily.

"The painting became the seed from which our world grew."

Apollo threw a handful of dust at Zeus's air sketch, and the circle darkened until it resembled an odd-shaped planet.

"You mean this world was made by people's art?" Alex asked.

Zeus nodded. "Let me continue. The twin boys painted many caves in their lifetimes, bringing countless joy to their tribe. But not everyone shared in this joy."

"Bartholomew can relate to this story, can't you, bud?" Alex nudged him.

Bartholomew laughed. "Those words are an understatement. Mr. White says painting is nonsense, and Mother thinks it's filth."

"As it has always been." Zeus said, walking around the floating planet between them. "One fierce hunter, Kandart, was afraid of the changes in his village. He argued how these creations were dangerous. In truth, he was jealous of the attention the twins received. He wanted it stopped, but few listened, and he grew angrier by the day." The god's eyes narrowed.

"Finally, his envy consumed him like a devouring flame, and he decided it was time to strike out. At night while the rest of the village lay sleeping, he stole quietly to a nearby cave where a tableau of man and beast danced on the walls. Emptying his water-filled goatskin onto the dirt floor, he stirred and squeezed the muck in his hands. He took handful after handful of mud and smeared it over the twins' painting. All the while, he cursed art and all its creators."

Zeus waved a hand in front of the air sketch, and it slowly spun. He let out a long sad sigh.

Bartholomew leaned forward. "What happened then?"

"Kandart gave birth to an evil race of creatures." Apollo shuddered.

"It was the genesis of the Shadow Swine," Zeus added.

"Shadow Swine? What are they?" Alex asked.

"They are the destroyers of Artania. They live below."

"If they destroy, how did this place ever get here?" Bartholomew asked.

"Fortunately, the twins' ideas inspired others. In caves and huts and longhouses, people found joy in creation. So Artania had a beginning. We had animals, people, the sun, and stars." Zeus walked behind Apollo and placed both hands on his shoulders. "And family." The two gods exchanged warm smiles.

"However, the Anti-Artist Army waits beneath the soil," Zeus continued. "Whenever a human curses art or destroys its beauty, the Shadow Swine gain power, and a death occurs here." Zeus took off his leafy crown and set it atop the suspended world. The cave outline faded, and the planet shrank by a third. He removed the crown and put it back on his head.

"The Swineys reach out their muddy arms and take our sweet children beneath to Subterranea." Apollo punched his fist into the center of the still shrinking sphere, and it burst into a thousand dark pieces to rain down at his feet.

Bartholomew stared at the gathered dust and stiffened. The creature, Sludge, must have been one of those Shadow Swine. A kidnapper and a dream invader? Scary.

"Do they ever come back?"

"When one of our kind disappears, it is forever. Even if the creators were to chisel a new sculpture, it would not bring the lost Artanian back. Unless… but only the Deliverers have such power. We can only hope the future will bring more to life."

Bartholomew stared thoughtfully at the gods. This was unbelievable. Every art piece alive? His sculptures? Alex's paintings? The pieces in the museum? Amazing. Still, one thing was bothering him. "What does this all have to do with us?"

"Yeah, we're just a couple of kids." Alex nodded.

"It's not as if we were famous artists or anything," Bartholomew said.

"Whoever told you fame was a requisite for being an artist?" Zeus asked quietly.

Bartholomew shrugged, not knowing what to say.

"Come," Zeus said rising from his throne. "I have more to show you."

They made their way down a long rectangular hallway until they reached the central chamber, or naos, of the Greek temple. Bartholomew stood at the columned entry to the room and peered inside. White marble with bending patterns of gray covered the walls and floor of the nearly empty room. They all led to the center where a half-moon stone tablet stood. It was about three feet wide, carved with weird ancient writing, and gave off a faint glow.

"This is the Soothsayer Stone," Zeus said, laying a hand on it.

"The letters look odd." Alex said as he stepped past Bartholomew toward the floating stone.

"Hey," Bartholomew blurted, practically jumping out of his pants. "It's Greek!"

"Of course. What else would it be?" replied Zeus.

"Yeah, Richie. What else would it be?" Alex muttered under his breath.

"But sir, we can't read Greek," Bartholomew said, ignoring Alex's sarcasm.

"Then my son shall translate it for you."

As he moved closer to the tablet, Apollo's face glowed as if someone put a lantern under his chin. He gave a quick nod and laid a hand on the stone. "These words contain a prophecy sacred to all Artanians. Listen, young ones." His voice rang strong and sweet.

Our world was born from the magic of two,
The smiling twins whose creations grew.
They painted walls with ideas anew,
Until the dark day we came to rue.
When one jealous hand used mud to undo,
And the life of many too soon was through.

"Hey, that's the story you just told us!" Bartholomew said. Apollo nodded, then continued.

But listen to this prophecy with open ears,
To know what happens every 2,000 years.
The Shadow Swine will make you live in fear,
Bringing death to those whom you hold so dear,
For they will open the doorway so wide
That no one will find a place to hide.
And the Creators will stop
As their dreams are drained,
Before 12 moons wax and wane.

Apollo pointed at Alex and Bartholomew.

But hope will lie in the hands of twins
Born near the cusp of the second millennium.
On the eleventh year of their lives
They will join together like single forged knives.
Their battle will be long with 7 evils to undo.
Scattered around will be 7 clues.
And many will perish before they are through,
But our world will be saved if their art is true.

Chapter 24

Alex held back, crossing and uncrossing his arms as if an invisible wall stood between him and the others. Should he be a part of this? He thought finding the button was a good omen; it would help to heal Mom. Now, he was beginning to wonder. "I don't get it," he said shaking his head.

"You are the twins reborn," Zeus replied.

"We're not twins. We're not even related." Alex closed his eyes. *It can't be true. I'm going to wake up in my own bed and find this was just some weird dream.*

"Alex?" Bartholomew's voice grated at his ears like fingernails on a chalkboard.

Why can't he leave me alone? Alex squeezed his eyes shut tighter. *I am in control. I will make this dream go away.*

"Come on, Alex." Bartholomew laid a hand on his shoulder.

"Stop it!" Alex roared as he shoved Bartholomew away.

"Hey, Alex. It's all right."

"To you maybe. What have you got to lose? Nothing! My mom needs me," he said, his lower lip quivering.

"But they said time stands still while we're here."

"How do I know it's true? Maybe these are bad guys trying to trick us. Did you ever think of that, Mr. Clean?"

Zeus stepped between them.

"How did you feel when I rode the waves for you?"

"I don't know." Staring at his feet, Alex shoved his hands deep in his pockets and felt for the smooth button.

"Look at me."

Alex slowly raised his gaze. There was the kind face and soft beard he painted all summer. He glanced at Apollo, whose warm hands had rested on his shoulder and warmed his worries away. *Were* they tricking him?

"Now, answer me true. What does your heart tell you?"

He thought for a moment. Did they act like the Sludge creature he'd met? No. Apollo and Zeus were more like friends.

"You're all right, for a cartoon."

"Then observe."

Zeus waved a strong hand causing a faint mist to swirl and condense into a single ray of light. Then, like a spotlight opening a hole in the floor, it created a window to the world below where scattered towns peppered the multi-colored landscape.

The scene focused on one medieval village where realistically painted people went about their daily business. A butcher sold meat in the town square; two knights jousted in a field, and a rustic horse-drawn cart carried a pile of hay. An aproned woman in a long brown dress held a stick-figure child's hand as they made their way across the dusty street.

Alex smiled when he saw them. Mom used to hold his hand the same way.

Suddenly, the ground rumbled. The villagers ran for hiding places. They ducked behind barrels, dashed into stables, and slammed doors shut. The only ones left were mother and son who stood frozen to the spot in the road.

A crack appeared in the ground next to the boy, and a mud-dripping arm emerged. It grabbed his foot and pulled him downward.

"Mama!" he screamed.

The mother grabbed the child's arm "No! Not my baby!" She dug her feet into the soil.

Alex clenched his fists.

The child's leg disappeared into the hole. Sweat poured from the mother's pale face as he strained to pull it back up. Then, she was on her knees, being dragged toward the fissure.

Alex thought of Mom. All alone. He remembered how busy he'd been.

"No!" The mother tugged and heaved but in the end was too weak. The boy went under. All that remained were little fingers wrapped round hers. Then, like a ship descending into a dark sea, they too sank below.

Tears streaming down her cheeks, the mother dug furiously, flinging handfuls of soil into a heap behind her until she'd dug a grave-sized hole.

But her child was gone.

She squeezed two clumps of earth to her chest and crumpled into a heap as the villagers came out of hiding, gathering round to comfort her. Their grim faces told Alex this was not the first time they'd witnessed such a scene.

"So?" He jerked away, erasing the vision. "What do you want me to do about it?"

"You will know when the time is right. Fear not, young one. Put your faith in the Soothsayer Stone."

Alex looked up into the wise face of the Greek statue. He thought of his mother in the hospital. *The poor lady. To see your own kid disappear. If she'd been Mom…*

"Okay," he said. "Time better be stopped in our world, or I'll…I'll…"

"You may singe my beard with lightning if my word is untrue."

"Then, let's get started." He turned to Bartholomew. "Are you ready, B-Three?"

"According to this Soothsayer Stone, I was born ready. Just like you. Twin." He giggled and gave Alex with a playful nudge.

They turned to Zeus who with a wave of his hand, sent them hurtling toward their first task.

Chapter 25

Bartholomew couldn't contain his curiosity any more. He tapped Apollo on the shoulder. "Excuse me, sir, but where are we headed?"

"The hieroglyphs, sculptures, and papyrus paintings have need of us. The Egyptians of long ago suffer. You shall begin your quest here. In fact, we have arrived." As he tugged back on the reins, the fiery stallions whinnied and tossed their heads.

"Giza." Bartholomew gasped when he saw the trio of pyramids in the white sand below. "Wow!"

There stood one of the wonders of the ancient world, casting triangular shadows onto the sand. The Great Pyramid of Khufu towered protectively above the other two, while nearby, the Nile River twisted and snaked with wooden sailboats peppering its waters. On the other side, the Great Sphinx rested his lion body on the earth with pharaoh eyes staring off into the distance.

"Look!" Alex cried pointing at the Sphinx.

The great beast lifted its stone head, shook the sand from its royal headcloth, and yawned. Hot sticky wind blew back Bartholomew's hair as Apollo guided the chariot to a landing.

"Yuck. Lion breath," Bartholomew said, waving a hand in front of his face.

Apollo raised a hand to the massive sculpture. "Greetings, oh, Sphinx," he called, yanking on the reins to calm the snorting stallions.

"I, in turn greet you, son of Zeus and Leto," the huge statue boomed in reply. "You have brought the Deliverers?"

"Yes, and I give them over to you, for I hear your need is great." Apollo gave the boys a gentle push.

Bartholomew and Alex stumbled toward this magnificent being. Neither spoke. Alex crossed his arms and surveyed the monolith while Bartholomew bowed his head in reverence.

"So these are the prophesied ones. It is hard to believe how creatures so small could have birthed my brethren and me. Still, The Thinker knows much, and to him our future is entrusted. Thank you, Sun-god."

The Sphinx extended a single claw. Apollo took it in his hands and shook it before turning to Alex and Bartholomew. "Farewell, young ones."

Bartholomew gulped. "You are leaving us?"

"I return to Olympus, but fear not. Your visions will lead you."

"How can ideas help us here?" Bartholomew's face blanched thinking about those horrible monsters.

"Remember," Apollo said. He placed a warm hand on Bartholomew's chest. "Your power is here. Trust in it. Follow the creative flow wherever it may lead you." With a gentle smile, the fair-faced god hopped back in his carriage and snapped the reins.

The stallions stomped their hooves and instantly each silvery mane burst into flame. The horses gave a lurch before galloping into the air. The chariot rose higher, growing ever brighter until the golden chariot and the sun were one.

Bartholomew would have liked to take a moment to breathe it all in, but Alex cocked his head at the Sphinx and demanded, "Okay, now what?"

The great stone statue yawned. "You go forward. I'm going to take a nap." Resting his head on his paws, the Sphinx closed his eyes and immediately began snoring.

"Now we're stuck here with no help. Great," Alex said. "Any ideas?"

Staring at the three pyramids in the distance, Bartholomew shrugged.

"A lot of help you are," Alex grumbled.

Bartholomew was about to retort a defense when a light wind blowing the Sphinx's striped head cloth picked up the sand in front of its left paw. Swirling, it took shape until it turned into a mini-tornado. Even now. the Sphinx didn't wake but kept on snoring and snorting in long, even breaths.

The whirling sand rose higher, blowing grit into their faces. Alex sputtered. Bartholomew shielded his eyes, but he didn't look away. It was too amazing. The tornado lifted into the sky, turned in the direction of the Great Pyramid, and formed a pointing arrow.

"I suppose it means we should follow it," Bartholomew said.

"Oh, I don't know. Maybe we're supposed to go in the opposite direction."

"Really?" Bartholomew asked, missing the sarcasm.

"Not!" Guffawing, Alex cuffed his shoulder with the back of his hand.

Bartholomew blushed even as a grin formed. "Oh, I get it."

Alex smiled back "Come on, B-Three." He turned to follow the sandy arrow in the sky.

Bartholomew's heart soared. This teasing was just like what he'd read best friends do. Beaming, he skipped along as they made their way toward the Great Pyramid of Khufu.

Chapter 26

Bartholomew felt as insignificant as an ant when they arrived at the square base of the pyramid. It was huge, stretching out at least ten acres and looked nothing like the photographs he had seen. Instead of time-worn blocks, the polished limestone gleamed and shone like silvery glass. He stepped closer and bent to see if his reflection showed up in one of the stones.

"It was called 'Ikhet' or 'glorious light' by my people," a feminine voice behind him said.

He turned to see a beautiful Egyptian woman dressed in a formfitting linen dress. She wore a tall crown with a bronze sun disk between two cow horns. Her black, shoulder-length hair and bangs framed her high cheekbones perfectly. But it her eyes were what drew him in. They already shone like black pearls, but the kohl eyeliner made them absolutely mesmerizing.

"Greetings. I am Isis, goddess of love and protectress of little children. Wife to Osiris and mother of Horus. I bid you welcome."

"I know about you! We just finished studying about you in school. Your husband, Osiris, was attacked by his brother who chopped him up and scattered his pieces throughout Egypt!"

Isis nodded sadly. "A day I will always rue."

Bartholomew read how a brokenhearted Isis gathered up all the pieces of Osiris and brought him back to life. Wow, what loyalty. Would he do the same for Alex? He figured he would and was about to open his mouth to say so when Alex broke in with a clearing of his throat.

"Excuse my friend. He doesn't get out much." He bowed deeply. Then, raising his eyebrows, Alex gave Bartholomew a warning stare and said under his breath, "Watch what you say."

Bartholomew's smile vanished, and he bit his lower lip. "I didn't mean to bring up sad memories."

"It was long ago," Isis said. "Life is wrought with both joy and pain, but now there is much to do, and time grows short. Come." She tilted her crown toward the triangular entrance high above them and quickly scaled the pyramid, glancing back from time to time with an encouraging smile.

Alex followed first while Bartholomew studied his every move. He knew Alex used to rock climb with his parents when they lived in Colorado, so he was probably an expert. Shielding his eyes against the noonday sun, Bartholomew watched Alex closely to see how he placed his hands. Alex took a deep breath first. Okay, now grunt on stone three. Pull, bend, climb.

Glancing down at his cream-colored pants and shirt, Bartholomew hesitated before tackling the pyramid. Would he stain his clothes?

Imagining himself copying every deft movement, he took a similar deep breath and placed his fingers in the same place Alex had. He pulled. Yes! One stone conquered!

Bartholomew waved a hand in triumph, lost his balance, and fell back to the sand. "I'm all right!" he called with a nervous laugh.

He stood and eyed the pyramid. Digging his fingers between the cracks in the limestone blocks this time, he twisted his body sideways. He inching upward, pretending to be a spider: creeping, crawling, heaving. Success!

For all of five seconds. Then he was flat on his back again.

"Come on, Bartholomew! Just because time is standing still here, doesn't mean we should!" Alex called in an exasperated voice.

"I'm trying! It's slippery," Bartholomew retorted as he sprang to his feet. Brushing off his pants, he was determined to make a running start when he heard a rumbling and turned.

A jagged crack was opening in the earth behind him.

"The enemy senses your presence. Quickly, Deliverer!" Isis called down.

Sand flew from under his feet as Bartholomew scurried toward the pyramid. Granules blinded him for a moment. Trying to gauge the distance, he leaped.

It felt as if he were suspended in the air. Heart pounding, he reached out, praying for a firm handhold.

His fingers scraped the pyramid, ripping one nail to the quick. Bartholomew fell backwards and hit his head. A throbbing ache pounded his skull.

The crack opened wider, and a spiked head emerged from the fissure.

Horrified, Bartholomew backed up against the pyramid.

"Climb! Now!" Isis cried.

Pivoting, he pressed against the stone seeking any foothold he could find.

There were none.

A muddy face emerged from the sand. And glared at him with yellow eyes. "Human," it rasped.

"I-uh, umm, help?" he croaked

"I am coming," Isis called. She lifted her arms and instantly, long white feathers sprouted. She unfolded her freshly-grown wings and flapped them twice. Then, leaning forward, Isis dove to his side.

Black cloaked shoulders and a hunched back surfaced. One clawed hand shot out, brushed Isis's linen dress.

"No!" Isis said, kicking Sludge's slimy fingers aside as she dragged the shaking Bartholomew away. Then she lifted him onto her shoulders as easily as if he were one of her feathers.

Gaping at the monster shaking a fist below, Bartholomew clung to her crown as she rose higher. How did Captain Sludge find them?

When Isis landed at the doorway, Bartholomew slid off her back trying to keep his sandy feet from touching her pretty dress. He mumbled some thanks and stared at the angry creature below.

"Go home, Deliverers!" he snarled.

Alex shook his head while Bartholomew thought of all their nightmares: Alex's, Mother's, his own. If he couldn't even climb a few feet, how could he stop such power?

The boy felt his confidence slip away like desert sand through his fingers.

Chapter 27

"We are safe here. But keep yourselves bent at the waist. The ceiling is but four feet in height," Isis called over her shoulder as she ducked into the triangular doorway.

Alex gave Bartholomew a comforting pat on the shoulder before following Isis inside. "It's all right. Come on, bud," he said, not really believing his words. It wasn't okay. It was full blown freaky. These Shadow Swine were more powerful than Zeus let on. If they could invade dreams in one world and track humans in another, how was he supposed to keep his buddy safe?

"It's so dark," Bartholomew whispered, halting at the entrance. "I can't see the end."

"That is because the distance is so great, some three hundred forty-four feet," Isis explained.

She snapped her fingers, and a line of flaming torches lit the corridor. Their eerie glow seemed to go on forever like lampposts on the world's longest street. Bending at the waist, Isis glided down the narrow corridor, her feet barely touching the floor.

But making his way down wasn't so easy for Alex. The low ramp was only a few feet wide, and he kept scratching his arms on the stone walls.

Bartholomew had it worse and kept stopping every few steps. Alex felt sorry for the poor dude. He wasn't used to doing this physical stuff. Even when he got down on all fours, it didn't help much. Alex could hear him bumping into the walls. By the time they reached the bottom, his jacket was torn, and two scratches were oozing red beads from his hands.

At the dead end, Isis stopped and bent her crown toward the wall. As soon as the horned tips touched stone, the air sizzled and jagged sparks jumped from one antler to the other.

Alex heard a pop as the sun disk in the center of her crown glowed pink then red, filling the chamber with radiant heat. When the disk turned white-hot with blinding light, Alex extended one arm in front of Bartholomew pushing him back.

The stones groaned and slid apart, revealing another dark chamber beyond. In the same moment, Isis's crown dimmed to normal. Then, cool air rushed up to meet them, and Alex took a deep breath.

She lifted her head, stepping through the newly formed doorway. "Come. We are nearly there."

Inside the chamber were two beings unlike any he had ever seen, even in this strange world. Alex turned to exchange a glance with Bartholomew but the goof was doing toe touches. *No way.*

Bartholomew twisted right and left totally oblivious to Alex's raised eyebrows and warning glare.

"Ahem." Alex tapped Bartholomew on the shoulder.

"What? My muscles are all cramped up."

"Look!" He pointed to a green-skinned man in front of them. Wrapped like a mummy, he wore a tall white crown of soft cloth with a cobra in the center and sat on a golden throne. The long rectangular beard jutting from his chin pointed to a striped crook and flail in his right hand. Next to him was a hawk-headed boy. Alex did a double take. Hawk-headed boy?

Isis glided forward and bowed her head. "Dear husband and son, I present Bartholomew and Alexander, the men-boys whose hands shape our destiny. Deliverers, meet Osiris and Horus." She embraced her husband and stroked her son's cheek with the back of her hand before taking her place on the empty throne to Osiris's right.

"These younglings possess power? Hmm." Osiris searched their faces as if trying to find where it could possibly be.

Alex sniffed indignantly. He'd show them powerful.

"But, Father, did I not avenge your murder? Did I not defeat Uncle Set? Did I not use magic to help Mother find all of your dismembered parts?"

"You did, dear son, but these times are different. The Shadow Swine grow in strength. Our very world lies on the cusp of death. It is not only I who suffer. It is all of our kind."

"Excuse me, sir," Bartholomew began, "but the Soothsayer Stone said—"

"Silence! Do I, Osiris, Lord of the Underworld, know nothing? Who are you to instruct me? I have seen death and returned stronger. I am the god of eternal life and resurrection. I do not need a lesson from a child."

Alex was ticked. "You guys brought us here to do whatever. Meanwhile we're getting chased and threatened by freaky monsters. But still we're here, ready to work. So why not get on with it?"

Bartholomew gave a shy nod of agreement. Osiris eyed them before pointing his crook at Alex.

"Sickhert and the *monsters* you speak of have kidnapped our twelve greatest pharaohs." Osiris shook his head as the torchlight made strange shadows on his green skin.

"These kings symbolize the power that sustains the Land of Antiquities. Without them all of Egypt will vanish," Horus added.

"We pray for their safe return, but although sun follows moon time and again, each throne remains empty," Osiris said.

"We have already lost three villages on the Upper Nile. Every home beneath the sand is fodder for the Shadow Swine." A tear grew like a jewel in the corner of Isis's eye. It rolled down her cheek and made a round blotch on her linen dress.

Horus leaned to lay a hand on his mother's knee before speaking. "If the pharaohs don't return, even the pyramids will turn to dust. We need you to free the trapped twelve."

"Are they serious?" Bartholomew grabbed Alex's arm.

Alex unhooked Bartholomew's hand. Good. Now he'd be doing something to help. *Not hurt like–* He clenched his jaw to stop the thought. "Tell us how," Alex said.

The torches flickered and went out. Long seconds passed in silence. Alex was about to demand an explanation. when suddenly in a puff of red smoke every wooden stick burst into flame. When the smoke cleared, Alex gasped. Linking arms with Isis, Osiris and Horus were twenty more Egyptian gods.

They stepped forward in turn introducing themselves.

"Bastet, cat goddess and eye of the moon," a feline-headed woman said. She slung a longbow and quiver of arrows over her sleek fur-covered shoulder and bowed.

A giant hooded snake flicked its forked tongue at them and hissed, "Wadjet, cobra goddess. Protector of Egypt."

"Sobek, god of the Nile greets you." A crocodile headed creature snapped his toothy jaws twice and bowed.

His man-legged companion wagged a furry tail. "Hello, I am Anubis the Jackal, god of embalming."

Alex grinned at Anubis. He remembered seeing a terrifying half-dog with the same name in a movie long ago, but this god wasn't scary at all. With his tongue lolling out and perky ears, he reminded Alex of Rembrandt wanting to play ball.

When the last in line said her name, they all cried in a single voice, "With our help! With our help, you will drive back the Shadow Swine!"

Chapter 28

"Darn!" Bartholomew cursed after the fourth time he dropped his stylus. He sure as Saniscrub didn't want to make a new one. They took forever. First gathering reeds from the Nile's shore and chewing on each yucky one to make its end soft like bristles. Then he cut them to size but broke a dozen before getting even one right.

Alex glanced up from painting symbols on the scroll. The Egyptians still hadn't told them what the long sheet of papyrus was for, but it was obviously pretty important since one god or another checked on its progress every hour or so.

"It's all right. You didn't mess anything up. No big deal," Alex said.

"Easy for you to say. You're not the klutz who had to be carried like a baby."

Alex set the reed pen back down on the stone palette. He was careful and didn't drip any paint anywhere. "I've just done more stuff than you. I'm not perfect. Believe me."

Bartholomew thought Alex was only being nice. Again. He had helped countless times over the last few weeks, first at school and now in Artania: Demanding answers from these gods. Protecting him from those monsters, which thankfully hadn't shown up for a few days. Working by his side. He shrugged. "A heck of a lot more than me, but thanks."

"Come on. Let's finish this." Alex drew his eyebrows together and returned to painting his half of the sheet.

Bartholomew knew enough to be quiet now. Alex liked to focus his whole being on a task without chitchat. This job had taken too much work to mess up now. First, they cut triangular stems from papyrus plants and soaked them until they were soft. After dividing them into strips, they beat and flattened the fibers for hours before layering them over each other. Then they waited two days for the squares to dry under heavy weights of stone. Finally, they wove it all together to make this long roll of papyrus.

Bartholomew smiled appreciatively at their work. The fibrous sheet now had twelve hieroglyphic cartouches spaced evenly from one end to the other.

He held the stylus aloft, imagining how the final touches would look before dipping it into the red cake of paint. As he applied the crimson to the hieroglyph, the tickling shiver he always got while creating tingled up his arm. He dabbed two more splotches on the fabric when a faint wind ruffled his hair. Horus, in hawk form, swooped down behind him.

"Ahh! I see Thoth has taught you well these past few days. You could be scribes yourselves in Pharaoh's court."

"It would have been amazing," Bartholomew said, leaning back.

"Ready?" the god asked.

"Not really." Alex gave the hawk-god a long stare. "But do I have any choice?"

"We all have choices, Deliverer." Horus shook out his wings and folded them behind. "I have chosen to battle the Shadow Swine rather than hide. You have chosen to help us and fulfill your destiny."

"Destiny? Yeah, right." Alex stared blankly into Horus's face. "Sure I'm here, but not by choice. You creatures tricked us into coming, led us through some crazy labyrinth, and now we've been working for days, not knowing what's up or when we can go home. This is no destiny. This is just the cry of some dying world so desperate they brought in a couple of kids to save it."

Bartholomew was used to Alex's skepticism but still was curious to hear Horus's reply. He slowed his painting and listened.

"Ah, I see. A nonbeliever. Events are too few for you to believe in destiny."

"I am in control. I make my own choices," Alex said.

"I, too, thought I had power over my own fate. Until my father's death."

"You really fought for him?" Bartholomew changed the subject hoping to lighten Alex's mood.

"Yes. For eighty years, I battled Uncle Set. When I finally I defeated him, I realized I'd been fulfilling my destiny."

"I don't believe in some predetermined fate." Alex shook his head. "Some things just suck."

Horus raised his wing and brushed a feather against Alex's cheek. "It is terrible to see a parent suffer. I, at least, had a foe to fight. Sickness is an invisible enemy."

Alex recoiled from the god's touch. Angrily, he brushed the wing away with the back of his hand. "Well, what's the plan?" Alex asked.

"Forgive me. I digress. It is time for the gathering."

"Finally," Alex said.

Bartholomew glanced down at his hands. Pain caked them like chalky gloves. He couldn't face the gods like this!

Obviously, Alex felt the same way because he'd already kicked out of his shoes, ripped off his shirt, and was sprinting toward the Nile. As soon as he reached the bank, he stripped down to his boxers and cannon-balled into the river.

"Come on in. The water's great!" he called.

Bartholomew grabbed a towel from the pile Thoth supplied them for swimming and draped it over his shoulder. Tiptoeing after Alex, he hid behind some papyrus reeds to undress, first tucking each sock inside a shoe, then folding his clothes in a perfect rectangle before placing them neatly on top of a flat boulder.

He ventured a single toe into the river. Brrr. Remembering what his swimming coach taught him about the dangers of diving into shallow water, Bartholomew bent his knees and executed a graceful racing dive. He bobbed to the surface and swam a few strokes, reveling in stretching his cramped muscles. Then he rolled over and let the morning sun warm his face as he floated peacefully on the river.

He didn't know it then, but it was the last serenity he'd have for a long, long time.

Chapter 29

Alex stooped and touched one corner of the long papyrus sheet. Good, it was dry. Careful not to damage the fabric, he rolled it loosely and cradled it in his arms.

He glanced up to see Bartholomew finally dressed but still dabbing his face with a linen towel as if his neat freak mother were scrutinizing his every move.

"Are you sure you're clean enough?" Alex asked with a smirk.

Bartholomew's face blanched. "What? Is there still paint in my hair?"

"Oh, yeah. You have a big red blotch on top of your head." Alex replied, trying to keep a straight face.

Bartholomew reached up. "I do? Where?"

"Right there." Alex pointed at Bartholomew's forehead.

"Darn! Darn! Darn!" He hit his thigh with his fist. "I'll be right back." He turned toward the riverbank.

"Come, Deliverers. It is time." Horus called beckoning them to follow.

"In a minute. I won't be long," Bartholomew replied.

"Gotcha!" Alex punched him in the shoulder.

"Hey!" Bartholomew got a puppy grin on his face and hit Alex back before jogging to catch up with Horus.

Cradling the fabric again, Alex trailed behind, watching his goofy friend bob up and down, asking Horus a million questions. "Watch out for that–"

Alex spoke too late, and Bartholomew tripped on a rock. Down he went, nearly knocking Horus over in the process. He struggled to his feet and turned back to see if Alex had seen. With a shrug of his shoulders, he gave Alex a toothy grin.

Alex shook his head and laughed. Bartholomew's smile reminded Alex of all the times Mom had acted silly to relax him. Like the first time she took him swimming. She'd put on a whole show doing pratfalls into the pool just so he wouldn't be afraid of the water. It worked. He jumped right into her waiting arms. Man, they'd had fun that day.

His smile faded. Not anymore.

He clenched his jaw in grim determination and focused on the hike. Sweat beaded his upper lip, but he didn't wipe it away. Instead. he breathed in the hot wind of the desert and marched forward. Heat waves rose from the sand. Staring at the distant hills, he swung the papyrus sheet over his shoulder and quickened his pace to close the gap between with the others.

When he drew near, Bartholomew said, "Alex, remember what Isis said. You can create whatever you want."

Alex knew full well what Isis told them. It was trick she'd taught them the first day.

"You are creators," she'd said. "You have only to think of water, and your thirst will be quenched. Imagine coolness, and it is so."

But right then, he didn't want to feel cool and comfortable. He needed to sweat and feel his heart pounding against his chest. It kept his mind from his mother. He passed Bartholomew and trudged on in silence.

The distant cliffs jutted like a pharaoh's beard on a desert sand face, growing larger until the features blended back into the mountain. When they got to its base, Horus pointed to the gray summit above them. "The gathering is beyond yon ridge."

Alex began his ascent quickly, trying to match Horus's pace. But soon, he slowed. This path was steeper than it looked. Within minutes, both he and Bartholomew were creeping along as slowly as scarab beetles. The only sounds in the still air were their panting breaths and shoes crunching over the pebbled path.

"Horus, could you slow down?" Bartholomew gasped. "I am about to collapse."

Horus said nothing.

Alex wondered if they were being tested somehow. Maybe if they passed this test, they could go home. *Well, I'll show them. If I can beat both Mom and Dad to the top of a high mountain, I can do this.* With three deep breaths, he prepared his mind. He would not show doubt or disbelief. He would create by sheer will. He imagined a flat walkway, and suddenly it felt like level.

A final leap put him at the crest of the cliff. What lay below was like something out of a movie. On one side, stood a large village dotted with mud brick houses and open courtyards. The other had tombs etched into the mountain. Egyptian men in loincloths and women in single-strapped dresses trotted back and forth. Some carried baskets, while others balanced large urns on their heads. They passed in and out of the openings cut into the cliffs as they must have back on Earth thirty-five hundred years before.

"Welcome to the Valley of the Kings," Horus said with a wave of his hand. "Tomb of the pharaohs."

Alex stared at this giant cemetery where a barren pocket of desert-gray paths led to low stone walls. The light bricks barely contrasted against the rocky hills, making the man-made doorways hard to see.

An arid wind seeming to come from eons ago blew against Alex's face. He licked his dry lips. It was so was so quiet he could hear insects scuttling over the rocks.

Bartholomew must have remembered to create an easy hike in his mind because when he joined them at the top of the hill, he wasn't out of breath anymore.

"Wow! The Valley of the Kings. I read about this. Did you know it was Pharaoh Thutmose the First who decided to find a safer place for mummies? He wanted to stop all of the looting going on." Bartholomew dipped his head toward the valley. "Its remoteness sold him on this place. See?"

Alex sighed. There he goes again. You'd think this was a classroom.

"Yes," Horus said, "with only two ways in, it was easier to protect the pharaohs."

"I know." Bartholomew nodded. "Soldiers stood guard to keep robbers from stealing the treasures inside."

"Like those," Horus pointed below where twenty painted sentries stood at attention on either side of the path.

As the three of them approached, all the soldiers turned, held up their spears, and crossed shafts with a clicking of wood. Alex skidded to a stop to avoid their spiked tunnel.

"Halt! Who dares approach the Valley of the Kings?" the first kilted soldier demanded.

"In the name of Osiris, let us pass," Horus called out. "I bring the Deliverers on their appointed mission."

"All hail the Deliverers." They lifted their spears to the sky. "May the Pharaohs be freed!" Bowing deeply, they waved the trio through.

Bartholomew puffed up his chest, but Alex just stared straight ahead. He was here to do a job and hopefully keep monsters out of Mom's dreams, not to be flattered.

As they made their way toward the limestone cemetery cut into the mountain, Horus told them there were more than sixty tombs in the Valley of the Kings—a haven for the Ka and Ba spirits of the mummies.

"But," he warned, "if we are not successful, this entire valley and all who reside here will turn to dust."

Alex grew quiet. He was afraid to speak here, where so many lay buried. A pit in his stomach, he glanced at the shadowy doorways etched in the gray hillside.

Horus waved his feathered hand and ducked into one of those dark entrances, while a fact-chattering Bartholomew followed him. Alex shivered as he passed through the stony opening. Immediately, the creeping shadows of the passageway played tricks on his mind. He imagined the ghosts of all those people floating toward him. So many dead in these tombs.

He felt small and insignificant. This was quite an about-face for someone who always felt larger than life. He was a kid who could do things, wonderful things: 360s on his skateboard, paint robot-creatures that soared in his mind, or sketch pterodactyls in the blink of an eye.

Until Mom's heart attack. What good had his art been then? It hadn't helped her heart to beat any better. He saw her face on that day. Bloodless, pale. Like this graveyard. He didn't want to go any deeper into this place. He wanted to go home.

"Wow! Do you see the writing?" Bartholomew pointed his chin toward the wall of hieroglyphs at the end of the sloping corridor.

Alex ignored him. How could he be so excited in this death-filled place? The gloomy stone corridors were bad enough, but with the rubble in every corner, it made this place a regular prison.

"We enter the sacred place where the Litany of Ra sings. It is time for the gathering. Ready yourselves, Deliverers," Horus said.

They all passed through the halls as the flickering torches made grotesque shadows on their faces. At one point, Alex thought Bartholomew looked like the cobra goddess, Wadjet. It somehow made the boy look stronger.

Strange music floated toward them. With haunting flutes and distant drums, it sounded like a funeral dirge in an old movie. The words, "Sun-God, Raa, Osiris," filled the air.

They stepped down into one of the many sunken chambers. On the back wall, brightly painted hieroglyphs framed a scene. The half-jackal, half-man Anubis held up a mummy while two priests touched its face and other parts of its body with a fish-tail knife and a hooked tool. Singing softly, they repeated this action again and again.

"It is the Ritual of the Opening of the Mouth they act out, our way of preparing the dead for their journey into the Underworld. They are trying to call the trapped pharaohs home," Horus said.

Isis raised her arms and cried, "Gods of wood and clay. The time of the Gathering is nigh. Come!"

The torches flickered as the walls shook. When sand swirled at their feet, Bartholomew drew closer to Alex who gave him a reassuring smile. The room darkened in a familiar pattern, so it was no surprise when the torches burst back into flame to reveal Egyptian gods and goddesses.

A few he recognized from earlier, such as green-skinned Osiris and cat-headed Bastet, but there were others Alex had never seen. Some looked almost human, whereas others looked like the leftovers from a taxidermy experiment. One had a hippo's head, lion's feet, and a crocodile's tail. Another was a mummy holding a necklace with a loop-shaped end. Alex had to cover his mouth to keep from laughing when he saw the fat cow with shiny star eyes.

"Silence all," Osiris ordered as he stepped from the crowd and held up his staff.

The murmurings ceased, and all eyes turned to the God of the Underworld.

"As you know, Sickhert is gaining in strength. As we speak, he mounts an army for our demise. Yet there is still hope. Thoth, is it true the trapped pharaohs were able to send a message?"

The bird-headed god nodded while Alex cleared his throat to keep from chuckling at Thoth's funny rhyming speech: "Do I. Toward walls turn eyes. Portions from Book of the Dead. Appear now above your head." With these words, Thoth waved his hand and the frozen hieroglyphs on the wall began to move and rearrange themselves.

"*Save us, oh, gods. We are trapped. If we do not return before the sun rises and sets our Ka and Ba will be no more. Sickhert will remold us in mud.*" They sang in one voice.

"Not Mudlarks!" cried Bastet, her silky cat fur raised on end.

"Yes," Osiris spoke. "If we are not victorious, these kindred spirits will be ours no more. Those who once flew as free as larks from sarcophagus to the land of the living will be de-formed and re-formed into Mudlarks."

"What are Mudlarks?" Bartholomew asked.

"They are twisted creatures who do Sickhert's will," Isis explained.

"But they weren't always such. Once they were one of us," Horus continued. "A he or she, not an it. A creation in Artania. Part of our family who danced and sang or even flew."

"Until Mudlark Maker grabbed hold," said Thoth. "With twisting magic that morphs and molds."

"We can't let it happen again!" Alex protested.

"I was hoping you would say so, young one," Osiris said. "Once begun, to stop this is only possible with help from the Deliverers. But your art must be true. There will be no turning back once the trap is set, and we will only have one chance to save them."

"We'll try, sir. Whatever we can do." Bartholomew draped an arm over Alex's shoulder.

"You have done much already. Thoth tells me the papyrus is good and strong."

"We painted those cartouches just like you told us." Alex patted the large rolled sheet still tucked under one arm.

"But I still don't understand the plan," Bartholomew said. "How is this going to help?"

"A cartouche is more than a mere name," Osiris explained. "It is a symbol of a person's spirit. It contains his name enclosed by an oval circle of rope. This oval represents the outline of all that the sun encircled or the king's domain."

"You mean these are the trapped king's names?" Alex asked.

"Yes." Osiris replied.

"And it has magical powers?" Bartholomew raised his eyebrows and grinned.

"It is our hope," Osiris replied.

"We will use this to recapture our kin. Even so, you must use great care," Isis warned. "Our plan is to lure the Shadow Swine into opening a doorway between our worlds."

Thoth waved his hands in a circle. "But you Deliverers need to be standing by for magic to free."

Alex looked from god to god. Each with hopes pinned on him. Even though the responsibility weighed as heavily as a pyramid, he found himself standing straighter. He felt stronger than he had for a long time and couldn't wait to fight those Shadow Swine.

"You understand that only your presence at the doorway during the spell will release them from Subterranea...that place where Sickhert rules," Isis continued.

Osiris stepped next to his wife. "Should you fail, Sickhert has power enough to make all Egypt-art fall. Then we will be no more. Our life forces will become his."

"Only the chosen two can stop it," Horus added.

"Join together like single forged knives," Bartholomew quoted from the Soothsayer Stone.

Alex nodded quietly and clenched his jaw. For Mom, he would become steel. He stood before the gods and goddesses with but a single thought: *Words alone won't drive back these creatures. Only a battle will. It is time to wage war.*

Chapter 30

"Remember to lie perfectly still until Osiris gives the command," Isis said as Alex climbed into the stone sarcophagus. "Never forget you are a Creator. Air, water, food…it is all at your command. You have only to dream it."

Alex listened intently. Sure, it was easy for her to say. She wasn't lying in King Tut's coffin. So what if this single block of quartzite stone was beautiful? Who cared if it had carvings of goddesses in each corner and was the one untouched tomb discovered in the twentieth century? It was still a dark box she was closing him up in.

Emptied now to make room for Alex, this coffin had contained two other sarcophagi fitting inside each other like nesting dolls. At its center had been the amazing 22-carat gold form of King Tut, and since he was a sculpture, here in Artania he was alive. The young pharaoh's face had shone like sun on the Nile when they'd met earlier.

"Thank you, Deliverer," he'd said. "It is most brave of you to take my place as bait for the Shadow Swine. I, for one, fear them."

"No problem. Let's just kick some Swiney butt."

The yellow gold of the boy-king's face rippled and his lapis lined eyes crinkled into a smile. "May you triumph over the Anti-Artist Army."

Such amazing work! Alex wanted to reach out and pet the vulture nuzzling the cobra on the headcloth. He wondered what it would be like to have golden skin and wave around the crook and flail inlaid with lapis-blue stripes. The necklace he could do without since it seemed like a girly collar all set in red and blue glass.

Alex gave him a thumbs-up before saying goodbye.

Now squirming inside the sarcophagus, horribly cramped and even a little scared, he still was glad the real King Tut was tucked safely away. Soon Isis would come to close the coffin. Then he would be alone in the dark under a huge granite lid.

Sandaled feet shuffled across the floor, and Alex peered over the side to see the disk-crowned goddess approaching. When she began to seal him in, Alex placed a hand over her wrist to stop her. "Why do I have to be bait? Why does Bartholomew get to hold the papyrus while I'm stuck in this death box?" he asked.

"Your mind is so filled with thoughts of death that even Lord Sick-hert will be fooled into thinking a mummy is here." Isis said. "You must face this fear, or you will be of little use to us. Remember the guardians in each corner of the sarcophagus are here for you."

"Fear not. We are by your side," the four goddesses whispered. They beat their outstretched wings against the side of the coffin and cool air met Alex's face.

He looked away, not knowing how to reply.

"Ready?" Isis asked her dark face full of concern.

Alex nodded. Like a diver preparing to descend, he filled his lungs and lay down. He knew he could create more oxygen, but it still made him feel better to gulp a few mouthfuls first.

Several gods joined her to help push, and the coffin lid closed. Waves of darkness splashed over him. Alex put his hand in front of his face. He couldn't see a thing; he squeezed his eyes shut and tried to think of happy things. He thought of sailing in a harbor on a bright summer's day, but the boat began to sink as if a sea were closing in on him, entangling his arms in seaweed ropes.

Alex gasped for breath. He was drowning.

"Our world will be saved if their art is true," the protecting goddesses whispered in unison.

"Get me out of here! I can't breathe."

"Our world will be saved if their art is true."

He grasped his throat, searching for a last pocket of oxygen. It was gone. His chest tightened as if an entire ocean were pressing down on him. Alex coughed. Choked. Gasped. Sucked at empty space.

"Art...Art... Art..." they chanted. He felt a small hand reach through the coffin and unclasp his fingers from his throat. When he finally relaxed each digit, the goddess drew shapes in his palm.

As she drew, Alex remembered a paintbrush in his hand, a blank canvas before him, and his studio in the garage. He ventured a small breath. A bit of cool air flowed into his mouth. He sucked in more, letting his lungs fill with sweet oxygen.

He must have drifted off because the next thing he knew he was dreaming of home. Mom was standing in their sunny kitchen making his favorite: spaghetti and meatballs. He liked it because you didn't just eat it, you could make designs with the long noodles, too.

"Wash those hands, Rainbow Kid," she said, smiling at him.

Returning her smile, he looked down at his hands. They were covered in brilliant paint shining like Las Vegas lights. Each finger was a different colored spotlight. He wiggled them, pointing beams of red, blue, and green on the walls. Giggling, Mom danced between them like she had danced in a rain shower back in Boulder.

He was ready to join her when a sound awoke him. It was the gurgling of a familiar voice. "I smell him. Come minions."

Alex's eyes shot open. Sludge!

"Yes, sir," several voices rasped.

"We have waited too long for the stars to be exactly right, and now is our time. Soon we'll have their precious Tutankhamen. With the thirteenth pharaoh, all of Egypt will fall," Sludge said.

"And Sickhert will reward us goodly. Right, sir?"

Sludge cackled.

Scum! Alex put his fingers in his ears. He knew their howling laughter all too well. It had echoed in his dreams for weeks. Every night since Mom's heart attack. He pressed harder trying to shut it all out, digging his nails in deeper until they almost cut his skin.

Then he heard the muffled sound of fists pounding on the coffin, and he remembered the plan. Steeling himself, he unplugged his ears and listened for the signal. He tried to think of what to do if they opened the lid before the gods were ready.

It would take time for the Shadow Swine to move the heavy lid. It weighed over a ton, and it sounded like there were only a couple of Swineys there to move it. Then Sludge would call more in to help. Even if they opened it, Alex had time. There were still the stone relief goddesses to contend with. And by then the army should attack.

Clenching and unclenching his fists, he waited.

Chapter 31

Hugging the papyrus, Bartholomew crouched farther behind the gilded wooden screen surrounding King Tutankhamen's sarcophagus. Even though Alex lay as bait inside the coffin, Osiris, Isis, Bastet, and several Egyptian soldiers lined up ready to help. It was still scary, but he felt a little better knowing this shrine went all the way around the casket so the Shadow Swine wouldn't see them until it was too late.

Along the corridor and in the adjoining antechamber were scores of Egyptian soldiers, waiting for Osiris's signal. Their green-skinned general stood at the head of the line, sword raised, cloth crown cocked to the side.

Earlier, Bartholomew spent some time getting to know a few of these beings. He'd felt a little shy at first until a young warrior named Thutma demonstrated a few moves with his long sword. Soon, the two were practicing thrusts and lunges just like old friends.

When Bartholomew glanced at Bastet to his right, the cat-headed goddess winked at him. He felt his cheeks redden. Twitching her whiskers, she purred a giggle, so he turned away, only to have Horus in boy form grin at him.

Then Bartholomew heard a shuffling sound. "Are they coming?"

Horus put a finger to his lips and pointed to a crack between two of the walls. When Bartholomew peered inside, he had to cover his mouth. There, lined up on one side of the coffin, were six hunchbacked Shadow Swine—all pushing against the lid with their slimy hands.

Horrible Captain Sludge was in the front, urging them on. His muscular shoulders bulged through his dark cloak as he pressed against the coffin. Bartholomew held his breath, praying the lid would stay in place.

"Curses!" Sludge growled and pounded the stone with his fists. Pulling a mud-encased stick from his long coat, he raised it skyward. "Shadow, muck, and whither wall. Listen servants to my call. A waging war is ours to win. I call for help from my minions."

Instantly, the floor shook. Eyes glued to the scene, Bartholomew took a step closer, but he didn't see Bastet's quiver of arrows on the ground until it was too late. Tripping over them, he fell against the wooden shrine which leaned inward.

It teetered.

"Careful, Deliverer," Horus rasped as he reached out and steadied the wall. "Surprise is our greatest ally."

Blushing again, Bartholomew nodded and sat back on his haunches. The view from there would be just fine.

As the hole in front of the coffin widened, dark slimy faces with slit pupils emerged. Bartholomew shuddered as the staircase secreted muddy head after muddy head, all with flaring porcine nostrils. Snuffling sounds chafed his ears, and their matted hair made him reach for the hand sanitizer in his pocket. One had a hump so large Bartholomew wondered how it could walk upright. More came. Their dark cloaks rustled against the flooring as they snaked their way upward. Bartholomew counted them: Two, four... twenty.

The doorway to Subterranea was open. Just a few moments more. Bartholomew rubbed in the sterilizing gel.

"Sloven slaves," Captain Sludge sneered. "What took you so long?"

"We had long way to go. We was bathing at Swallow Hole Swamp. It—"

"I don't care if you were at Sickhert's Stalagmite. We are at war. Stand at the ready!"

"Sorry, Captain," the Swiney with the large hump mumbled.

"Get along that side," Sludge growled irritably and pointed to positions beside the granite sarcophagus. "There and there."

The creatures rushed into place. Half put their claw-tipped fingers on the lid and leaned forward. This rest clapped their hands onto the hulking backs in front of them.

"Watch your nails," a Swiney in the first row grumbled to the one standing next to him.

"You watch yours!"

"Silence idiots!"

The monsters swayed back and forth angrily but followed their captain's orders.

Bartholomew never saw such a disgusting group of creatures. Not as if he'd seen many creatures in his isolated life. Even a trip to the zoo was more than his mother would ever allow. Too much filth. Of course, he'd never owned any pets. He did capture a spider once, which had sent Mother into a cleaning fury lasting for weeks.

Even the pictures of animals were nothing like these Shadow Swine. They were almost human with those huge piggish nostrils flaring at every breath. But their skin was so different. It was shiny and covered in dripping slime. Bartholomew hated their eyes. Those yellow snake eyes took him to nightmares he wished he'd forgotten.

The Swineys locked their arms straight in place and leaned forward.

"Heave, ho! Heave ho!"

Ropey throats quivered as they strained against the stone. Muddy beads of sweat pooled on their heavy brows. It dripped onto their dark coats, leaving ugly raised splotches. Thankfully, the lid didn't budge.

"Harder you fools!" Sludge cried. "Push!"

Osiris lowered his curved sword. "Attack!"

Before the Shadow Swine could say "Sickhert," the Egyptians were upon them. Like an avalanche of rolling rocks, they rushed forward, weapons held high. Caught off guard, several monsters fell before realizing what had happened.

"It's a trap!" Sludge cried, pulling a battle-axe from his ebony cloak. "To arms!"

The Shadow Swine drew swords, clubs, and chains from the folds of cloaks and the tops of jackboots. The sound of metal against metal filled the air. Biting his lip, Bartholomew crouched farther out of the way. Sludge swung his battle-axe at the soldier Bartholomew met earlier. It missed Thutma by mere millimeters.

"Come on. Beat him," Bartholomew whispered.

The soldier raised his sword and thrust but met only air. The two adversaries planted their feet firmly and stared into each other's eyes. Sludge feinted left, raising his axe-wielding arm at the same time.

"Watch out!" Bartholomew cried.

Thutma jerked to one side. Still, the axe fell. He crumpled to the stones, and Bartholomew's Egyptian friend was no more.

"No," Bartholomew moaned, swallowing the sick bile in his throat.

Bastet mewed angrily, baring her sharp teeth at the nearest Shadow Swine. With a flick of the whiskers, she raised her bow. She nocked an arrow while the Swiney opposite her ducked and charged. Butting her with his shoulder, he knocked her off balance, and the shaft hit the ceiling.

The monster grinned, showing rows of jagged teeth as he reached for her throat. Big mistake, Bartholomew thought.

Bastet pulled a gold-hilted dagger from the belt around her waist and with a single thrust, turned him to dust.

Behind her, a column of growling Shadow Swine took up their cudgels, daggers, and spears. Surging forward, they knocked one of the gilded panels over. Bartholomew ducked, thankful his wall was still standing. Bastet turned with her arrow already nocked and dropped two in quick succession.

With a howling trumpet from another muddy creature's horn, more Shadow Swine stormed up the steps and ripped into the awaiting Egyptians. Swords met spears, and lances met clubs.

"Gilded gods! Advance!" Osiris cried, holding off two Swineys with his curved sword.

The second battalion of Egyptians sprang from the wooden panels. Dwarves, lions, and jackals tumbled toward a gaping Shadow Swine who didn't seem to know which way to turn.

"Apis!" Osiris called. His back was against the wall. He swung his scimitar again at the pair of Swineys advancing on him.

The bull leaped from his place above the hieroglyphs and galloped toward Osiris. Lowering his head, he charged at the two Swineys who'd cornered the god. When he rammed, they toppled over, and Osiris finished them off with his sword.

Holding the papyrus to his chest as he'd been ordered, Bartholomew continued watching from behind the only remaining wall. He shivered, knowing it didn't make any sense in this place. He wasn't cold. He wondered if the strong Alex was doing the same inside the coffin.

It looked like Sludge had little chance of winning. His soldiers were dropping right and left. But oddly, he didn't look defeated. If anything, his yellow eyes shone with victory. After felling several Egyptians with a single swing, he vaulted onto the ledge of the great stone sarcophagus.

The lid was too heavy to open, wasn't it?

With a quick glance over his shoulder, Sludge thrust the butt of his axe into the fissure between the lid and the coffin. Using the handle as a lever, he leaned over to drive a wedge between top and base. The lid slid open and fell beside the sarcophagus with a crash.

Bartholomew's jaw dropped. This hadn't been part of the plan. They were supposed to win before the coffin was ever breached.

"Now I have you, King Tutankhamen," Sludge gurgled, dropping his axe. As he peered into the sarcophagus, the captain's jagged smile disappeared. He threw his head back and roared with anger. "You! What trickery is this?"

"Get away from me," Alex growled.

"Orders from a child?" Sludge sneered and pointed a single clawed finger at the boy. "An unarmed one at that."

My friend! Bartholomew's eyes darted to and fro. All the gods were busy fighting. He felt sick. No one could see what was happening to Alex.

The rising bile in his throat forced his mouth shut on his warning cry. Swallowing hard, he watched Alex draw up his knees and kick the Swiney with both his feet. It was horrifying how the creature didn't even budge.

Alex kicked again. Still nothing. Sludge grabbed Alex by the collar, lifted him into the air, and shook him. Alex's body flailed about like a cloth doll in a windstorm.

Bartholomew stood. Curling his fists in anger, he punched the gilded panel which clattered onto the floor. Blind to anything but saving Alex, he stumbled over the fallen wall and leaped onto Sludge's back.

"Get off, human!" Sludge dropped Alex and jerked around, but Bartholomew held fast.

"Go, Alex! Run!" Bartholomew cried, trying to maintain a grip on a slippery neck.

"Bartholomew! What are you doing? You don't know how to fight."

"Hurry. I can't hold him for long."

Sludge reached around to grab Bartholomew, but the boy ducked to the left and scraped his leg against the inside of the coffin. Snarling, the Swiney shook his hunched shoulders, scraping Bartholomew's leg even more. He cringed but refused to let go.

Alex wriggled out from under them and had just cleared the top of the sarcophagus when Sludge said, "Oh, no you don't." He drew his fist back and punched Alex square in the face.

Alex fell back, holding his bleeding nose in his hands.

Bartholomew saw red. "Don't you hurt my friend!" he screeched, biting into the muddy neck.

"Yowww!" Sludge tried shaking the boy off, but Bartholomew only clamped down harder. Sludge arched his back, grunted, and smashed Bartholomew against the stone sarcophagus.

Bartholomew dug his teeth in. A toilet water taste filled his mouth as blow after blow knocked him against the coffin. Knotty bruises swelled on his back, but he willed himself to hold on.

Then came the blow even friendship couldn't withstand. The huge Shadow Swine growled and twisted to the side, smashing Bartholomew's arm into the stone. He heard a sickening crunch. Blinded with pain, he unclenched his jaw, slid down the hunched back, and crumpled beside Alex.

"Stupid humans." Sludge cuffed Bartholomew's head before plunging back into the fight.

Shards of pain shot up Bartholomew's arm. His head throbbed. Globs of slime matted his hair and dripped down his face leaving an acrid taste in his mouth. "Swiney sweat. Disgusting," he spat.

"Hey," Alex leaned over Bartholomew and wiped the slime out of his hair with one corner of his t-shirt. "Thanks."

"Sure," Bartholomew said, trying to sound strong through the waves of pain flooding his arm.

"Are you okay?"

Bartholomew tried to straighten his elbow. Wincing, he ventured a glance. His arm was bent and twisted. Spots appeared in front of his eyes as he started to swoon.

Alex shook him. "Remember what Isis told us. See it and it will be."

"I can't. It's ruined. I will never sculpt again."

"Come on, B-Three. Don't be a baby." Alex grasped Bartholomew's shoulders and stared him straight in the eye. "You can do it."

Alex's deep brown eyes made Bartholomew believe in his powers. He took several long breaths.

"Yes. Breathe in and out. Imagine your arm healthy. Straight. Strong. Whole."

Bartholomew exhaled slowly. "Hey, it work—"

"Duck!" Alex cried, shoving him to the left.

The blade missed, but when Bartholomew looked up, three Shadow Swine with raised swords were perched on the sarcophagus frame above them. This was it. Death was imminent. He covered his head.

Like Apis the Bull, Alex went from a crouch to a leap, butting the first Swiney right in the gut. It teetered and knocked the other two off the edge back onto the floor.

"Come on!" Alex cried, grabbing Bartholomew by the wrist.

One Shadow Swine was already getting back up and swinging its sword. Air rushed past Bartholomew's right ear. He pointed, frozen in place, mouth opening and closing in silent protest.

"Let's go!" Alex half dragged him out of the coffin.

The boys scrambled over the wooden panels, trying to dodge the Shadow Swine who seemed to be everywhere. Zigzagging away from swords, they ran to and fro, seeking escape. Bartholomew felt like a jerboa mouse running from a pack of hyenas.

"What do we do?" he cried, jerking away from yet another Swiney's claws.

"Let's try in here." Alex ducked through an opening, Bartholomew right behind him.

They found more of the same in the antechamber. Here a wooden couch in the shape of a leopard smacked a fat Swiney, sending his dreadlocked head backwards. Canopic jars hopped around like hot sparks until one bopped the shorter Swiney on the head, and a satisfying crack filled the air.

"Come on!" Alex pointed to a hole in the wall and crawled inside.

Bartholomew scrambled through, hoping no Swineys followed him.

Bartholomew stood. The fight hadn't reached this small room. No wonder. Where would they find space? Hundreds of reed baskets and pottery jars were stacked high in one corner. A heap of royal furniture, urns, and clothes were piled in the other.

Alex squeezed his way behind some stools. He picked up some linen cloth and draped it over his body. "Hurry, hide."

Bartholomew realized where he was. *King Tut's annex!* He would have shouted it if Alex weren't waiting with imploring eyes, so Bartholomew pushed past the dusty furniture and took his place at Alex's side. *It's the great discovery of Howard Carter and Lord Carnarvon back in 1922... the most intact tomb ever found. Wow.* He didn't say any of this to Alex, keeping thoughts to himself as he crouched and pulled a corner of the linen cloth over his head.

The battle raged on in the next room.

Chapter 32

"Retreat!" Captain Sludge's muffled voice came through the wall. Then Bartholomew heard a whoop of triumph rise from the Egyptian army and heaved a cautious sigh of relief.

Alex tossed the linen blanket aside and gave him playful jab in the shoulder. "Cool, B-Three. It worked."

Bartholomew carefully made his way out from under the jumble of furniture they'd been hiding behind and followed Alex back through the doorway. He got a lump in his throat as they made their way through the litter of bodies and piles of dust. Moments before, those people had been smiling and laughing with him. His friends, magical chairs dancing in battle moments before, now were timber and twigs in heaps. A wooden cobra lay in a corner, curled up and still.

It all made him think. *Since we are the creators, we did this carnage, going from wonder to death in the blink of an eye.* It was no longer some abstract painting or sculpture in his mind. These creations were real. In many ways, more real than any people he'd ever known.

As he tiptoed back to King Tut's shrine, he looked around furtively, unconvinced that all the Shadow Swine were gone. To make sure, he peered down the dark staircase to see if any were hiding there before standing next to the sarcophagus with Alex as the medics in white linen robes attended the wounded.

A much smaller army gathered around it this time. Bartholomew chewed on his lower lip and tried not to think about the cost.

He saw Thoth among the survivors and noticed though many had fallen, most of his newest friends remained. A bruised Bastet checked her quiver of arrows while Horus and Isis leaned against each other for support. Osiris looked grimly over the company with Anubis, the jackal-headed warrior, at his side.

"Friends." Osiris raised a green hand waiting for the murmurings to quiet before continuing. "You have battled well, and for your sacrifice, I thank you, but our task is not yet complete."

"Yes," Thoth continued. "Time for the papyrus spell, the clock it ticks, and pharaohs' lives soon it will fix. Young Deliverers, bring papyrus to see, and kindred souls we will free."

"Yes, sir." Alex rested a hand on Bartholomew's shoulder.

Bartholomew felt the blood drain from his face.

"What is it?" Alex asked, grinning. "You're as white as a mummy."

Bartholomew's mouth opened and closed but no sound came out.

"Quickly, young one. The door left by the Shadow Swine remains open but a short time," Osiris said.

Bartholomew's stomach lurched as looked around wildly. He mumbled.

"Hurry up, B-Three," Alex urged.

Leaning in close to Alex, Bartholomew whispered, "I can't. I lost it."

"What?" Alex cried.

All eyes turned to Bartholomew.

"I…lost…it…during…the battle," he stammered. "I must have dropped it."

"Quickly, search the room," Osiris ordered.

They all scrambled. Bastet and Anubis went one direction turning over chairs and peering into corners. Thoth hopped in another, using his ibis's legs to kick apart the piles of Swiney dust. Horus morphed into hawk form and flew overhead. A scowling Alex stomped to the gilded panels and rummaged beneath them.

Bartholomew's search was the most desperate of all. He retraced every step from annex to antechamber and tomb to treasury. Guilty knots twisted his gut as he peered under stools and baskets and groped inside ebony and alabaster chests. He ransacked coffins and canopic jars, tossing aside cloth, weapons, and armor.

Refusing to meet any of those accusing eyes, Bartholomew went over every square inch of the tomb, going back to the same place two, three, four times. While the rest of the company sadly returned to King Tut's sarcophagus, he searched, refusing to believe the sad truth.

And kept on.

Osiris's firm hand on his chest blocked his way. "It is gone. The Shadow Swine must have taken it."

Crumpling next to the sarcophagus, Bartholomew buried his face in his hands. "I am so sorry."

Solemn and resigned, the gods and goddesses nodded. Many turned to go, but a glaring Alex stood over him. "Get up. Find it." He shoved Bartholomew's shoulder.

"There is no hope, young one," Osiris said. "And there is no time to make a new one."

"Why did I come here then? To watch you blow it, Richie? No way. We have to do something."

"Don't you understand? The Shadow Swine will not be tricked into opening the doorway again. Our kindred are beyond reach in Sickhert's realm," Bastet said.

"So?" Alex asked.

"Our power wanes in Subterranea. We can be turned to Mudlarks below," explained Isis.

"How about us?" Bartholomew asked, raising his head "Can we be turned into Mudlarks?"

"This I do not know." Osiris stroked his long straight beard. "So few of your kind have ever visited. Thoth?"

"Back in days of millennium four. In the time of Egypt gone before. There said was a Deliverer true, who did walk a doorway through. Caw! Caw! Believe the boon saying how you Deliverers are immune," Thoth said hopping to Bartholomew.

"Okay, then." Feeling a glimmer of hope, Bartholomew stood. "It's what I'll do. I will go underground and get the papyrus back."

"You?" Alex stared at him as if he were a stranger. "You worry if your pants get dirty."

"I can do this. I know it."

Alex pointed at the dark hole in the floor. "How are you supposed to find anything?"

"The same way I found Grandfather's studio. My instincts."

"Yeah, they've worked really great up till now."

Remembering how his father had drowned in strange circumstances, Bartholomew looked Alex square in the eye. "But we have to defeat Sludge. You know why."

Fear clouded Alex's face. "The nightmares. Mom's heart," he whispered so low only Bartholomew could hear. Then he turned to the surrounding gods. "He's right."

"We cannot trust those young ones to go alone," Bastet argued with a twitch of her whiskers. "They are ignorant and inexperienced."

Isis nodded, her motherly voice full of concern. "Even though one Deliverer made it through Subterranea, that doesn't mean these boys will. Sickhert may have figured out a way to morph Deliverers."

"If the Deliverers become Mudlarks, all will be lost," a soldier from the crowd called out.

Many chimed in with echoes of the soldier's fears. It was a dangerous idea. These boys were the chosen ones. If they were remolded in Sickhert's realm, Artania would be no more. But if the pharaohs were not rescued, Egypt will surely fall. Arguments bounced off the walls like leather balls volleying in an ancient game.

"Silence!" Osiris commanded, holding his staff above him. Next, he climbed atop the sarcophagus and pointed his staff at the crowd. "Arguments are in vain. Do we follow the Deliverers and try to save our home? Or do we give it up to Sickhert and let our kindred souls be forever encased in mud?"

"But what of the doorway?" Isis asked, her sun disk glowing yellow. "How much time do we have before it closes?"

"Unknown," Osiris replied. "Thoth?"

The ibis-headed god was already reading the etched hieroglyphs on the sarcophagus. A split second later all the writing rearranged itself and grew by a third. Thoth ran a finger over the writing. "Here lies an open door, but magic lasts only hours four." The bird-god said bobbing his beak in time to his rhyme.

The gathered group grew quieter. Many stared into the dark opening. Bartholomew blinked. Four hours? Could they rescue these pharaohs and escape in just four hours?

In the silence, Osiris circulated again, capturing the gaze of every soldier, god, and goddess in the crowd. He tapped the sarcophagus with his staff. Once, twice, three times, then repeated the thrumming again.

The crowd stomped its feet in unison with the staff, beating out the rhythm of hope.

"As for me," Osiris said, his voice strong and deep, "I say we stand shoulder to shoulder with the Deliverers. Are you with me?"

Bastet stepped forward, holding her bow across her chest. She raised it in the air and took her place behind Osiris. Thoth hopped up beside her. The jackal-headed Anubis touched a hand to his heart in tribute. Horus and Isis took flight and hovered in the air on either side of their green-skinned leader.

When the room quieted, Osiris spoke. "We stand ready to embark upon a dangerous journey. But remember hope lies in creation, young ones. Go forth, for pharaoh and fate."

Trying to proceed nobly, Bartholomew took a single step into the dark opening. "For pharaoh and fate," he whispered.

It would, he knew, take a great deal more than hope to make their way through Subterranea. It would take all his creative talents and more.

Chapter 33

With Osiris and the rest of the gods and soldiers behind them, Bartholomew and Alex descended the slippery stair the Shadow Swine had left.

Bartholomew tried to walk lightly, afraid the thin granite stilts supporting the twisting staircase hugging the cavern wall would snap with too much weight. If it crumbled, there wouldn't even be a handrail to cling to. This slimy trail into Subterranea seemed to drop for miles, zigzagging ever downward into darkness. He stared at the ropey stream of water trickling from each step and shivered.

Bartholomew was silent, his shame pressing on his mind.

If only he hadn't been so stupid! He'd only had one job; hold the papyrus until Thoth gave the signal. He couldn't even do that right.

But I'll get it back. They'll see, he thought. Then his shoulders slumped. *Who am I kidding?*

A few steps below, Alex marched down the stairs, slim shoulders held erect, dark curls like a knight's helmet in the torchlight. Bartholomew longed for such valor. Even if it put him in harm's way, Alex always trudged onward.

If I hadn't messed up, he'd be on his way home now.

Bartholomew only looked away for a moment, but it was enough for disaster. His foot hit a mossy patch. Slipping, he reached out, but met only air.

Legs flailing, he slid backwards down the stony stair. "Ahh!"

Arms outstretched, Bartholomew collided with Alex. His friend tumbled into his lap and they became a backward bobsled skidding, slipping, and bumping downward.

Smack! They hit bottom, a jumble of arms and legs. Bartholomew clung to Alex gasping for breath.

"Get off me!" Alex shoved him.

Bartholomew rolled clumsily to the left, his knees digging into Alex's gut.

"Oomph!" Alex coughed and wrapped his arms around his stomach. "Did you take a numbskull pill today or what?"

Bartholomew didn't reply.

"I'm talking to you, Richie."

Bartholomew just stared into the blackness wishing he could disappear.

"I said, did you take a pill today? Or are you just stupid?"

"Shut up."

"Must be yes."

"I am not."

"Could've fooled me."

"You better stop," Bartholomew warned.

"Yeah, like you could really make me, Richie. If it weren't for you I'd be home by now. Stupid Richie."

"Shut up!"

"Richie, Richie, stupid Richie." Alex stood up and shoved Bartholomew's shoulder.

For the second time, Bartholomew saw red. He leaped up. "Didn't you hear me?" He pushed Alex back. "I said shut up!"

"Yeah? Make me." Alex raised his fists.

Bartholomew charged, but Alex sidestepped at the last moment, and Bartholomew fell to his knees. "I'll knock you off your cocky feet!" he yelled. He jumped up and lunged again, this time pulling Alex's ankles out from under him. Before he could get back up, Bartholomew straddled Alex's chest and tugged on his ears.

Raising his hips, Alex bucked his assailant to forward, then butted with his head, and Bartholomew yelped, covering his nose. Alex wriggled out from under.

"Oh, no you don't," Bartholomew said, pinning Alex's wrists to the floor.

Alex kicked, knocking Bartholomew over. Now he was on top, but not for long.

Bartholomew jerked to the right, pulling Alex with him. Like rocks tumbled by the Nile, they rolled over and over. Each tried to wrestle for control, but neither could get the upper hand. In desperation, Bartholomew grabbed a fistful of Alex's hair.

"Oww!" Alex grimaced. Then narrowing his eyes, he dug his fingernails into Bartholomew's arms.

Bartholomew pulled harder. A few hairs came loose in his hand.

Suddenly, Osiris appeared in the gloom and thrust his staff between them. "Cease! Do you wish for us all to become Mudlarks?"

Bartholomew froze, his anger dissipating like mist in the desert. Biting his lip, he let go of Alex and slowly stood. In what was becoming a familiar posc, Bartholomew hung his head and mumbled an apology.

"Foolish children." Osiris held up his hand. "Words are meaningless. Only actions speak." He turned away from the boys.

"Yeah, stupid Richie," Alex hissed under his breath.

With a heavy sigh, Osiris turned back to face Alex and Bartholomew. "We are now in Sickhert's realm. Be ever on your guard." He raised his crook at the ibis-headed scribe. "Thoth, as the reckoner of years, do you know where we must go?"

Thoth nodded. "Have, I do. Though writings are few. That long tunnel leads, to the place Mudlark Maker feeds."

Next Osiris called for the torchbearers whose flames revealed they were in a cave with limy sandstone walls. A few stalactites hung menacingly from the ceiling some twenty feet above. Half a dozen stalagmites grew on the floor. Like a ticking clock, water dripped rhythmically from the rocky formations above to the ones below, leaving ghostly deposits of calcite.

They reminded Bartholomew of sobbing children. He thought the dripping water must be tears from all those lost creations turned to Mudlarks over time.

The torchbearers circled the room in search of exit tunnels. They found two at opposite ends of the cave. Thoth laid a stylus flat in the palm of his hand. It twisted to and fro like the needle on a compass not pointing to either one.

"Which do we choose?" Isis asked.

"Believe I downward we must go," Thoth said as he rubbed his feathered head. "Yes, I recall writings told it so. Beware the tunnel going south, for it leads to Swallow Hole's mouth."

"You must lead the way." Osiris placed his hands on the boys' shoulders. "Remember, as creators only you have powers here in Sickhert's realm. But they have limits, so be wary."

Bartholomew's heart raced. This place felt so evil. He fell in line behind Alex, pausing at the entrance. "Lava tube tunnel," Bartholomew said, reaching out to feel the black walls around him.

"I know. I saw the volcano video, too," Alex retorted in a less than convincing voice.

Thoth stepped forward. "Rivers of lava did this land make. Please, care take, or plunge into a fiery lake."

Bartholomew shuddered at the thought. "In our world, these things can collapse quite easily," he said. "We should all be careful."

He took a deep breath and followed Alex into the dark tube.

Chapter 34

The light from the torches cast eerie ghost shadows as it crawled up the walls. All Alex could hear was the light slapping of leather sandals, the rustling of linen tunics, and Bartholomew's shuffling feet.

Bartholomew sidled closer to him, his eyes wide. "You don't suppose shadows come alive here, too?" he asked in a low voice.

"Fear not, young one," Osiris said from behind them. "Sickhert's army does not hide. You will know when they are nearby for stealth is not one of their talents."

Alex couldn't help but smile. He shook his head. "Those guys are nothing. You just had one for breakfast."

"I know." Bartholomew spat. "I can still taste it. Yuck." He shuddered.

Alex laid a hand on Bartholomew's shoulder.

"Sorry about the fight back there. It's just—"

"I know. Home. How's your head?"

"Good as new. See?" Alex raised one eyebrow, then the other. Grinning, he wiggled his ears.

Bartholomew chuckled. Alex was about to join in when he heard an echoing sound and held up a finger for silence. There it was again, like a den of whispering snakes. Craning to listen, he cupped a hand to his ear.

With a wave of his staff, Osiris signaled the company to retreat. He bent over and leaned closer to Alex.

"We will wait here while you investigate," he whispered.

"No worries, guys," Alex said in a low voice. "We've got this covered, don't we B-Three?"

Bartholomew nodded

When the torchbearers marched out of sight, darkness fell upon Alex like a shroud. Far off in the distance, he could see a pinhole of light and headed toward it, groping along with a clinging Bartholomew shuffling behind.

The hole grew wider until a shaft of light appeared in the floor. At the same time, the muffled hissing changed into voices. Alex could even pick out a word here and there. "Sickhert…powers…Mudlarks…No!"

That "no" stopped him dead in his tracks. It was not the wolfish rasp of a Shadow Swine. It was the regal voice of a king. Like torches flooding the tunnel with light, hope washed over Alex. The pharaohs hadn't been turned into Mudlarks yet!

He put a finger to his lips and tiptoed forward, stopping a few feet short of the hole in the floor. Now the words clearly echoed up the tunnel.

"You dare to defy the captain of the most powerful army in Subterranea? Second only to Sickhert himself?" a familiar voice sneered.

"I am Ramses, conqueror and builder of Egypt. I will never bow to your will."

"You don't have any choice, king."

Alex knew it was risky, but his curiosity got the better of him. Dropping to all fours, he crawled to the end of the tunnel. Bartholomew started to argue, but when Alex ignored the protests, his friend quieted.

The round hole cut into the floor was large enough for five men to fit through. Or, Alex thought with a shudder, two of those Shadow Swine with their monstrous hunched backs. Alex peered down through the opening glowing like a single cobra's eye. A wooden ladder hugged one side of the obsidian wall.

"Bartholomew, check this out," he whispered, motioning with one hand.

Bartholomew crawled forward slowly, then craned his neck over the empty space. "Holy dust bunnies!" he gasped, his fingers digging into the damp soil.

They were suspended above one end of an enormous cavern. A stalagmite forest as thick as papyrus marshes on the Nile lay directly below. In the glow of multiple torches at the far end, Shadow Swine were gathered around a wooden platform. Alex did a double take. Squinting, he could just make out the see-through-figure of a crowned man in the center of the raised stage.

"I think I see one of the pharaohs," he said.

"It is?" Bartholomew asked. "Oh, look. You can see right through him. I guess it's from the trapping spell, like Thoth said."

"It's Sludge." Alex jabbed a finger at that ugly monster, remembering every inflection of the evil voice haunting his nightmares for weeks. With a clenched jaw, he scrunched up his face and lowered his tone into an imitation of the Swiney. "I am captain of the most powerful army in Subterranea. Second only to Sickhert himself."

"I still don't see how you copy him. It's real enough to give me the heebie jeebies."

Alex shrugged, but just then the real Captain Sludge cackled, and both boys craned their necks to see why.

"You will not easily destroy me. I have monuments in Karnak, Luxor, and Thebes," the pharaoh cried.

"Ha! You think so? Watch." Captain Sludge raised his voice to a commanding roar. "Bring forth the cat!"

Alex was horrified to see a Swiney dressed like an executioner carrying a cat mummy up the platform steps. Struggling to free itself, the pitiful thing had ripped off most of its linen wrappings and was clawing in vain at the monster holding it by the scruff of the neck. Extending the cat to his leader, the hooded one bowed in front of Captain Sludge.

"No!" Ramses jerked right and left. "Not my pet! You can't," he pleaded.

"Of course, I can, and I will. Observe." Sludge pointed a large club at the pharaoh before touching the cat with it and calling, "Arise, Mudlark Maker. Rise."

Sludge stepped to the edge of the platform and lowered his club until it touched the mound of soil below him. When the ground swelled, a single strand of mud anchored onto the wooden club. Sludge slowly raised his arms as the muddy fibers grew wider. A head arose, and long tentacle-like arms sprouted. Bulbous lips swelled. Soon the mud became a legless creature with long ratty hair.

"A mud monster, gross," Bartholomew said.

"Yeah," Alex said as the entire cavern vibrated with the creature's sigh.

"I am Mudlark Maker. I make any Artanian a slave." Its rippling arms seized the cat and held it up in front of its huge face. "Aww, a snack. Yum."

With these words Mudlark Maker's body melted away while its mouth kept growing larger until it was as big as an elephant's grave. Soon all Alex could see were two boggy arms holding the mewling cat. Then Mudlark Maker raised the poor creature directly over its mouth and dropped it in. The giant lips closed. Next came a loud swallow that shook the walls.

Alex clenched his jaw. Sweat beaded on his upper lip as long seconds passed. He exchanged a glance with Bartholomew.

The mouth opened with a huge belch, and a spray of steam spewed out the cat, which landed at Captain Sludge's feet. Now, a muck-covered feline crouched in place of what once was a beautiful mummy. Its red eyes flashed like jewels from hell as it stretched its mouth into a yowl. Alex wished he could block out its evil mewing. Then he heard the terrifying orders.

"Attack Ramses. Scratch his eyes out."

Hairs rose on the cat's arched back. It hissed and crouched, ready to pounce.

Chapter 35

Alex grabbed Bartholomew by the collar. "We have to do something."

Raising his eyebrows, Bartholomew glanced at the dripping walls. "Okay. We create, right?"

"That's what I'm saying. We create a way to help him."

Bartholomew felt moisture soak through the knees of his slacks and leaned back. Yuck! Then he saw the depressions in the soil and wondered. Could it work? He closed his eyes and focused on the image. Scooping up a handful from the floor, he turned to Alex. "Do this. It has to be big enough to scare a cat."

"I should have thought of it," Alex said, plunging his hands into the mud. He plopped some onto Bartholomew's pile. Then more and more.

The two boys molded the clay into an animal shape. Without a word, they both knew where to place their hands. They scooped, pulled, and smoothed as if their minds were one.

Bartholomew realized his powers as his hands tugged and pressed, sculpting faster than ever before. A leg appeared. Then another. Paws. A larger-than-life head. Soon, they were moving at the speed of light.

One final pinch, and the sculpture shimmered. Fur sprouted all over its body. Two silvery eyes looked up at them. Bartholomew sat back on his haunches and smiled. "Glorious."

"Cool, B-Three." Alex gave Bartholomew a high five before turning to their sculpture. "Wolf, down to the cave. Protect Ramses."

The great wolf, its newly-formed coat glistening in the dim light, hunched its muscular shoulders and gave a quick nod before leaping down the hole. It landed behind the stalagmite forest on the cave floor. With its head swaying to and fro, it skulked among the shadows, then skirted the cave walls. As Wolf neared the platform, its lips curled back, and the hackles on its back rose.

By now, the Mudlark-cat was on Ramses's head, clawing at the defenseless pharaoh while the regal king tried to fend it off.

With a ferocious snarl, Wolf pounced, landing on all fours next to Captain Sludge.

"What's this?" he cried.

Wolf flattened its ears and charged, knocking Sludge onto his hunched back. Teeth barred, it stood over the captain, one paw on his chest while the cowering Swiney hid his face in the crook of his arm.

"Yes!" Bartholomew cried, ready to give Alex another high five.

None of this deterred Mudlark-cat. With a casual glance, it raised its right forepaw and swiped at Ramses's face. Long claw marks on the pharaoh's cheek bled.

"No!" Bartholomew punched the ground.

Wolf snarled and leaped. Sailing over the pharaoh, it snatched the cat up in his jaws. When it landed growling on the edge of the platform, it rattled its head as if trying to shake the spell out of the cat. The Mudlark clawed furiously, but Wolf held fast, clenching ever tighter until the once-beloved pet of Ramses crumbled in his jaws.

With a sigh, Bartholomew leaned back.

"Come on. Let's make more," Alex ordered already sculpting a second animal.

Like wheels of the same chariot, their hands worked together. Faster and faster they rolled clay, each mirroring the movements of the other. Alex molded one eye while Bartholomew formed the other. Bartholomew pulled a horn on the left side while Alex coaxed one from the right. A sheep-like body formed. Then another.

In less than a breath, two shimmering rams became fur and flesh. They pawed the ground next to them; horns curled back like spiral seashells over their wooly necks. The sheep stood aside as a new animal took shape.

Bartholomew thought of Ursa Major as he dug into the clay-like soil. Imagining the Great Bear Constellation, he piled clay ever higher. Was Alex sharing the same vision? Did he see the black fur, long snout, and deep-set eyes? He must have, since a heartbeat later it took shape. Immobile clay one microsecond, in the next a bear was chuffing and nuzzling Alex.

He gave Bartholomew a knowing look and pushed Bear away before beginning the last animal. Bartholomew saw it immediately in his mind's eye: an African lion with a mane of golden fur. Hands plunged into the mud and blurred. A few touches later, Lion also transformed from sculpture to glimmering life.

"Go, join Wolf below," Alex said. Like phoenixes in flight, all four animals dove through the hole. Not a one made the slightest sound as it hit the ground behind the stalagmite forest and galloped across the cavern floor.

Bartholomew hung his head over the opening, watching the fight with fascination. This was even better than the time Aleea Von Violet, the daughter of one of the Borax board members, threw up all over Mother's shoes at his ninth birthday party. Lion leaped onto a Swiney's back while the rams butted three others with their heads.

"Get 'em!" Bartholomew cheered.

"We're ready!" Alex called down the tunnel.

"Come." Osiris's voice filled the air. "The Deliverers have paved the way."

As the fight escalated below, the Egyptian army gathered round Alex and Bartholomew. Osiris placed a hand on each boy's shoulder and looked out at the assembled company. "While this end of the cavern is still in shadow, let us to descend. But be wary. Victory will be ours only if silence is our guide."

One by one, they slipped through the hole in the floor and down the wooden ladder. Bartholomew made sure to grasp the rails tightly as he descended. He didn't want to stumble and take a header here. When the wood creaked under his weight, he held his breath, but the rungs held, and soon they were all in a tunnel behind the stalagmite forest.

Thoth hopped up on his ibis legs and pulled an hourglass from the leather pouch slung over his shoulder. "Hours three is all we hath. For job to do and exit path." He placed the hourglass with most of the sand still at the top in a crevice on the cave wall.

Only three hours? A soft murmur went through the crowd.

Placing his fingers to his green lips for silence, Osiris signaled for half of the soldiers to line up behind Alex. "You take the right flank with Isis, Thoth, and Bastet. Bartholomew will lead the rest of us the other way. The medics will wait here until needed."

Bartholomew felt like a deer frozen in the spear's sight. *Me?* "Sir, I don't think—"

Osiris gave him a look to clamp his jaw shut. "You are a creator," he said.

Trying to muster up courage, Bartholomew nodded gravely.

"I'll create a diversion," Alex whispered in his ear. "You get your group ready to attack. Okay?"

Bartholomew smiled weakly. Alex punched him lightly in the arm and winked. They both looked up again as Osiris silently waved his flail in the air. The green-skinned god gave a quick nod, then spoke in low tones as everyone craned their necks to listen.

"Today we fight for our kings and homes. Our very existence is at stake. Remember we have the power of creation on our side. We will find the papyrus and free the twelve. Now go forth for pharaoh and fate!"

The crowd raised their fists in the air. And although they were silent, Bartholomew could have sworn he heard thunderous cheers in his mind.

"See ya, Deliverer," Alex said after everyone lined up behind each of them. He gave Bartholomew a quick salute, waved his battalion off to the right, and disappeared into the labyrinth of stalagmites.

Bartholomew stood for long moments watching Alex and his squadron go. He purposefully avoided looking at Horus and Osiris. Why did they have such confidence in him? He was just a screw-up.

"Our weapons are useless here. Ideas, young one?" Osiris asked.

Because only he and Alex had powers here didn't mean Bartholomew could quickly come up with ideas. If anything, responsibility drained them away.

Chewing on his lower lip, he glanced at the jackal-headed Anubis who clasped an ankh in his left hand. Ankh, the symbol of life, a T-shape surmounted by a loop. A handle and… Bartholomew's gaze shot up at the stalactites hanging nearby. Maybe?

He rubbed some hand sanitizer in and conjured up the image in his mind. Then he reached up and broke off several of the soda straw stalactites hanging from the low ceiling of the tunnel. Ignoring the crowd around him, he drew his mind inward. He tried to visualize the swords he had read about. What shape were the handles? How long should a blade be? What was the best weight for his army?

He brushed his hands over one of the broken stalactites, trying to force it to change like he and Alex had done with the mud moments before. But when he glanced down, the stick-shaped stone only crumbled away.

"Junk!" Bartholomew tossed the stalactite aside and let out an exasperated sigh.

Anubis wiggled his jackal ears playfully at him. Bartholomew's face reddened. Turning away, he tried to pretend he was all alone.

Taking a breath, he let his hands search for another. It had to have just the right feel. When he found it, he knew immediately. It was warm and sent sparks up his arm. He carefully broke off the long piece and rolled it between his palms. Flatten and sharpen. Smooth and shape. His hands became blurs as he went faster and faster.

"Ouch!" He jerked away and dropped the sculpture. Bewildered, he looked down at his bleeding finger. Then he saw it on the ground beside him. The blade was long and sharp. He had done it!

Bowing, he handed the first sword to Anubis. The jackal-headed god licked his chops and gave everyone a wide grin before slicing the air dramatically. Then Bartholomew set to making more. Time sped up again. His hands moved beyond the speed of light. In a matter of moments, all of his squad was armed and ready.

"Just one more," he said, snapping off a final stalactite.

He wanted to create something of true beauty for himself. He thought back to the Persian scimitars he read about. The razor-edged blade would be a crescent moon, and the grip would fit perfectly in his hand.

Three breaths, and it was done. Bartholomew ran his fingers over the flat of the curved blade. Its silver shone in the faint torchlight of the cavern. He twisted his wrist, and the steel reflected the flames like a signal mirror. The soldiers lined up behind it, their swords held at the ready.

All was set to go. He just hoped Alex was ready.

Chapter 36

Setting his jaw, Alex trudged through the maze of stalagmites. On the other side of the cavern, the oomphs and cries of battling Shadow Swine muffled the sound of his battalion's shuffling feet. Even though he'd created more sculptures in a few moments than during his entire life, it did little to ease the worry at the back of his mind.

He shook his head. *No time. Focus, Alex.* Somehow, he had to wrench the papyrus away from the Shadow Swine, and he'd need to be fast. Zooming fast.

His battalion followed him to the edge of the stalagmite forest where water pooled in small puddles. He held up a hand to halt them. "I have an idea."

Bending down, he scooped up a handful of mud, flattened it into a thick oval, and set it aside. Four more lumps of clay he formed into balls and attached them to the base. Time for truing the wheels. He spun each one until it stopped clunking. Then the thing changed. It was no longer a rough sculpture but a chariot made especially for a goddess.

Alex rolled the skateboard back and forth before motioning for Isis to give it a try. She listened carefully while he demonstrated how to stand with one foot on the board and kick off with the other. Nodding, Isis mounted and rolled forward. While Alex coached, she spread her wings and soon was gliding easily around the stalagmites.

"Good! Now for the rest of you."

He grabbed more handfuls of clay and repeated the process, his fingers flying like hummingbird wings over air. Alex was no longer part of time but creating outside of it. Faster than you could say flip-kick, a score of skateboards were at his feet.

Alex didn't take time to admire his work but beckoned Thoth, now in ibis form, to try. Long bird legs bending backwards, the god toddled to the boy and placed a clawed foot onto the back of the board. It popped into the air hurling into a stalagmite.

Thoth pitched forward landing in a puff of feathers.

Trying not to chuckle, Alex cleared his throat. "Just try again." He jogged to the board, grabbed it, and brought it back. "Put your foot in the middle. Easy now."

Beak twisted into a ridiculous grin, Thoth set his right foot on the deck. The board slid out from under him. Thoth toppled over, legs and wings all akimbo.

"Umm, maybe..." Alex rubbed his chin.

The ibis-god shook a feather at him. "Fear not, creator boy. I shall master this new toy." He brushed the dust off and hopped back up. But as soon as he lurched forward, he tripped again.

Thoth fell several more times before he could even roll a few feet. When he finally got going, everyone gave a silent cheer. With his wings held out stiffly and beak bobbing up and down, his head spun in circles.

"Dizzy, dizzy is my brain. Fear have I for more pain." His eyes crossed, and he toppled. Alex rushed to grab him before he fell.

"Umm. Why don't you follow at the rear?"

"To be last is good, yes is it. Coordination to skate I not yet get," Thoth said moving to the end of the line.

Although Thoth struggled more than any preschooler Alex saw at the park back home, the rest of the gods caught on quickly. Isis led the way, while Bastet and the others formed a rolling line behind her. When she weaved around a stalagmite, they followed like thread on a loom. She flew over a slanted boulder with the string of gods, soldiers, and mythological creatures trailing perfectly behind her. All except Thoth, of course. It was all he could do to keep from falling.

The skateboarders rounded a stalagmite and formed three lines facing Alex. How strange it would have looked to Zach, Gwen, and Jose to see these Egyptian gods on shiny brown skateboards. The only one they would have been able to relate to was Alex. He stood in front of the gods, arms crossed, as if he were ready to take on anyone in an extreme sports challenge. He supposed this was like the challenges in the skate park back in Santa Barbara. The only difference was if he lost here, the consequences were much greater than a few friends laughing at him. If he blew it now, Egypt would be gone forever.

While wheels warmed beneath their feet. Alex wondered how to signal Bartholomew. He looked at the smooth walls of the cavern which seemed to say, "Come on, Skater Boy, show us your stuff."

Alex muttered under his breath, "Heck yeah." He set his board down and waved to his battalion. "When I give the signal, charge!" He kicked off, furiously building speed and dropped into a crouch position. As he reached the place where the wall sloped upward, he straightened his legs to gain speed. Thrusting a hand out, he grabbed a stalagmite, increasing momentum as he spun around. Then he let go and became a slingshot's stone.

Dodging stalactites right and left, he went up the cavern wall. His ascent felt smoother than an empty swimming pool ride. When he reached the long stalactite, he punched and sent it hurling toward the ground.

The sound of crashing rock echoed throughout the cavern. For long moments, everyone was silent. Then he heard Bartholomew's war cry from across the room. "Attack!"

"Skateboarders, charge!" Alex shouted, still rolling along the wall. "Full speed ahead."

With a whirr of wheels, they sailed forward, threading their way through the stalagmites.

Alex came to the clearing and slowed his skateboard. Craning his neck, he searched for Bartholomew. When Alex saw him running along a side wall with a sword, he shook his head in disbelief. "You go, B-Three."

Chapter 37

A wry grin twisted Alex's lips when mayhem broke out at the far side of the cavern. None of those Shadow Swine seemed to know what to do. Cool.

One slime monster batted furiously against Lion's head only to get tangled in the bushy mane. Lion immediately clamped down on his arm and dragged the kicking and screaming creature to Mudlark Maker's open jaws. When he dropped the Swiney in, the huge mouth closed. The ground rumbled as Mudlark Maker swallowed one of its own.

While the confused Mudlark Maker tried to transform the Swiney, Lion leaped. Diving toward one of the monstrous eyes, the great cat dug into the gelatinous orb. Mudlark Maker squeezed its eyelids shut, but the claws only went deeper. The creature roared in pain and sank back into the soil.

Alex turned to Isis. "I hope he gets a gnarly stomach ache."

"My wish is he ceases to exist, without pain." The crowned goddess's words were clipped and disapproving.

He wondered why she sounded so judgmental. Did he sound mean? Was she mad at him about the fight with Bartholomew?

"I wasn't saying I want him to suffer. I just—"

Captain Sludge's angry roar from across the cavern stopped Alex in mid-sentence. "Get back into lines I say!" he cried from atop the platform.

As Sludge raised his fists and backed up, Wolf snarled and snapped at him. The Shadow Swine kicked, but the canine dodged it easily. The captain darted right where Wolf's barred teeth blocked his escape. Retreating to the edge of the platform where Ramses stood, Sludge pulled out a dagger from the folds of his black cloak.

When he saw the dagger, Alex forgot all about waiting and wheeled straight for the platform. Isis flanked him, her outstretched wings blurring like oncoming storm clouds.

Captain Sludge shoved the guard out of the way and leaped over Wolf. Before Alex could stop him, he'd grabbed Ramses's arm, twisted it behind his back, and raised the dagger to his throat. Now poor Ramses stood quivering in the evil captain's grasp.

Alex blinked. What gave this slime bucket the right? He rolled up a boulder and flew over Mudlark Maker, landing directly opposite Sludge. "Let him go," Alex snarled, wheels skidding across the wood.

"And who will make me? A boy whose dreams I so easily invade?" Jerking Ramses with him, Sludge took two steps back.

"I'm warning you." Alex waved Wolf to his side.

The Swiney captain laughed, but Alex knew it was a bluff. He could see the slimy sweat rolling down his ugly face. Sludge took another step.

Now one foot perched on the platform while the other rested on the top stair.

When he saw Ramses's imploring eyes, Alex's breath caught in his throat. Mom had that same look when she'd had her heart attack.

For a moment, he faltered, his mind clouded with the awful memory. This was the opportunity the Shadow Swine had been waiting for. He bolted down the steps, half dragging, half carrying the struggling Ramses. Immediately, a line of Swineys closed in behind him and raised their battle-axes.

"Hey!" Alex cried. He ran after them but just as he reached the edge of the platform, Isis landed an aerial in front of him and blocked his way.

"Wait." Isis held her golden hand to his chest.

"Get out of my way." He tried to push past her.

"It is too dangerous. Look at their weapons."

Alex didn't care about the Shadow Swine's shaking axes. He could fly over those creeps. He placed a foot on his skateboard, ready to kick off, but Isis positioned her sandaled foot atop his.

"We must wait until the time is right. Then, when he least expects it, we will strike," she said.

"But what if I–"

"You have no weapons, and Sludge's dagger is poised for death."

Alex knew she was right. He shook his head gravely. *You just wait slime bucket,* he thought. He might not get to rescue Ramses, but he could still do some major damage. Alex turned to his squad before kicking off.

"Skateboarders! Use the animals. Destroy."

Isis gave him a nod of encouragement, then joined Bastet below. The rest of the Skateboarding Squad darted in and out of the groups of Swineys, their bodies little more than a blur. With each pass, they punched, kicked, or slapped their muddy foes. Howls of pain filled the cavern.

Alex bumped over the wooden slats, picking up speed. When he reached the edge, he shifted to the back of the board, launching straight for the nearest hunched back. His wheels hit a dreadlock-twined head, knocking the creature to its knees.

With a satisfied grunt, Alex crouched into a landing and turned his board back into the fray. All around him the Shadow Swine flailed their muscular arms to stop the onslaught, but they were too slow for Alex's skateboarders. Every angry swing met only air.

Alex punched a tall monster and drove him back. Then another. One more pig-nose stumbled.

But these attacks were doing little more than slowing the enemy. Not even one fell. With another ineffectual rabbit punch to a Swiney's gut, Alex worried. He didn't have anything but his fists to fight with. They needed swords and axes, but there wasn't time to make any now.

He wondered what was taking Bartholomew so long. *I hope he made some good weapons. We're not doing so hot here.*

Chapter 38

If Bartholomew knew what Alex was going through, he would have plowed straight into the battle, but he had no idea, so he was taking it slow. With multiple entrance tunnels the Shadow Swine could pop out of, he figured it was safer to keep his battalion close to the walls and creep forward inch by inch.

"You are a creator," he whispered Osiris's words. They became his mantra, his song, the aria propelling him onward. Yet at the edges of his mind, another tune threatened to play, and it was thunderbolt loud. This was the song of his life.

You can't. It's too dangerous.

He slowed even more, pressing his body against the wall until he came to a full stop. Pulling out his hand sanitizer, he rubbed it into trembling hands. Behind him, shuffling sandals whispered to a halt. Bartholomew looked back at the green face of Osiris and almost shouted, *Why aren't you the one in front?*

But he'd disappointed them enough for one day. Losing the papyrus. Fighting with Alex. Having to be carried like a baby. Swallowing hard, he forced his feet to move, skirting along the edges of the rocky wall until he found a shallow cave large enough for his battalion. Signaling the others, Bartholomew ducked into the shadows.

"What do you think?" he asked, leaning toward Osiris and Horus. Bartholomew hoped they'd say, *Hide until Alex saves everyone.*

"Now is a good time to attack," Osiris replied. He obviously didn't share Bartholomew's concerns. "My wife and the other Deliverer have created a diversion."

"I thought, maybe…" Bartholomew cleared his throat and pointed toward a lava tube tunnel behind the platform. "… if we came from behind over there, maybe we could surround them and perhaps they'd surrender?"

"Good thinking, Deliverer." The hawk-headed Horus nodded.

Oh, I'm good at it, he thought. *I've spent my life studying and planning. But implementing?* He stared at his shoes. They were so dusty and scuffed. He should polish them.

"Ready young one?" Osiris asked.

He shrugged. "I guess."

"No suppositions. The lives of the pharaohs are at stake. You must be certain."

"Yes, Deliverer," Horus said. "Doubt cannot enter your mind. When you strike, it must be without hesitation. Remember my Uncle Set."

Bartholomew swallowed hard. "Let's do this."

Horus waved the rest of the soldiers in closer and explained how they would swing right. He warned them all to be on the lookout for skateboarders and to assist them in any way they could.

"The Deliverer will lead us," Horus said, bowing to Bartholomew.

With a shaking hand, Bartholomew raised his sword to his forehead and saluted Horus. The hawk-headed god returned the gesture. Bartholomew turned to Osiris and slowly lifted his blade to his nose.

Arms of bronze, clay, and basalt raised their swords in unison. Although still shaking, seeing those raised scimitars made Bartholomew feel a little taller. He took a deep breath and counted to three silently. "For pharaoh and fate. Charge!"

It came out more like a croak than a trumpet, but they marched anyway.

Swinging his sword right and left, Bartholomew picked up speed while his linen-skirted soldiers fanned out behind him. Their marching feet clattered over the cave floor faster and faster. With every step, more power coursed through Bartholomew's veins.

When they reached the platform, the monsters were not in one little group like he'd expected. They were everywhere! The skateboarders zig-zagged in all directions, drawing them off toward exit tunnels, around Mudlark Maker, even back towards the stalagmite forest.

Gawking, Bartholomew raised his scimitar but couldn't decide which way to point it. He tried right then left. "This won't work," he said, shaking his head.

"Then we'll fight them one by one!" Osiris shouted, thrusting his sword at a fat Swiney opposite him, turning the creature to dust.

"Soldiers, scatter," Horus ordered as he rushed headlong into the fray, pecking, jabbing, kicking.

Bartholomew gulped. Hand-to-hand combat? His legs went numb. Wheels rolled past him. Bastet dodged, Anubis punched, and Isis soared. Swirling dust rained down upon him, but he stood still, frozen, crumbly mist peppering his sword.

Osiris's green brow furrowed. He faced Bartholomew and gave him a meaningful look. "Let go of doubt. Never forget you are a Deliverer." Instead of waiting for a reply, the god saluted and disappeared into the dust.

Bartholomew didn't feel like a Deliverer. Instead, he felt like a fly surrounded by hundreds of swirling swatters. "Better not move. Too dangerous," he told himself.

Ahead, he saw two hunchbacked Swineys dragging a shackled figure. The prisoner was transparent with a long rectangular beard and square head cloth. One of the captured pharaohs!

Bartholomew's knees threatened to buckle beneath him. "Umm, Horus? Osiris? Someone should help that guy."

No gods in sight.

The taller Swiney tugged on the rusty chain attached to the prisoner's wrists. The king tripped and fell to his knees. Even though the trapping spell made his body as transparent as stained glass, Bartholomew could still see the pain in his eyes.

He glanced around. Not a single Egyptian was near. Bartholomew bit his lower lip and took a step, then stopped. "Maybe Horus will come back."

Suddenly. the tall Shadow Swine kicked the pharaoh in the ribs ,and both Swineys laughed.

Bartholomew cringed. It was up to him. Holding his breath, he shuffled forward until he was face-to-face with the pharaoh's tormentors.

Looking the boy up and down, the taller Swiney raised one eyebrow and nudged his wide-nosed comrade. Both monsters flared their piggish nostrils and guffawed.

"Let him go," Bartholomew said, forcing himself to speak. With a wobbly hand, he raised his sword over his head.

The creatures burst into laughter. But the king's eyes filled with hope. Bartholomew managed another croaking command. "I said, let him go."

The taller Swiney pushed Bartholomew's chest. "Make me."

Bartholomew couldn't believe it. This was not like they said it would be. Osiris made it sound so easy. He was a Deliverer. These creatures were supposed to be afraid of him. Then he wondered. Could humans be killed in Artania?

The other Swiney shoved his right shoulder. Bartholomew took a deep breath and waved his sword again, but the Swineys only watched him in amusement. Their yellow eyes rounded as if he were putting on a show.

Bartholomew ignored their mocking faces. Trembling, he swung at the tall one. The sword whistled over the creature's head. He adjusted his grip and jabbed at the other. His thrust fell short. Bartholomew shifted his weight to his hind leg for leverage.

"He think he tough," Pig-nose snarled.

"We show him what tough is." His partner pulled a dagger from his belt.

Before Bartholomew could stop him, the Swiney thrust his knife into the pharaoh's chest. The Egyptian king began to fade, his life force ebbing like fiery embers immersed in the sea. The last to disappear were his eyes. Sad, tortured eyes.

"No!" Bartholomew cried. Swinging wildly, he ran headlong into the Swineys, twisting his sword in crazy directions, oblivious to whether he connected or not.

The tall one was the first to fall. His body shrank and dried like a prune shriveling in a fire.

"Argh!" Battle axe raised and black cloak flying, the second one rushed forward. Grasping the sword handle in both hands, Bartholomew thrust, piercing the creature's chest.

His sword glowed. For a split second, the inside of the Shadow Swine was illuminated. Bartholomew saw black ink splashing around his heart and lungs. The dark liquid boiled. Then steam poured out of each nostril and misshapen ear. The body shriveled and crumbled into a heap of dry dust.

Bartholomew stared down at the two gray mounds of dirt at his feet. He wished it brought him more satisfaction, although nothing would bring the pharaoh back. He kept seeing those brown eyes, imploring and suffering, so full of hope.

Why did I hesitate?

A grinding sound made him turn to see, Alex approaching through the misty dust. His dark hair blew back to reveal a strong jaw and steady eyes. His face was focused, every movement deliberate and smooth. Alex waved and turned. Then, shifting his weight to the back of the board, he skidded to a halt.

"Nice sword," he said.

"Thanks." Bartholomew couldn't meet his eyes.

"Looks like you know how to use it." Alex pointed at the heaps of dirt on the ground.

Chewing on his lower lip, Bartholomew considered telling Alex everything. He opened his mouth, but "I am learning" came out instead. *Alex doesn't know, and it's going to stay that way.*

Chapter 39

Bartholomew seemed self-conscious, so Alex changed the subject. "Have you seen the papyrus?"

Bartholomew shook his head. They both scanned the crowd. Shadow Swine and Egyptians scuffled in fistfights and swordplay all around. Even if one of the monsters were holding a bundle of fabric, the battle was kicking up so much dust they wouldn't have seen it.

"Alex?" Bartholomew ventured.

"Yeah?"

Bartholomew opened his mouth to speak when a Shadow Swine ran at him grunting something indiscernible. Instead of quivering into jelly, Mr. Clean heaved a sigh."Get away. I am working here," Bartholomew muttered, whacking it with the flat of his blade. The creature's yellow eyes crossed, and it tottered. Bartholomew gave the Swiney a quick shove, and it fell over.

Alex cleared his throat and stared. Who was this stranger? Had someone cloned Bartholomew and replaced him with a superhero version?

"Could I get on your shoulders?" Bartholomew asked, glancing casually at the unconscious Shadow Swine. "You could skate around so I can see if the papyrus is anywhere."

"Maybe," Alex sized his friend. "We're about the same height and weight, but I'm not promising anything." Widening his stance, he steadied his board with one foot, placed his hands on his knees, and stooped. "Hop up."

Bartholomew got behind Alex, wrapped his arms around his torso, and did a little jump. Falling short, Bartholomew dug his foot into Alex's side as he crawled up.

"Ow! Watch it!" Alex cried, twisting around. Nope, Bartholomew had not been replaced with a clone. Same old clumsy kid.

"Hold still, Alex," Bartholomew said. nearly toppling over and taking Alex with him.

"You are heavy," Alex complained. His wiggling friend's full weight made his back ache.

"Only if you believe I am. Make me a feather."

Alex closed his eyes. Instantly his breath came easier. His shoulders relaxed, and his back straightened.

"Good," Bartholomew said. "Now pass me my sword."

"Be careful with it. I already had a haircut this week." Alex handed up the scimitar and stepped onto his skateboard. "Hold on," he commanded as he rolled toward the stalagmite forest.

Bartholomew may have been good at giving out advice, but following it was a different story. Every two seconds, he changed his body position. First, he'd twist right, then jerk to the left, making it nearly impossible for Alex to control his board.

"Watch it!" Alex grunted giving Bartholomew's foot a backhanded slap.

"Sorry!"

"Try using your sword as a balance pole," Alex suggested.

Bartholomew extended it over his head, stopping the wobbliness. "I don't see the papyrus anywhere," he called down.

"Hold on. I'm gonna try something." Alex shouted over the sound of whirring wheels. He turned into the lava tube tunnel and rolled up the curved side to pick up speed. Shifting his weight, he cried, "Now look!" before scaling a wall.

"No! It's too high!"

"Hurry. I can't hold this much longer," Alex urged.

"I think I see something! Over there by the tunnel…" He leaned to one side and aimed the tip of his sword. The sudden weight shift sent them both tumbling to the ground. Groaning, Alex stood, rubbing his sore shoulder.

Bartholomew was a few feet away, pointing, his mouth agape. "Over there. Two Swineys have it!"

The Shadow Swine ducked inside a side tunnel. Alex could just make out a bundle of fabric in the second one's arms. He raised his eyebrows at his friend. "Well, what are we waiting for, B-Three? Hop on."

Chapter 40

Bartholomew smiled as the wind whipped through his hair. He was getting better at riding double. He learned how to position his legs so he didn't wobble so much. Alex glided effortlessly below him. It was amazing at how his friend could dodge stalagmites in this dark tunnel so easily, even at this speed. He must be going twenty miles per hour. The damp cave air filled his nostrils with moisture. Still, he breathed it all in deeply. He didn't care if he drowned in its dank smell.

He was riding atop his friend's shoulders on a quest. They were soldiers, comrades, chums and pals, side-by-side. He thought of noble friendships he'd read about. Aslan and Peter. King Arthur and Merlin. Dorothy and the Scarecrow. Wilbur and Charlotte. A lump rose in his throat.

He wanted to explain it all to Alex. How much his friendship meant. How Bartholomew would do just about anything for his buddy. But he knew what Alex's response would be. *Yeah right, Richie. I'll send you a love note when we get home.*

Perhaps Alex's stoic ways helped here in Artania. He didn't get caught up so much in his emotions, so he acted quickly, decisively, and got things done. He really had it together. Bartholomew could see why he was the chosen one.

But why was I chosen?? He thought. *I can sculpt and sketch. But brave is another thing.*

A flash made him blink. "I think I see something up ahead," Bartholomew called down between cupped hands.

"I see it, too." Alex shifted his weight and slowed. "Flickering lights." He ground to a halt. "Hop off, and let's check it out."

Bartholomew shimmied down Alex's back and put his ear against the tunnel wall. He turned, but his friend was already gone, running toward a pinhole of light in the distance.

"Wait for me!" Bartholomew rasped as he jogged to catch up. Pebbles flew out from under his feet and hit the walls, their clattering sounds echoing throughout the cavern.

"Shh!" Alex hissed putting a finger to his lips. When Bartholomew skidded to a halt, Alex motioned with his hand and readjusted the skateboard tucked under his arm. "Follow me."

Pressing their bodies against the tunnel walls, the boys crept forward, step by step. Bartholomew kept his gaze on every rock that might betray him, vowing to be as quiet as possible. Then, some fifty feet ahead, he saw them.

Shadows dancing in the torchlight. He stopped dead in his tracks.

"Now what? Now what? Now what?" a Shadow Swine bleated.

"The captain said we protect this thing. So we protect," a second voice rasped.

"They have it!" Alex whispered giving Bartholomew a thumbs-up sign.

Heart skipping a beat, he cupped a hand to Alex's ear. "What do you think? Shall we jump them?"

"Nah." Alex stroked his chin. "Too risky. We don't know what sort of weapons they have."

"Douse their lights?" Bartholomew suggested.

"Then we couldn't see."

"We need to fool them somehow," Bartholomew said.

"Shouldn't be too hard. They are so stupid, doing whatever Sludge tells them."

Great idea! He laid a hand on Alex's shoulder. "Remember when you did your Captain Sludge impersonation?" Bartholomew quickly outlined his plan, pointing up and down passages while Alex's grin widened.

"Yeah, it just might work. Let me focus." Alex took a step away and scrunched up his face. Taking three deep breaths, he hunched his shoulders and cleared his throat. "Idiot scum!" he bellowed into the tunnel. "Why do you just stand there? Your captain is present."

"Captain Sludge?" a Shadow Swine squeaked.

"Who else? Stand at attention!"

"Yes sir."

"Ready yourselves for inspection! Hands at sides, chests out, and....and...close your eyes."

"Close our eyes?"

"Don't argue with me!"

"But we never do this before," a second voice chimed in.

"Has it never occurred to you how our enemy might approach in darkness? Now eyes shut!" It was amazing. Alex had Sludge's gravelly rasp down pat. He sounded exactly like the monster.

Bartholomew peered around the corner to see what the Swineys were doing. Both slimy creatures had their eyes squeezed shut and were shaking in their muddy boots. One had a nose so big that Bartholomew wondered how it could stand upright. The other Swiney was short and squat, with a triangular hump making it look like it was carrying a mini-pyramid beneath its black cloak.

With a finger to his lips, Alex grabbed Bartholomew's shoulder and set a leg next to his. In unison, they stepped forward, glued to each other's sides so it sounded like one person was approaching, not two.

When Bartholomew saw the papyrus on the ground next to Elephant-nose, his legs nearly buckled. He pointed and Alex nodded. Barely breathing, Bartholomew tiptoed closer. Just when he reached the cartouche printed fabric, one of Pyramid-back's eyelids fluttered. Bartholomew gulped.

"Eyes shut! Don't you know how to follow orders?" Alex cried, his squeaky voice nearly giving them both away.

Bartholomew froze, hoping the little quaver hadn't betrayed them.

Afraid to even breathe, Bartholomew bent down and wedged his hands under the papyrus. When he secured his grip, he gently lifted it. Although the papyrus was rough and scratchy, in that moment, it seemed as soft as a rabbit goddess's fur. He rubbed his cheek against it, nuzzling its imaginary softness. Hugging the magical scroll to his chest, he stepped backwards. One step. Two. Three.

"Name and rank. Now," Alex barked, his voice more commanding now Bartholomew and the papyrus were safely by his side.

"Private Slimy Smith, sir." The monster's eyes were squeezed shut so tightly Bartholomew thought his eyeballs would shoot out the back of his head

"I'm watching you, soldier. Careful, or you'll be on report."

Smith barely managed a gurgling yes.

"Any orders, Captain?" the huge-nosed one asked, sniffing the air like an elephant with a cold.

Bartholomew covered his mouth trying to hold back his giggles. With a snigger, he whispered in Alex's ear.

Ha! Alex mouthed silently and nodded.

"Captain?"

Backing up slowly, Bartholomew extended each of his fingers in slow succession. One…two…three.

"I want you to recite the formula for the area of a circle fifty times!" Alex blurted out with a burst of laughter.

"What?" Pyramid-back gasped.

"It's a trick! After them!" his partner cried.

The boys dashed away, laughing, and Alex called over his shoulder. "It's not a trick. It's Pi r-squared!"

Rounding the corner, Alex threw his skateboard on the ground and Bartholomew leaped onto his shoulders. He glanced back. The Swineys were right on their tail. "Go, Alex!"

They rolled forward, picking up speed, and it looked like they might escape. At first.

Bartholomew had just heaved a sigh of relief when it was cut short by a sharp tug on his hands.

"Hey!" Bartholomew cried, tugging back.

"What now?" Alex groaned beneath him

Bartholomew glanced down to see a dripping arm clutching a corner of the papyrus. Oh, no! He'd let it dangle behind him, and now Pyramid-back had it in his clawed grip.

Bartholomew curled his hand into a vise as the fabric stretched out more and more. He shuddered to imagine what would happen when there were no more coils.

A moment later, the Swiney gave a mighty tug to almost unseated him. The cartouches vibrated on the tight folds of the fabric, but Bartholomew clung desperately to his corner. "Go Alex!" he urged.

Alex kicked furiously, but they were stuck. The creature had dug his heels in, bringing them to a dead stop. Bartholomew tried flicking his wrist but those muddy hands weren't as slippery as they looked. He jerked the papyrus right, but the Swiney held on. Then Elephant-nose lumbered to them and grabbed the other corner.

"Hop down!" Alex ordered.

Keeping a tight grip on the fabric, Bartholomew slid off Alex's back and handed him the opposite corner. Both boys leaned back in a face-to-face duel with the Swineys.

"Don't let go," Alex said bunching a little more fabric into his fist.

"I won't," Bartholomew said, beads of sweat collecting on his upper lip.

"Give it back," Elephant-nose gurgled.

"No," Alex grunted.

Pulling ever harder, Bartholomew clenched his teeth so tightly he bit his cheek. He flinched, almost letting go.

Torchlight flickered in those yellow eyes, ugly glares never blinking.

Straining against the weight, Bartholomew fought to stay upright. By now, sweat was streaming down his face. What he wouldn't give for a cool handkerchief. It took everything he had to keep from reaching into his pocket to wipe it off.

Resist. He warned himself as long moments passed in this frozen tug-o'-war.

His shoulder cramped. Even with Artania powers, he didn't know how much longer he could hold on. He looked to Alex and was surprised to see his friend smirking.

"What?" Bartholomew mouthed.

"Follow my lead," Alex whispered.

A confused Bartholomew nodded as his buddy counted backwards from three.

"Now!" Alex shouted.

Bartholomew blinked.

"Now!" Alex repeated.

"Oh…" Bartholomew let go.

The Swineys fell back and landed flat on their ugly hunched backs with a crash. A cloud of dust belched around them.

"Yes!" Alex cheered with a fist pump.

Pyramid-back struggled to get up but slipped on his comrade's long cloak instead.

"Ow," Elephant nose groaned, clutching his gut. "Ga-off fatty," he bellowed through his vacuum tube of a nose.

Bartholomew gathered up the folds of the fabric and ran.

"Get on my back!" Alex cried as he threw his skateboard on the ground.

Bartholomew shimmied up a boulder and leaped, landing square on Alex's shoulders. "Oomph." His legs buckled but didn't fail. He kicked hard against the ground, and zoom, they were off, air rushing past their smiling faces.

"Yes!" Bartholomew whooped. He unsheathed his sword and held it high in triumph as he and his buddy wheeled through the tunnel.

Chapter 41

Bartholomew jerked up and down so much Alex could barely stay on his board. He groaned. You'd think B-3 was some circus cowboy doing lasso tricks the way he was waving his sword in circles.

"We did it, Alex! You and me!" Bartholomew cried.

"Careful," an annoyed Alex said, backhanding Bartholomew's knee.

"Sor-ry," Bartholomew said. He was quiet for two blissful moments, then bent closer to Alex's ear and sang, "We got it. The amazing Deliverers. Yeah!"

"Would you cool it? We're not done, you know."

"Okay, grump." This time he barely paused before crying out, "But we did it!"

Alex smiled and rolled his eyes. *Goof.* He slowed and turned back toward the tunnel to see if they were still being followed. Nope. The creatures were nowhere to be seen. Double-checking, he cocked his head and listened. Nothing. They had left those Swineys far behind.

The boys rode on together until they rounded the final bend with a circle of light ahead. There, Alex stopped to let Bartholomew off. After his friend shimmied down, Alex pressed one foot on the back of the skateboard launching it into his waiting hands. He tucked it under one arm and turned to Bartholomew. "When we hit the cavern, have your sword ready," Alex said, holding out his hands. "Give me the papyrus. I'll head straight for Thoth."

Without a word, Bartholomew placed it into Alex's arms. Alex considered saying something encouraging right then, but babying Bartholomew wouldn't make him the soldier he needed to be.

At the entrance to the cavern, Alex stared into the still raging battle where Swineys crossed swords with gods, and Mudlarks traded blows with Egyptians. Dust blew in his mouth, giving Alex a gritty taste in the back of his throat. He spat to get rid of it.

Crumpled bodies lay everywhere. Alex wished he could rush to each one, but sympathy wasn't his job. The medics who had accompanied them were already tending to the wounded. Priests in white linen robes bent over the groaning soldiers, wrapping injured limbs in bandages and placing amulets over more serious wounds.

"It's getting worse," Alex muttered.

"Horrible." Bartholomew shook his head.

Alex looked away. This was no time for tears. His gaze fell upon a crowned figure standing next to Osiris at the far end of the cavern.

"Look," Alex pointed. "I think they found one of the pharaohs."

"I wonder where the other ten might be?" Bartholomew mused.

"Ten? What do you mean ten? I thought there were twelve."

Bartholomew looked exactly like he'd been caught robbing King Tut's tomb.

"Oh. Umm. One was killed."

"No way! When?" Alex demanded.

"Earlier."

"But why didn't you tell me?"

Bartholomew shrugged. The hilt of his sword suddenly became very interesting. Why did he keep tapping on it?

"I don't get it." Alex said. "I thought the Swiney's plan was to make them into Mudlarks."

Bartholomew shrugged again.

Alex stared at him. There was something Bartholomew wasn't telling. What would he hold back? The kid shared everything. Sometimes too much.

"I want to know what happened," Alex said evenly.

Bartholomew's face blanched, his eyes fixed on his sword. "Like I said. One of them was murdered."

"You said killed earlier." Alex's eyes narrowed.

"Killed, murdered...what's the difference? He's dead, isn't he?" Bartholomew pushed past Alex and trudged ahead.

"Bartholomew, stop. What's going on?"

Bartholomew kept walking, ignoring Alex's questions. Alex skateboarded around him to block his way, but Bartholomew turned left and ran.

"What's up with you?" Alex cried when he caught up again.

"Superman wouldn't want to know." Bartholomew crossed his arms and glared at him. "He's too brave and perfect."

"Superman? What?"

"Yeah," Bartholomew exploded. "You're Superman, and I'm a failure!"

"You are not a failure, Bartholomew. You're doing a good job. Under the circumstances."

"Don't patronize me. I am not stupid."

"Whoever said you were?" Alex asked.

"You."

"Well, I was ticked off. You know me. I get mad and say things."

"It's not in what you say. It's how you are." Bartholomew pointed his chin at the papyrus in Alex's arms. He bit his lip and blinked repeatedly.

"What do you mean?" Alex was genuinely perplexed.

"Always plunging ahead." Bartholomew crossed his arms defiantly. "No fear."

"I get scared."

"Not like me. You are afraid others will be hurt, like our moms or one of the Egyptians. But me, I'm afraid of...of everything."

"Come on." Alex gave him a gentle punch. "Tell me what happened. "

And it all came out. The shackled pharaoh. The Shadow Swine taunting. The knife too soon at his throat. Alex listened and tried to be understanding, not judge, and imagine what he would have done in Bartholomew's place. "It's okay, B-Three." Alex chose his words carefully. Bartholomew needed confidence if he would be of any use. "You didn't know they were going to kill him."

Bartholomew just stared at his shoes. Those preppy dress shoes—usually so clean you'd think they'd just been dipped in bleach—were now as gray as the surrounding dirt. His shoulders sagged, and he refused to look at Alex. Comforting words weren't enough. He needed to know for certain that everyone makes mistakes.

"You're not the only one who hesitated." Alex began. "I did, too. With Ramses."

"No, you did not. You are just making it up."

"I did. I swear."

"Really? When Captain Sludge had him?" Bartholomew gave him a tentative glance.

"Yeah." Alex met those insecure blue eyes with a steady gaze. "I started to follow, but Isis stopped me. She said it was too dangerous. Sludge might hurt him. I don't know if I did the right thing or not. He ran off into one of the side tunnels." Alex paused, then said thoughtfully, "Hey, Bartholomew. If you were going to hold some pharaohs captive, how would you do it?"

"I suppose I would put them in some sort of prison."

"Exactly," Alex said holding up a finger.

"So do you believe the pharaohs might be jailed nearby?"

"You got it."

"But where?" Bartholomew glanced around.

"Captain Sludge dragged Ramses into the tunnel over there." Alex indicated a passageway opposite them. Hopeful thoughts rode over him. He squeezed his skateboard tightly under his arm. "We could free them in one swoop."

"We will require assistance."

"We've got a whole army." Alex scanned the room to map out the best path. He bent down and said, "Come on."

Bartholomew didn't hop up. Instead, he crossed his arms and shook his head.

"What if I fail again?"

Alex tried not to sigh in exasperation. They had a job to do, and Bartholomew was feeling sorry for himself.

"Then you just erase it in your mind and draw it again."

"Easy for you to say."

"Bartholomew, we don't have time for this pity party. I need your help. Get on my back and be ready to fight Swineys, or I'm leaving your sorry butt right here!"

Bartholomew looked like someone slapped him. His mouth hung open and color rose in his cheeks. Alex didn't know if he'd pushed too far, but without a word, Mr. Clean jumped up on his shoulders.

Trying to make up for lost time, Alex imagined him as light as a feather as he raced across the floor. Faster and faster he threaded through the axe-wielding Swineys. "Hold on tight!" he cried as he shifted his weight to pick up speed. Then he headed straight for a slanted slab of stone, rolled up, and they both were airborne.

Chapter 42

"What is that awful smell?" Bartholomew asked, holding his nose.

"Ugh, yeah. Like rotten eggs," Alex said.

In front of them, Osiris was crossing swords with a ratty-looking Swiney whose hair hung down in long choppy strings. It reminded Alex of the moldy rag doll he'd seen in Gwen's backyard. Even for a Shadow Swine, this one seemed extra dirty. Its clothes were in tatters, holes peppered the army cloak, and its clawed fingertips were jagged as if he'd been biting them.

"The reek you notice is from this offensive creature," the green-skinned Osiris said, thrusting his sword again. It clanged against the monster's dull blade.

"It is horrible. Like a sulfur spring I drove past once," Bartholomew said.

"How you know where I born?" the Swiney asked.

Alex exchanged a glance with Bartholomew, and they giggled. "I guess he's proud of his stinky origins," Alex said.

"I not smell. You smell." The Shadow Swine pouted. He jabbed at Osiris with his sword but missed. Stinky crouched on his haunches and pulled into a low defensive position.

"I think Osiris might need our help." Alex grinned. "What do you think, B-Three?"

"I don't know." Bartholomew's sword whistled as he pulled it from its sheath. "I hadn't planned on sullying my blade again just yet. But if you insist..." With a dramatic wave of his scimitar, he took his place next to Osiris.

Alex felt a little sorry for the quivering Shadow Swine as Bartholomew and Osiris moved closer to him. Every time Stinky backed up, the duo matched him step for step.

As the Swiney's head twisted around, his long dreadlocks whipped him in the face and left muddy patches on either cheek. He swung wildly at the grinning pair, but his aim was far enough off for Alex to think he must be nearsighted. Or panicked. Taking another step back, Stinky stumbled on a rock and fell to his knees.

Bartholomew flicked his sword in circles. Alex couldn't resist. Tucking the papyrus safely under his arm, he raced into the fray. "Hugaboo!" Alex raised an arm as if ready to pounce.

Osiris, Bartholomew, and Alex stood back chuckling while the Swiney scrambled to his feet. He tottered away with rising stink waves trailing behind. "Ch-Chaw!" Alex guffawed, giving Bartholomew a high five.

"I see you have recovered the papyrus." Osiris said with a wry smile. "Excellent, but time grows short, and we have yet to find our kin. Unfortunately, Hatshepsut knows nothing of their whereabouts." He nodded at a young pharaoh who stood behind them in the shadows.

The ghost-like apparition of Hatshepsut stepped forward, her transparent body indicating she was still under the Swiney's spell. She wore a tall red crown and had a false beard on her chin. She acknowledged Alex and Bartholomew with a slight bow.

"We were all chained together at first," she said.

"Hey, I know who you are!" Alex blurted out. "We studied you in school. You were a woman pharaoh."

"The human counterpart who birthed my creation was, yes. She had herself crowned king, not content with her role as regent for her brother, Thutmose III."

"Pretty gutsy for those days," Alex said.

"It was, but I digress. They separated me from the rest when they saw my female form. They must have thought me not a pharaoh. Then they tied me to a stalagmite and marched the rest away. I was trapped there until dear Osiris freed me."

"Where are the rest?" the mummy-wrapped god asked.

"We think we might know," said Bartholomew.

"Yeah, I saw Captain Sludge take Ramses into that tunnel over there." Alex jerked his head to the right. He turned to Hatshepsut. "Did you say all the pharaohs were together in one group?"

"As far as I could see, yes. But they were headed in the opposite direction when I saw them last." She pointed to a distant lava tube tunnel.

"Then Ramses isn't with them!" Alex growled, punching his palm twice. "I should have saved him when I had the chance."

"Worry not. You have done well, young one," Osiris said.

Alex hiked up the papyrus shifting under his arm as Ramses's face flashed before his eyes. *I have to save him, somehow.* Lost in thought, he absentmindedly stroked the fabric until he noticed the others staring at him. "So now what?" he asked, uncomfortable with the attention.

"Thoth will perform the spell. But all others must be present." Osiris pulled his crook and flail from the folds of his robe and beat out the rhythm of war. He tapped on a boulder. Thrum. Thrum Thrum. The pulses echoed from ceiling to floor to tunnel. Thrum. Thrum Thrum.

The battle stopped, and all at once, gods, goddesses, and Egyptian soldiers turned. Marching in time to the rhythm, they gathered before Osiris. Even the animals Bartholomew and Alex had sculpted earlier lined up. They all stood silently waiting for orders.

"Watch the papyrus magic hold back the Shadow Swine," Osiris said as the confused Shadow Swine army who tried to follow found themselves blocked at the opposite end of the cavern as if held back by an invisible hand.

"Whoa," Alex whispered

Osiris beckoned the crowd closer with a green hand. "From the time of creation, our people have used a secret language to hide our words from the enemy." He switched to the ancient language and lowered his voice. Alex was surprised when he could understand every word.

"Soon we will attack in the tunnel left of the platform. No! Do not look around! Guile is our best ally." He shook his flail at them. "We believe the pharaohs are held captive there."

Thoth cawed loudly. "Hatshepsut first freed will be. Anubis, ankh I need to see."

With a wagging tail, the jackal-god loped to them, changing form with every padding step. By the time he was next to Thoth, he was half-man again. He wriggled his dog-like ears and handed over the t-shaped amulet Alex recognized as the Egyptian symbol of life.

Like a performer taking center stage, Thoth held the ankh high as he stepped up to face the crowd. "Caw! Deliverers step forth, and you will see. The magic papyrus setting free. Each of you need to stand. With one corner in your hand."

Not knowing exactly what was going on, Alex picked up a corner of the Net in one hand while Bartholomew took up the other. Alex glanced at the twelve cartouches on the papyrus that he and Bartholomew had painted. Facing the crowd, he waited for Thoth to continue. "Now the Pharaohess Hatshepsut I do need. For Subterranean spell to set her free."

The see-through Hatshepsut glided forward. With a slight bow of her crowned head, she said, "I am ready."

"Now Deliverers, two must act as one. For bindings strong to be undone." Thoth, who was obviously enjoying the captive audience, waved the loop-topped ankh and cawed twice. "Stand and touch your own cartouche. And things unseen will be unloosed."

As Thoth explained the next steps Alex swallowed hard. *Bartholomew has to stare into my eyes the whole time Thoth does his magic? There's no way he can do that.*

"I know what you're thinking," Bartholomew said.

"Yeah?"

"You think I cannot do this thing, but you are wrong." Bartholomew turned to Thoth with a curt nod. "Go."

"Boy twin with thoughts so dim. Do you at last agree with him?" Thoth asked Alex.

"You're sure?" Alex asked searching Bartholomew's face.

"Let's do this."

"Yes. Go." Alex gripped the papyrus tightly as Thoth's directed them to hold the fabric taut so the designs were easy to see.

Hatshepsut's cartouche with a sun and a seated figure inside glowed and swelled as if filling with water. "Caw, Caw! Pharaohess. It's time to undo this mess. Touch hands both to your cartouche. And watch this spell be unloosed. While twin boys hold steady gaze. To release you from the Swineys' maze!" He raised both arms to the sky and drew a circle in the air with the ankh.

As Thoth cawed repeatedly, Hatshepsut stepped forward and placed her hands on her own symbol. The cartouche kept expanding, growing larger until the oval border was no longer a flat outline but a thick cobra rolling up and beyond the fabric.

"It is Wadjet! The Eye of Ra," Bastet cried while the gathered Artanians gasped at the cobra flicking its tongue and hissing at them

"Goddess Wadjet, we call upon you to free the pharaohess," Osiris called out.

The cobra glowed as if lava were coursing through her veins. Out of the corner of his eye Alex saw the fiery snake goddess coil around Hatshepsut once, twice, then three times.

"Snake, fire, rope, flame. Flaming rope and fiery dame," Thoth continued chanting.

Alex vowed not to look away. *I will hold his gaze. I will.* His mind kept time with Thoth's chants.

"Snake, fire, rope, flame. Flaming rope and fiery dame."

Wadjet glowed brighter and brighter. *Don't look away. Focus on the blue around his pupils.* The light grew so intense that Alex's eyes began to water.

"CAW! CAW!" Thoth's voice filled the air.

It burned as if Alex were looking right into the sun. He clenched his teeth. *If Mr. Clean can do it, so can I.*

"Caw!"

Tears streamed down his cheeks blurring his vision. Hot white seared his eyes.

There was a loud crack of thunder, and they were plunged into darkness. Alex covered his face.

"Caw! Caw! The pharaoh lovely who is a she. Can Deliverers thank for now she is free!"

Alex was afraid to uncover his eyes. Sure he was blind, he shook his head in despair. He would never see his mother's smile again.

Then he felt a hand on his shoulder. Slowly, he ventured a peek. There was Bartholomew giving him an understanding nod. He'd had the same fear and pushed through it. Maybe he wasn't such a wimp after all.

The torches flickered to life, and Thoth raised Hatshepsut's arm into the air. It was solid. The spell worked!

A cry arose, and the surrounding crowd rushed forward like the Nile surging into the sea. Hatshepsut embraced comrade after comrade in the flood of joy.

Alex looked down at the papyrus. All the cartouches were just as before, no snake or glowing lights. He glanced up through the maze of arms and bodies and winked at his friend. They both broke out into grins that stretched from Subterranea to the Valley of the Kings.

"Brethren quiet!" Osiris cried, his green mouth forcing down a smile. "We have many more to free and now with the force field gone, our enemy can approach. Divide into battalions. Hatshepsut, you will remain here in the safety of the stalagmite forest while Alex and Thoth come up with an escape plan. Deliverer Bartholomew will go with me."

Alex rolled up the papyrus and tucked it under his arm. He found his skateboard near a stalagmite, then turned to Bartholomew. "Are you ready?"

"Right-on, dude!" Bartholomew cried, putting his hand up awkwardly for a high five.

Alex chuckled. *That goof.* He slapped Bartholomew's hand.

"Then go rescue some kings!" Alex said. "For pharaoh and fate."

"For pharaoh and fate," Bartholomew repeated as he rushed ahead. He glanced back over his shoulder and gave Alex a thumbs-up signal.

"Hey, look out for that—" Alex called.

Still looking back, Bartholomew plowed into a stalagmite. He teetered for a moment then fell on his butt.

"—rock," Alex finished with a smiling shake of his head.

A red-faced Bartholomew got up and brushed himself off. He gave Alex a sheepish wave before running to catch up with Osiris.

As soon as Bartholomew turned away, Alex's smile disappeared. Should they be separated like this? When Thoth hopped to him, Alex's voice was full of concern. "Maybe I should go with him to make sure."

Thoth assured him that Bartholomew would be fine, but still Alex didn't know if it made sense to divide their forces. Then he realized Bartholomew was covered. He had the sculpted animals, Osiris, Horus, and Anubis on his side. Plus, lots of soldiers. Alex stared at the shrinking figures of Bartholomew's squad.

"Good luck, buddy," he said.

"Caw! Yes, hearts true, strong, and brave. Will be needed for all to save."

Chapter 43

Bartholomew wanted to kick himself. Why couldn't he watch where he was going? Just when Alex was beginning to gain a little respect for him, he blundered again. He chewed on his lower lip, trying to convince himself he was doing better.

Nonsense. He could hear Mother's words in his mind. You cannot do that. Cannot. Can. Not. He pulled out the nearly empty bottle of hand sanitizer and squeezed a bit into his palm.

Or could he? There were still ten pharaohs to rescue. Could he do the right thing when the time came? He had gotten the papyrus back, but only with Alex at his side. Now he was leading a couple dozen Artanians across this huge cavern and each was counting on him to do it right.

"Keep your scimitar at the ready, young one." Osiris pointed at the group of Shadow Swine directly ahead.

With a dry swallow, Bartholomew drew his sword. He gripped the hilt tightly in both hands, and the blade curved upward like a crescent moon. Osiris trotted faster, but Bartholomew's gaze stayed fixed to his blade.

Bartholomew called and pointed. "I'll go that way, and everyone else fan out. Okay?"

Bartholomew wished Osiris would reply, "Fear not, young one. We have your back." But he didn't. Instead he merely nodded, then plunged into the fray. Not even a good luck wave.

A snarling army of Swineys faced him. He shuddered.

For a moment, all was silence. He could hear the pounding of his heart and the steady blow by blow of his panting breath. For a brief second, he was in control. A cudgel-wielding Shadow Swine approached, yet Bartholomew felt no fear. He narrowed his eyes, aimed, and thrust.

"Yah!" he cried. And a heap of dust took the creature's place.

But his victorious moment didn't last. The next second had hands shoving from behind, and Bartholomew found himself flat on his stomach, sword trapped beneath his hips. He looked back to see an angry Swiney standing over him with eyes causing his blood run cold.

A glint of steel like burning papyrus ribbons flashed. The monster gave a short laugh. As cold slime dripped onto Bartholomew's face, he tried to reach for his sword.

The heavy arm swung. Bartholomew squeezed his eyes shut thinking, *Face down in muck just like Father.*

There was a whoosh and a groan. But no pain. Was he dead or alive? A ghost?

He unclenched his fists. They still felt solid. He ventured a peek, and there the Swiney froze in mid-air, a sword between its shoulders.

The hunchbacked figure crumbled to the ground.

Dazed, Bartholomew turned his head to see Osiris rushing off to his left. He mouthed a thank you, and the god gave a short bow before plunging back into the fight.

Bartholomew thought of following, but the memory of the axe blow held him down. It had been so close. He heard crashes, clangs, thuds, and cries. All he wanted to do was hide, not battle monsters with axes.

"Erase it from your mind and draw it again," he said, using Alex's words to steel himself. Bartholomew rose to one knee. "Get up. Now!" Trying to ignore the pit in his stomach, he stood. When he lifted his sword, he noticed the blade quivering in his hand. He squeezed tighter and took a cautious step forward. Then another.

The fighting kicked up so much dust that it was hard to see. Even if he squinted, he could barely make out figures forty feet away. He sniffed the air. No sulfur smells nearby.

A cry of pain made him turn. Through the misty haze, he saw Osiris lying on his side, blood seeping from his gut. Two jeering Swineys stood over him, one scratching Osiris's hand with a dagger while the other stood guard, javelin raised. Cackling, they switched places.

Where were Horus and Anubis? Was all his battalion hidden in the dusty haze? Bartholomew wiped his eyes, but no one was around.

The shorter Shadow Swine kicked Osiris in the gut. Then with an evil grin, it poked him with the point of his javelin.

"The jerk is toying with Osiris!" Bartholomew swallowed back the bile in his throat and charged. His quivering legs felt like rubber. "Go," he said, willing himself to greater speed, but he didn't seem to be getting any closer. Instead, it was as if the distance stretched with every step.

The shorter Swiney kicked Osiris again. If Bartholomew didn't hurry, the god would soon bleed to death. Bartholomew sprinted, finally closing the distance between them. He raced behind the larger Swiney and swung.

When the monster dropped, his runty companion turned and lunged with his spear. Bartholomew stepped aside but too slow. The point sliced open his shirt. Feeling muggy air sticking to his chest, Bartholomew stared down at the flapping fabric.

Mr. Runt hunched over and stood back on his haunches, eyeing him.

Trying to sound like Alex, Bartholomew called, "Is that your best shot? I'm not even wounded."

Swiney jabbed again. Bartholomew feigned left and thrust, hitting the creature square in the chest. It crumpled to dust.

"Thank you, young one." Osiris managed a feeble smile. Bartholomew knelt at the god's side. His green face was bruised, and one eye already swelled.

"I am sorry I was not here sooner. I got—"

"Frightened," Osiris said, completing his sentence. "Bravery is not lack of fear, young one. It is action in the face of it."

"But I..."

"... you acted is all that matters." Osiris tried to sit up but his green face paled, and he fell back. Although blood was no longer gushing, the six-inch wound still oozed. He clutched his side and winced.

Bartholomew cringed along with him. Mud! He wished he had powers to heal others. But Isis had already explained the magic only worked for Alex and him. He put a hand behind Osiris's head.

"Are you all right?"

"I will heal, but I cannot lead. It is up to you now, Twin Deliverer."

Bartholomew nodded solemnly. The battle raged around them, but they were unnoticed for the moment.

"We have to get you to safety." He stood and glanced around.

As if on cue, galloping hooves and padding paws drummed over the cavern floor. Lion, Bear, Wolf and the rams returned from wherever they were fighting and skidded to a halt in front of him. Bowing, they waited for instructions. He knew Lion would protect Osiris well. He'd made sure to sculpt each claw to a fine point.

"Lion, carry Osiris to the stalagmite forest," he told the great cat. "Do not let him fall. There you will find Alex and Thoth."

The lion lowered its great head. Bartholomew ripped a long swath of fabric from the bottom of his dress shirt and wrapped it around Osiris's waist to slow the bleeding. Then he put his arm around the god's torso and helped him onto the feline's back. Osiris grimaced yet held his head high. "Go forward. Free them." He grasped the lion's mane and raised his crook and flail. "For pharaoh and fate."

Bartholomew gave him a curt nod as he watched them go. Lion picked up speed, leaping over several pairs of dueling soldiers before disappearing into the safety of forest of stalagmites. "For pharaoh and fate," Bartholomew whispered.

Chapter 44

Alex rubbed the brown button in his pocket between two fingers as doubts clouded his mind. He was about to say something when a flash of movement between two stalagmites caught his eye. Leaping in front of the papyrus, he raised both fists. "Isis!"

The goddess darted to him. Alex barely had time to point before a bushy mane came into view.

He gaped. Someone rode the great cat's back, head buried in the mass of fur. Lion's tail was wrapped around the rider's waist, not hiding red blotch spreading on his robe.

"Husband?" A sob caught in Isis's throat.

Alex flew to the injured Osiris's side. Trying to be a gentle as possible, Alex tucked an arm under Osiris's and lifted. He pulled him off Lion's back and helped him to the nearest stalagmite.

"My husband, you are hurt." Isis kneeled at his side and propped him up against the stone.

"I will be fine."

"Let me be the judge of your injuries."

"This small cut is nothing. I have survived much worse," he said, winking.

With shaking hands, Isis undid the cloth bandage around Osiris's waist and opened the folds of his blood-soaked robe. When she saw the large gash in his side, her kohl-lined eyes filled with tears leaving black trails down her cheeks. She immediately tore a corner of fabric from her gown and picked up her goatskin bag. Using her teeth to yank out the stopper, Isis poured half of the water onto the cloth. The other half pooled at her feet.

Dabbing at the wound, she sopped the blood before opening a small leather kit and threading a needle. Alex wished he could think of something to say as she nursed her husband, but all he could do was watch.

"Dear wife," Osiris grunted. "I know your medicinal skills are great, but could you use a slightly lighter touch?"

Isis paused to pat his hand. Shaking her head, she continued sewing closed the edges of his wound.

The pit in Alex's stomach grew, gnawing at his intestines. If Osiris were this hurt... "Hey, where's Bartholomew?" he blurted.

"In the tunnel."

"Alone?"

"Ouch!" Osiris glared at Isis. "Worry not, he had the animal creations with him."

"I knew I should have gone with him." Alex buried his head in his hands.

"I will say to you exactly what I said to your celestial twin." Osiris waited for Alex to raise his head. "Bravery is not lack of fear. It is action in the face of it."

"We're doomed."

"Have faith. He will act. I know it, just as I know my healing wife..." Osiris grunted and glared at Isis again. "...will save me from the world of the dead. He is a Deliverer."

Alex wished he shared Osiris's conviction, but Bartholomew had wimped out too many times. He knew a person couldn't change in just a couple days.

The sound of scrambling feet made Alex turn. Horus and Anubis were running toward them.

"What are you doing here?" Alex cried, trying to keep the panic out of his voice.

"We are too few. Our soldiers are dropping everywhere," Horus said.

"We tried to follow the Deliverer into the tunnel but were blocked at every turn." Anubis shook his jackal head.

"We need more warriors," Isis said before biting off one end of the thread. She wrapped a piece of linen around Osiris's waist and tied it securely with its frayed edges. Gently she pulled the folds of his robe together and brushed his cheek with the back of her hand.

"Yes, we do." Osiris stared at Alex.

"Of course. The Deliverer," Isis said with a smile.

Horus joined his parents. "Yes, you can create help for us. Make it so."

"What? Make an army?" Alex asked incredulously.

"Certainly." Anubis wagged his tail. "He who makes animals and rolling chariots could easily sculpt soldiers."

Alex sighed. It was no use to argue with four gods. He took a few steps away and rounded the corner of a stalagmite, shielding himself from view.

He bent down near a cluster of small formations and tried to remember how he and Bartholomew formed the animals. He broke off a piece of a small stalagmite, then scooped up some soft soil moistened by the dripping stalactites overhead. *See it. Believe.*

His hands moved faster and faster. The limestone rounded and took shape. In two breaths, it was done. The miniature soldier in his hand raised a spear.

"What is your will, Deliverer?" a tinny voice called out.

Alex pointed to Isis. The doll-sized soldier marched to her and saluted.

Isis stooped to look at the shin-high sculpture.

"He is perfect. Just like the foot soldiers of old, but why so small?"

"Surprise. The Swineys won't be looking down at their feet for an attack," Alex replied, breaking off another stalagmite to work with.

This just might work. He thought slowing his breath to stretch time.

Chapter 45

When Bartholomew and the sculpted animals reached the mouth of the dark tunnel, he tried to peer into the darkness but only saw shadows. He craned his neck to listen for Swineys inside but couldn't hear a thing over the echoing din of battle.

"Stay quiet and follow me," he said, waving the animals into a line before stepping into the darkness. He wished there were torches in the walls so he didn't have to feel his way along. Why didn't this stupid magic include making electricity or fire? His newfound confidence slipped away like Swiney sweat dripping to the ground.

Squinting, he groped forward. He did okay for about five steps. Then he tripped on a pebble and splatted face down in a mud puddle. *Just like Father!* He struggled to his knees, sputtering and coughing. Heart pounding, Bartholomew spent long moments catching his breath.

Finally, he crept forward again. The moist ground felt like wet sandpaper over his knees. He winced and slowed his pace giving the animals time to catch up. When he heard the faint padding of Wolf's paws, he stood and felt his way along the wall.

Just as he was breathed easier, he heard it. The unmistakable hiss of a Swiney's voice. Bartholomew froze, not even daring to draw another breath. He was almost on top of them and hadn't even realized it!

"Wuz that?"

"It's nothin," A deeper voice replied.

"I hear somethin' I tell you. Go check. Now."

There was the sound of a match being struck, and Bartholomew found himself face-to-face with a pig-nosed Shadow Swine, eyes glowing yellow in surprise. Behind him were at least fifty more, all standing guard in front of a makeshift wooden cage.

Bartholomew glimpsed inside. The pharaohs!

"Human! Get him!" the monsters shouted, raising their clubs.

Shadow Swine were closing in. Bartholomew looked right and left, trying to think. "Wolf, to the left. Bear, to the right. Attack," he barked. "Rams stay behind me."

Wolf barred his teeth, opened his mouth wide, and clamped down on the nearest Swiney. It crumbled in his jaws.

While Bear bellowed, Bartholomew grasped his sword in both hands and swung. He struck at the next one. Missed! He swung again, and his slime-covered foe dropped.

Three more Swineys rushed forward. Bear swiped with a great paw. Wolf bit. Bartholomew jabbed and pierced. Two more down.

"Yes!"

Forgetting his own orders, Bartholomew stepped in front of the animals to take out a couple more. He raised his sword, then heard a smack like a cracking walnut. He staggered backward. Bartholomew reached out and fell against one of the rams. His eyes fluttered as the light faded.

He must have passed out because the next thing he knew, he was flat on his back, his animal comrades around him. He rubbed a hand over his face and felt something sticky. Reaching up, he discovered an egg-sized lump on his forehead oozing blood.

He lay there, dazed, not quite sure of where he was or why. There were strange animals near him, and the sound of grunting all around. Shadows drifted over the torch-lit walls.

A wet tongue licked his face. Yuck!

"Wolf, stop that," he said over the waves of throbbing pain in his head.

Then he remembered. He was in Artania on a mission. And here he possessed powers. *You are a creator. This wound isn't real. You can create whatever you want.* He took a deep breath, held it for three seconds, and exhaled.

He closed his eyes. *Fight through the fear. Fight through the pain. Erase it.* First, he saw it in his mind's eye, imagining a healthy scalp. His heart rate slowed. Health. Strength. Creation. Suddenly, the pain was gone. Bartholomew sat up, opened his eyes, and ran a hand through his hair. No bump. Not only was it healed, but all blood had disappeared. Even his scalp felt clean.

"Amazing," he whispered.

Reveling in his newfound powers, he swung his sword in a wide arc and turned to face the growling creatures surrounding him. They shouldn't be so hard to battle.

"Wolf, Bear, attack!"

The animals ripped into the line while Bartholomew knocked over three with his scimitar. "Any more of you want a taste of this?" he taunted with a war whoop.

The Shadow Swine were clearly confused. Baffled murmurs drifted through the crowd. "He crazy," was repeated.

When Bartholomew heard this, a smile curled up at the corner of his mouth. He could use insanity to his advantage.

Trying to imagine a mad witch, he danced and cackled hysterically. Bartholomew moved his hips in wild gyrations and flung his head about in weird jerks. He probably looked more like a drunken cowboy than a possessed sorceress, but it was having an effect.

The murmurs increased, rising in pitch as the Shadow Swine backed away from him."Who this human?" one asked. "Why he not run away?"

Bartholomew stood on his head and leaped into a somersault. He hopped on one foot, then the other. He spun in circles as if casting a wild spell. "Hee hee hee! Beware of me!"

Grinning mischievously, he turned his back on them. With all the theatrics he could muster, Bartholomew raised his scimitar above his head. "Farewell cool…I mean cruel…world." He threw his head back and opened his mouth. Slowly he lowered the sword to make it appear as if he were swallowing it.

The Shadow Swine couldn't take it anymore. They were, after all, not very bright and prone to phobias. The hunchbacked creatures all turned tail and ran screaming into the nearest exit tunnel.

Bartholomew roared with laughter, watching the mud and pebbles fly from under those booted feet. One fat Swiney got stuck in a mud puddle flapping his stubby arms like a featherless duck. He squawked to his comrades, but they only kept running. Bartholomew was about to help the pitiful creature when it finally flopped its way out of the puddle.

A glimpse of wood in the corner of his eye reminded Bartholomew why he was there. The pharaohs. He turned and stared at the flimsily-built prison.

The acacia branches making the vertical bars of the cage looked like little kids put them there. They leaned in every direction and were lashed together with old frayed rope. Bartholomew was sure the whole thing might fall over at any minute.

The knots were tighter than they looked. After several minutes of frustration, he gave the padlock on the door a yank. It was shut tightly, too, and the key was nowhere to be found. A Swiney must have run off with it.

One of the pharaohs glided forth, his transparent body reminding Bartholomew the king was still under the trapping spell. He looked so strange because his jeweled eyes were still solid while the rest of him was see-through. The ghostly pharaoh peered through the bars of the cage.

"How is this possible? Artanians never go below unless kidnapped. Is this some sort of trick?" the Egyptian king asked.

"Oh, no, your highness, sir."

"Then how do you come to be here?"

"I am not one of your kind. I am human from Earth. When we received your message, we came."

"We?"

"Osiris, Thoth. Other gods. My friend Alex."

"Which message?" The pharaoh's eyes narrowed, as if doubting Bartholomew's words.

Bartholomew thought for a moment, remembering the stela. "Save us, O gods of ancient Egypt. We are trapped in the muck of the Shadow Swine."

"I sent that message!" A shorter pharaoh cried from behind the suspicious king. "I used the last of my powers to write it. He speaks truth."

"He could have intercepted it," the long-faced pharaoh said as he raised a finger.

"Oh, Akhenaton, your paranoia transcends all worlds."

"It does not."

"I seem to remember you accused me of flirting with Nefertiti."

"Well, Khufu, just because you had a pyramid built in your honor does not give you the right to wine and dine my wife." Akhenaton raised his fist, but another king with obsidian-eyes jumped between them.

"Khufu, Akhenaton. This fight is millennia old. Did you not see what just happened? The Shadow Swine fled, and this one knows the message."

Abashed, the thin-faced Akhenaton lowered his fist and turned to Bartholomew.

"What would you have us do?"

Glad he wouldn't have to do any more convincing, Bartholomew told them to stand back while his animals broke through the walls.

The spectral prisoners turned away, giving Bartholomew a good view of each crown. Some wore the white cap of upper Egypt, others the red of the lower realm. But three or four were dressed in a double crown symbolizing Egypt's unification.

Only Khufu wore a striped head cloth. It was pulled tightly across his forehead and tied in the back. Two squares of fabric hung down either side of his head like clipped elephant ears. The vulture and snake uraeus on his brow pecked and hissed at each other, wrestling for control of the highest perch.

"Everyone ready?" Bartholomew called through cupped hands. When the pharaohs and rams nodded, he shouted, "Okay. Go!"

The rams lowered their curled horned heads and charged, feet flying in a thunder of hooves. Crash! A crack split the air. Splinters shot in all directions, leaving a gaping hole in the prison wall. The rams skidded to a stop, rose on their hind legs, and butted heads in victory.

"Yes!" Bartholomew cried, wishing Alex were there to high five. He waited for the dust to settle, then called, "You can come out now."

Regally, the pharaohs stepped through the opening. One by one, they took Bartholomew's hands in theirs and introduced themselves.

Trying to imagine how an Egyptian would address his king, Bartholomew bowed to each one in turn. "Greetings, Montuhotep, he who is content. Greetings, Akhenaton, he who raised a temple in Karnak. Hail, Khufu, builder of the Great Pyramid of Giza." On he went, hoping he was giving each the honor of his station.

After a final bow, he addressed them as a group. "I need you all to stay close together. Wolf, Bear, and I will lead. The rams will guard your flank."

"Remember, though," the Pharaoh Khufu pointed to his transparent body. "We are not yet freed from the Spell of Subterranea. We are most vulnerable in this state."

Tall Akhenaton stepped in front of him and nodded. "We are in grave danger until it is reversed. Beware of Shadow Swine weapons and the twisting mouth of Mudlark Maker."

Bartholomew nodded grimly and pulled a torch from its niche in the wall. He knew although this flame might light the way now, the future was always fraught with darkness.

Chapter 46

Alex loved the moment of completion when he could stand back and admire his creations. Crossing his arms, he nodded appreciatively at the two dozen knee-high soldiers standing at attention and awaiting orders. Each wore a square loincloth and held a sharp-pointed javelin in one hand. *Nice job, if I do say so.* "Can you fly without being seen?" he asked, turning to Horus.

"My wings won't work in this place, and I have never had invisibility powers."

"I can change your wings but not get you invisible."

"I think I can be of some assistance there." Isis stepped forward and rested a hand on her son's shoulder.

After a few minutes of quiet conferencing, Alex bent down to explain the plan to his miniature soldiers. Next, he scooped up handfuls of clay, rubbed it over his two friends' unfurled wings, and used his creation powers to alter them temporarily. Now that Isis and Horus could fly, Alex handed each of them half of the tiny soldiers.

As soon as they took off, Alex turned to Anubis. "Be ready to strike with your sword. As soon as Isis flashes her crown, you will pave the way."

Anubis nodded his jackal head, then set off running toward the Swineys.

"Osiris," Alex said, "I know I said I'd hang back and protect the papyrus—"

"But things have changed," Osiris said, continuing Alex's train of thought. "They need you now."

"Maybe you should hold onto this," Alex offered the papyrus to the god.

"No." Osiris put his hands up in protest. "I would provide little protection should they come."

Alex looked down at the rust-colored stain on Osiris's gown. The god could barely stand, much less fight a Swiney. With a nod, he wrapped the papyrus tightly around his own shoulders. Satisfied he wouldn't drop it while skating, he called Lion forward. "Guard and protect," Alex ordered.

The great beast bobbed its head. It took two steps forward then sat back on its haunches directly in front of the god. Alex blinked. It looked just like that statue in front of Bartholomew's house. Funny, he hadn't noticed the similarity before.

"Good." Now where was everyone? "Thoth? Bastet?" Alex called into the mass of stalagmites. The skateboarding duo appeared immediately. Bastet rolled up like a pro surfer, but Thoth was still as wobbly as a first-timer. When he saw the awkward arms and the too straight legs, Alex had to clear his throat to keep from chuckling. "Ahem. Okay here's the plan," he said as they leaned in. He barely had time to explain and place the rest of the tiny soldiers atop the skateboards before a bright light flashed overhead. The sound of crashing bodies echoed throughout the stony cave.

Without a second to lose, Alex, Thoth, and Bastet raced across the cavern, punching at any Shadow Swine in their path. Luckily, most of the Swineys had been blinded by Isis's flashing crown, so they put up little resistance. It wasn't long before the trio arrived at the tunnel and unloaded the tiny soldiers. Then Isis and Horus landed in front of them and set the rest of the soldiers down.

Alex beckoned Bastet closer. He unrolled the papyrus and smoothed it out on the ground. "Can you remove only a few of the strands without damaging the cartouches?"

"I am as precise with my claws as I am with a bow," Bastet purred as she kneeled next to the papyrus. She barred those beautiful claws and carefully undid a few threads.

Alex thought over the plan as he braided the thin strands into rope. Attempting to anticipate where things could go wrong, he tried not to think of Bartholomew alone inside the tunnel.

Just then the jackal-god pranced to them, swinging two swords in figure-eight patterns. Thumping his tail, Anubis tossed them up, and the scimitars twisted and twirled like palm fronds in a sandstorm. Halfway into their descent, the god leaped up, snatched them out of the air, and tucked them under his arms. Lolling out his tongue, he made a sweeping bow. "Thought you might need this," he said handing a sword to Horus.

"Show-off," Horus muttered giving Anubis a begrudging look. He snatched his scimitar back before turning his attention to Alex.

"Okay, here it is." Alex passed the coiled twine to Anubis. "You both go into the shadows, then stretch the trip wire and hold it taut between you. Let my little soldiers take the Swineys out, okay? Only fight if you have to."

Anubis and Horus nodded as the grumbles drew closer. Alex glanced back across the cavern. The diversion had begun to wear off, and Shadow Swine were getting back up and regrouping into battalions.

Alex peered into the brave faces of his comrades, each so special: Thoth, with his ibis head and spindly legs. Bastet, the noble cat. Anubis, the practical joking jackal. And of course, the beautiful Isis standing taller than the rest, her wings rising and falling with each breath.

He could lose any one of them in this battle. But if this plan worked...no. Not if. *When* this plan worked, they would all be celebrating back in the Valley of the Kings.

"Anubis, Horus. Are you ready?"

With a quick salute, the duo nodded and dashed into the tunnel.

Alex faced the others. "Come on. Let's take out these Shadow Swine!"

* * *

"Hey, Swiney, Swiney!" Alex taunted a few moments later. "Come over here, you babies! We'll show you what a real fight is like."

"Are you afraid of my claws?" Bastet yowled.

"Or beak mine?" Thoth cried snapping his curved bill open and closed.

"No, I know what they're really afraid of," Alex shouted.

"What?" the gods asked on cue.

"That we're going to kick their butts!"

Now, you can say a lot of things to a Swiney, but threatening to kick his butt is not one of them. Shadow Swine, like all stupid bullies, think they can beat up anyone. They cannot, but they are too dumb to know it.

"Kick butts, huh? We show you!" a wart-faced ugly retorted, shaking his fist. He rushed forward, pounding his chest. More followed, hopping up and down like an angry troop of gorillas.

In any other situation, Alex would have burst out laughing. They all looked so ridiculous. But defeating these monsters was no laughing matter. Keeping his eyes on the advancing Shadow Swine, he backed into the dark tunnel.

"Let them come to you," he reminded his comrades.

The first line of growling Swineys marched to the dusky entrance, waving their fists and axes in the air. Alex and his squad matched them step for step, retreating until they were hidden in shadow. Then then they dashed farther inside and pressed themselves against the tunnel walls. The hawk-headed god and his jackal compatriot took up either side of the trip wire and stretched it across the ground while Alex stood nearby ready to give the order.

"Wait, wait..." Alex warned, steeling himself to do the same. "A few seconds more." The sound of heavy boots grew louder until they were almost on top of them. "Horus, pull now!"

Alex heard the snap of the rope being pulled taut. Then there was a loud thud and several grunts, followed by a rasping sound like miniature knives plunging into sand. The tunnel darkened even more as the toy soldiers cheered in tinny whispers. Alex peered toward the tunnel mouth. Swirling dust clouds were all that remained of the first Swiney row.

"Yes!"

The next line entered the tunnel, coughing and sputtering on the dust. Alex grinned as they approached. *They have no idea what's ahead,* he thought. "Anubis, again!"

The second row fell. More Swiney powder filled the air. *You'd think by now they'd have a clue about what's going on,* Alex thought as a third group marched directly into their trap. One moment their feet were pounding in unison, the next silence.

"Turnabout is fair play, huh? You ugly slime buckets." Alex sneered under his breath.

After the sixth line disappeared, the remaining Shadow Swine stopped at the entrance. Keeping pressed against the wall, Alex took a few steps toward them and ventured a peek.

"How far in are enemy? Where soldiers gone?" Confused murmurs rose and echoed up the cavern walls.

Some monsters hung back, pacing like panthers in a cage. A few jerked their heads right and left, not seeming to know what to do. A couple even charged forward, but were stopped by a grotesquely fat Swiney whose lumpy arm halted them short of the tunnel mouth.

Alex worried. With only a few Egyptians left, the only way to defeat the Shadow Swine was with trickery, and he didn't have time to make more clay soldiers. He simply *had* to get the rest of those Swineys into the tunnel. He stepped into the light of the opening. "What are you afraid of? The dark?" He laughed.

"We not afraid," Fatty hissed.

"Then come on," Horus cried, joining Alex's side. "Battle. If you dare."

"Yeah. You wimps!" Alex sniggered, thumbing his nose at them.

Don't ever call a Swiney a wimp. They go crazy. These were no different. In a rabid frenzy of shaking axes and swords, the monsters rushed forward.

"Uh-oh," Alex said, backing up. "Run, Horus! Grab the rope!" Alex dashed back to his waiting friends, the Shadow Swine mere paces behind. Only precious seconds remained to get the trip wire in place. "Pull, now!" he cried.

"Where is it?" Horus choked.

The Shadow Swine were closer. Soon they'd pass the trip wire. and the gods wouldn't stand a chance against them.

Alex shoved Horus out of the way and hit the dirt with a scraping skid. His mind raced as he groped about on his hands and knees. Thick dust hung in the air, filling his nostrils and mouth. It was so dark.

"Over here!" Anubis rasped.

Alex tried to go toward the voice. He felt something. No! Just a rock.

The footfalls drew closer. Fifteen feet. Ten.

It had to be somewhere. His frantic hands dug into the soil. Where was it?

Marching feet closed in. He could feel steamy breath thickening the air.

He flattened onto his stomach hands brushing in wide sweeps. Pebbles. Dirt. A stalagmite.

His fingers clutch something stringy.

He snatched up the rope. It was too dangerous to stand, so he put one end in his mouth and clamped down. Alex kept low as he crawled backwards. Gritty dust choked his every breath. Gross saliva drooled out one side of his mouth, but no way would he let his jaw slacken.

The drumming jackboots made Alex wish he could plug his ears. *Don't let go. Be strong.* Keeping the rope in his teeth, Alex scuttled to the wall.

The Swineys were inches away. He rose to his knees and jerked his head back.

The rope tugged on his mouth more than when Dad yanked his loose tooth with string. Managing to stand, Alex grabbed the rope in both hands. He pulled back, thankful Anubis had the presence of mind to keep his side tight.

He heard groans and a cry of surprise. A hiss.

Then silence. The rope slackened.

Alex waited. Man, his mouth ached. He circled his jaw and ticked off the seconds. *Five, ten, thirty.* He counted to be sure.

The dust settled. Now Alex could see the tiny soldiers holding their knife-sized swords up in the air. Beyond them, a panting Anubis thumped his tail up and down.

But not a single Swiney was in sight.

"Score!" Alex raised a victorious arm into the air. He leaped over piles of Swiney dust, scampered to the edge of the tunnel and gave everyone high fives.

He patted Anubis on the head and playfully tapped Horus on the beak. Isis smiled down at him like Mom did one time he brought home a good report card.

Chapter 47

In the pinhole of light ahead, Bartholomew could barely make out two silhouettes. One was a female with a large disk crown and the other a boy his size. Alex! He turned toward the pharaohs, and placed a finger to his lips. "Stay here for a minute. Okay?"

He tiptoed down the long tunnel as silent as a jerboa mouse until he was right behind Alex. This was great. Swallowing a giggle, he tapped him on the shoulder.

"Hey!" Alex jumped and jerked around. His brown curls were disheveled and his face streaked with sweaty grime. He raised a fist as if ready to fight, but when he saw Bartholomew, he uncurled it and cried, "You made it."

"I certainly did." Feeling like a victorious superhero, Bartholomew placed his hands on his hips.

"And the pharaohs?"

"See for yourself," Bartholomew replied, stepping aside to reveal the Egyptian kings making their way toward them.

Alex gaped and shook his head. "You did it!" He leaped in the air and gave Bartholomew a celebratory punch in the arm. Between whoops of joy, he cuffed his friend repeatedly until Bartholomew's shoulder was sore. He barely noticed. He was so proud Alex could have hit him with a brick.

"My kings!" Isis cried clutching her breast as she rushed into the waiting arms of her friends.

There was hugging and back slapping. Handshakes and high fives. Thoth hopped to Bartholomew and cawed his congratulations. Horus, now in boy form, darted figure eights around them while Anubis shook his tail so wildly a cool breeze ruffled Bartholomew's hair.

"B-Three, you did it," Alex said with a final punch.

Bartholomew felt his chest swell with pride. Everyone was talking at once. Bartholomew explained how he'd frightened the Swineys away by acting crazy while the pharaohs threw in a word here and there to fill in details. When everyone had quieted, Bartholomew turned to Alex. "What about the battle? Everything is so calm. Where'd all the Shadow Swine go?"

Alex opened his mouth to speak, but his words were cut short when Horus stepped in front of him. "We have defeated more than seventy Swiney due to the cunning of this boy."

"Really? How?"

"Oh, I made some helpers," Alex said, pointing to some miniature soldiers dancing in the shadows of the tunnel.

Bartholomew shrugged, not understanding at all.

"Mother and I flew them overhead." Horus chuckled

"And I shone my sun disk brightly to blind the enemy," Isis said.

"While they were blinded, we put the scale models in place," Horus continued.

"Meanwhile I unstitched a few strands of papyrus," Bastet barred her claws.

Alex nodded. "We needed trip wires, you see."

"Then Horus and I held the wire taut." Anubis wagged his tail again, and Alex patted him on the head.

"They stumbled right onto the lances of our small soldiers," Alex said.

Bartholomew raised his eyebrows. "Cool plan."

Thoth cut this conversation short. "Caw! Defeated now are seven powers. We must recall how short grow hours. Now is not the time for boasts. When Pharaohs remain in forms of ghosts."

With a nod, Alex pulled out the papyrus from its hiding place behind a loose rock in the wall. He gave one corner to Bartholomew and took the opposite in his hands. They walked apart until the fabric was stretched tightly.

Bartholomew exchanged a glance with Alex who grinned. The admiring look made Bartholomew feel as tall as the stony formations in the stalagmite forest.

"Okay," he called.

Thoth hopped toward them on his stick legs, adjusting the fabric until the hieroglyphics in every cartouche were clearly visible. With a caw, he called the pharaohs forward and pointed out different places on the papyrus. "Khufu, Akhenaton, here stands. Others places find between their hands." Each of the transparent pharaohs shuffled toward his own cartouche. It was so strange to see right through them and hear their feet make pattering sounds at the same time. "Goddess Isis, ankh have you? For magic freeing spell's work to do?

Isis pulled a large ankh from the folds of her dress and handed it to Thoth. She bowed, then stepped back to join the gathering crowd.

"Ready?" Alex asked Bartholomew.

Bartholomew nodded. He knew Alex believed him this time.

"Caw! Touch both hands to your own cartouche. And watch this spell quick unloose. While boys twin hold steady gaze. To release those trapped from Swiney maze!" He raised his arms to the sky and cawed rhythmically as the pharaohs placed their hands on the hieroglyphics, and the ropey outlines of each cartouche glowed.

Alex stared at Bartholomew and winked. With a nervous smile, Bartholomew winked back. The chanting grew louder and louder, and they held each other's eyes as Thoth directed.

The papyrus vibrated. Each of the cartouches turned different colors. First blue, then red. Soon orange and yellow. Several snakes like multiple twins of the cobra goddess Wadjet rose from the fabric and entwined each pharaoh.

The ropes brightened with each passing second, burning like white-hot suns. Bartholomew squinted against the glaucous glare. This time.

he knew how to keep the pain away with a single thought. He was a Deliverer.

A lightning bolt cracked.

"Forward step for all to see. Our pharaoh brethren now are free!"

Bartholomew glanced up. In place of the ghostlike apparitions were real pharaohs. They held their hands up in front of their faces turning them repeatedly in wonder, exchanging glances down the line at each other.

"I am whole again!" Khufu cried.

A cheer rose from the gathered crowd, starting a new round of hugs and backslaps while a grinning Bartholomew gathered the folds of the papyrus into his arms. The joyful group traded barbs and playful nudges as they made their way across the cavern. Isis's crown flashed a rainbow that shone through Anubis's furry tail like a multicolored flag while Alex and a laughing Bastet skateboarded circles around everyone.

Bartholomew shook his head at Khufu and Akhenaton who kept racing for the front of the line. First Akhenaton jogged ahead, but Khufu would grab his linen robe, pull him back, and take his place as the leader.

"Khufu! Stop that! I must be first." Akhenaton fumed. "I began a new era in Egypt...that of the sun god."

"No. I must lead. My tomb is the greatest in all the land."

"It is not."

"Of course it is."

"Not!"

Bartholomew jogged between the two arguing pharaohs as Akhenaton was ready to punch Khufu in the face. "Gentlemen, please," Bartholomew said, placing his raised sword between them.

The pharaohs immediately found their feet quite fascinating. Each stared at his sandals, wiggling his toes nervously.

Bartholomew exchanged a glance with Alex. Chuckling, Alex skateboarded in front of them and did a handstand to save them further embarrassment before grinding to a halt before the stalagmite forest.

They entered the stony glade and brought the pharaohs to a waiting Osiris and Hatshepsut. Bartholomew let out a long sigh. Now they could go home.

Chapter 48

Alex glanced at the reunion around him and smiled. It reminded him of the time he'd returned from summer camp to see his parents, two uncles, an aunt, Grandma, and a few cousins all waving Welcome Home signs. He remembered how happy his mom looked with healthy color in her cheeks and a wide smile. She was thrilled; all the people on her list attended.

Yep they'd all come. All fourteen. Not a one was missing. Everyone was there.

The word stuck in Alex's brain. Everyone? A cold prickle started up his spine. He counted. Eight, nine, ten. They were milling about, so maybe he missed one. He counted again. Nine, ten.

"No!" he gasped. The color drained from Alex's face. *It can't be.*

"Excuse me!" he called, shaking his head.

They ignored him.

"Hey! Everyone?"

The laughter continued.

Alex put his fingers in his mouth and let out a piercing whistle.

His friends froze.

"Where is Ramses?"

No answer.

"Ramses, are you there?" Alex cried, praying to see the tortured king Sludge had taunted with the cat, but he already knew the truth.

Bartholomew unfolded the papyrus. One cartouche remained flashing what was now undeniable. Ramses was still trapped somewhere in Subterranea.

"Sorry that I did not see. The final one we need to free." Thoth shook his bird head.

"How could we have missed him?" Bartholomew cried.

Cackling laughter echoed from the other side of the cavern in reply. "You missed him because you are fools!"

"I know that voice," Alex muttered, gritting his teeth.

"You thought you could defeat me? Ha! Don't you know my powers come directly from Sickhert himself? Stupid humans."

"Sludge." Bartholomew spat.

"I should have gone after him when I had the chance." Alex clenched and unclenched his fists until his nails dug quarter moon marks in his palm.

"No, young one. You did rightly," Isis said. "If you had followed him, he would have killed Ramses immediately, and the others would not now be free." She placed a reassuring hand on his shoulder.

"But what about Ramses?" Bartholomew asked.

"Monuments will be lost, yes, but as soon the ten reach Tutankhamen's tomb, the Land of Antiquities will be safe," Osiris replied.

"That's not good enough," Alex protested.

Thoth pulled the hourglass from a crevice in the wall and held it up to Alex. "If sands of time all outrun. Before pharaohs and tomb stand as one. The Land of Antiquities days will be done," the ibis god said.

Alex stared at the segmented glass. Most grains had trickled into the bottom, but it looked like about fifteen minutes remained.

"We still have time," Bartholomew argued. "You all go ahead. I'll stay and fight."

Alex gaped at Bartholomew. "I was going to say the same thing."

"You will be alone. Two young ones against all evil Captain Sludge can muster," Osiris said.

"No problem." Bartholomew draped his arm over Alex's shoulder. "We are the chosen ones. Remember?"

"Now you all get up the ladder," Alex said, shooing them along. "Quickly. We'll be just fine."

"I will stay, just right there," Thoth said, pointing to the bottom of the ladder where he would wait. "While others climb the stony stair. But don't forget Soothsayer's Stone. If you're feeling all alone."

Alex nodded. "I'll remember. Now go! We have work to do!"

"May good fortune be with you, young ones." A limping Osiris shook their hands in turn and led the Egyptians to the exit. Soon they'd all disappeared into the depths of the stalagmite forest.

"Cowards! I knew you would turn tail and run. Now Ramses is mine! Mine!" Sludge gurgled from across the cavern.

"Not if me and my buddy have anything to say about it," Alex whispered.

Bartholomew lifted his fist to the sky. Alex did the same.

The two friends stood side-by-side, their ideas flowing like rivers of paint from mind-to-mind. They were ready.

Chapter 49

Keeping his body pressed against the stalagmite, Bartholomew ventured a peek across the cavern. There Sludge was on top of the platform, cinching a rope around poor Ramses's waist. The slimy captain bowed his head and moved his lips as if he were chanting something important, but what he was saying was indiscernible.

Realizing what Sludge was doing, Bartholomew gasped in horror. "Mudlark Maker! He's waking him up!"

"Then, we'll just have to stop him, won't we?" Alex retorted with a savage whisper from his post behind the opposite stalagmite.

Bartholomew got a lump in his throat. Alex said, *we'll stop him.* Not *I* but *we.* No hesitation. Like equals.

He surveyed their remaining army. Wolf, Lion, Bear, the Rams, and the shin-high soldiers Alex sculpted were enough to surround Sludge—if they were smart and used the element of surprise.

"With Captain Sludge alone, this should not be difficult," Bartholomew said, crossing his fingers for good measure.

"Let's not get cocky and give it away," Alex warned, scooping up some of the tiny soldiers. "Keep quiet. I'll put as many on my board as can fit. The rest can go on my back."

"I'll ride Lion." Bartholomew beaconed the great feline.

Without pausing to look up, Alex gave a quick thumbs-up.

Bartholomew set his sheathed sword on the ground and stepped next to Lion. He cocked his head to one side and raised an eyebrow. He would have spit if his mouth weren't so dry. Trying to imagine cowboy stories he'd read, he grabbed Lion's mane and swung his right leg up. He actually got it halfway there before it slid back down. *Okay. Lion was taller than he'd first thought. Be an Apache. Run!* he told himself. Jogging back a few yards, Bartholomew sprinted forward and jumped.

He flew right over, overshooting his mark by a good three feet.

"Why not just ask Lion to bend down?" Alex crossed his arms and smirked.

"Oh, yeah." Trying to keep the embarrassment out of his voice, Bartholomew grabbed his sword, ordered the animal to kneel, and climbed on.

"Ready now?"

Bartholomew raised his scimitar in reply, and they were off. Immediately, Alex shot ahead, his five small soldiers grinning as they gripped the skateboard's nose.

"Come on, Lion," Bartholomew urged.

The great beast galloped faster, and the cavern walls blurred to gray. Lion's paws padded softly as Bartholomew's body rose and fell in perfect rhythm. The wind blew his hair back, and the lightness in his stomach tickled.

Hooves clattered over the stony ground, and Bartholomew glanced back. The rams were only a few paces behind, some of the tiny sculptures clinging to their backs. The rest of the mini soldiers rode atop Wolf and Bear. Good, Bartholomew thought. Almost there.

Twenty-five feet… ten.

Lion skidded to a halt short of the yawning Mudlark Maker. A steamy blast blew back Bartholomew's hair and filled his nostrils with a foul sulfuric stench. "Have you ever heard of mouthwash?" Bartholomew coughed, waving the air in front of his face.

Mudlark Maker blinked in confusion. One eye was now milky white and had long claw marks on it while the other was as dark as pitch. When the creature saw Bartholomew astride Lion, both eyes narrowed into long slits, and two tar-dripping arms burst out of the soil.

The mud creature swiped at him, and Bartholomew jerked Lion back, out of the monster's reach.

Alex rolled past the wooden platform, skating so fast Bartholomew couldn't tell where his body ended and the board began. He glided up one sloped wall and turned 180 degrees. The miniature soldiers held on tightly, giggling all the way. Alex surged over a slanted boulder like a lightning bolt headed straight for the platform.

He landed next to Sludge who still held the rope tied around Ramses's waist. The pharaoh was so transparent that he reminded Bartholomew of the conservatory's glass.

"Persistent, aren't we?" the evil captain sneered with a cruel tug on the line. The tormented pharaoh stumbled. All the proud nobility was gone from his fading face, replaced with a hollow look of dejection.

"Let him go, slime bucket." Alex's teeth were clenched so tightly Bartholomew could see the muscles in his cheeks.

"Yeah, we have you outnumbered," Bartholomew added from his place below them.

"You think so?" Sludge asked. He tilted his spiked head towards the tunnel to his right and clapped his hands twice. "Look now, idiot humans!"

Like ants marching to spilled honey, scores of the dark soldiers poured into the cavern. Bartholomew leaped off Lion's back and pulled his scimitar from its sheath. He turned around and round waving it above his head. But in less time than it takes to say *Land of Antiquities*, the two of them were surrounded.

Bartholomew felt like he was on a piece of jam-covered toast sinking into an insect-filled sea. Row after row of Shadow Swine lined up on every side him, advancing with pointed swords and spears, while double rows of the monsters circled the rams, bear, and wolf.

They were trapped.

Bartholomew stared at Alex's horrified face. He lowered his weapon and shook his head. *So close*, he thought. *We almost had them beat.*

"I warned you." Sludge grinned with teeth as sharp as knives. "But you would not listen. Now you will watch while the most powerful pharaoh in all of Egypt becomes my slave." Sludge licked his lips and yanked Ramses in close before punching the pharaoh savagely in the gut.

The king dropped to his knees, doubled over in pain; Bartholomew flinched as if he were the one smacked.

Alex rushed at Sludge, but the captain shoved him back with an outstretched hand. Bartholomew knew it was hopeless. Still, his friend backed up to try again. Before he could get a running start, two Swineys marched up the stairs and pinned his arms against his sides. Alex struggled against their clawed grip, but the monsters held fast.

"Soldiers!" Alex cried.

Spears raised, the tiny sculptures shimmied down his back and jumped off his skateboard before dashing across the platform. One pointed a javelin at the captain's leg and leaned forward to strike. Guffawing, Sludge kicked it into the air.

It landed next to a fat Swiney who raised his boot. With a stupid grin he stared into Alex's wretched eyes. Taunting him. When the fat beast brought his foot down, there was a sickening crunch.

"No!" Alex roared.

Bartholomew turned. Lion was at his side, but he couldn't think of how to use him against all those Swineys. *Think!* Grasping the hilt of his sword in both hands, he locked it into his gut and leaned forward. The slime-covered creatures opposite waved their gleaming axes.

"You try it, human, you die," the tallest one gurgled.

Bartholomew stepped back, ready to strike, whatever the cost.

"B-Three, don't," Alex implored from the Shadow Swine's grasp.

Bartholomew lowered his sword, but didn't let it go. He might find an opening yet if he stayed sharp.

Two more shin-high soldiers scurried to Ramses, scrambled up his linen robe, and sawed away at the rope around his waist.

Sludge gave the line a jerk, and the soldiers tumbled down, landing at the pharaoh's feet.

"Destroy them," he rasped at his cloaked soldiers. "I tire of this game."

Four more Shadow Swine lumbered up the stairs as the tiny men raised their javelins in unison. Small, brave, and ready to fight, they were no match for the hunchbacked monsters. Alex's beautiful soldiers didn't even get one jab in before the gleeful Swineys stomped and crushed them with braying laughter. Their horrible howls assaulted Bartholomew's ears and turned his stomach.

"Stop!" Alex wrenched to one side and then the other, but those hulky arms didn't loosen.

Bartholomew swung his sword wildly. He might not be able to get through that wall, but he could take out a few of those evil monsters. He jabbed one in the leg. It fell but did not die. Fueled by rage, he sliced at two more. They dodged his blows. "Hurt my friends, will you?" Blood rushed to Bartholomew's ears. He feigned left, waiting for the monster to duck. He thrust and the Shadow Swine crumbled away.

"Ha! That's what I'm talking about." Narrowing his eyes, Bartholomew swung again, not seeing the shield until it was too late. The next thing he knew, he was flat on his back, his sword at his side. Although dazed, he had the presence of mind to grab his fallen weapon.

Sword in hand, Bartholomew sat up and stared at the platform above him where the last two clay soldiers ran in circles desperately trying to escape the Shadow Swine on their heels. When they made it to the edge of the wooden stage, he thought they might get away. "Go, little guys. You can do it!" he urged.

But the clawed fingers were deadly precise. The Shadow Swine grabbed Alex's beautiful soldiers and flung them at the far wall. The small Egyptians shattered into a thousand pieces.

Howling, Bartholomew vaulted headlong into the sea of Swineys. They pushed him back. Grunting, he hammered right, then left. Two fell, but there was no way through that tsunami of mud.

He retreated to the center of the circle where Lion waited. He rubbed the thick fur and tried to think. With a pained shake of his head, he realized the truth. *Nothing can stop Sludge now.*

The captain wrapped one end of the rope tightly around his hands and leered at Alex, his serrated teeth glinting in the torchlight. Tugging, he forced Ramses to follow along like a dog on a leash. He reeled the pharaoh in closer and closer until the limp king was inches from his clawed hand. "You thought you could defeat me?" Sludge rasped, glaring at Alex. Drawing his hand back near the pharaoh's face, he waited until he had Alex's full attention. "You are nothing but a dream waiting to be twisted. Watch a *new* nightmare, Deliverer."

Never taking his eyes off Alex, Sludge slapped Ramses so savagely that it snapped the pharaoh's head back and knocked the uraeus on his striped headdress askew.

Although Ramses was in obvious pain, Bartholomew couldn't help but admire how regal he remained. No amount of cruelty could take away his dignity.

With a sneer, Sludge dragged Ramses to the edge of the platform, seeming to revel in the pitiful king's pain, feeding on it. Then he loosened a vicious kick launching Ramses into the air.

Bartholomew covered his mouth. Everything froze for a horrifying moment. Then as if in slow motion, the coils of rope unwound. Ramses plummeted toward the waiting mouth of Mudlark Maker.

When Alex choked out a scream, Bartholomew truly became afraid.

The rope shuddered and pulled taut. Ramses dangled just inches above those bulbous lips. One long bead of sweat traced a path down his cheek to his rectangular beard. It hung suspended, waiting to drip into the mud monster's mouth.

"You will not make me a Mudlark. I am pharaoh. I would rather die," the king shouted as he drew his sandaled feet further under his white tunic.

"Is that so, Ramses?" Sludge spat, backing up. Then as if he'd changed his mind, he stepped forward again.

Bartholomew shut his eyes and words appeared on back of his lids. What did they mean? He held his sword high and chanted aloud.

On the eleventh year of their lives,
They will join together like single forged knives.

Their battle will be long with seven evils to undo.
Scattered around will be seven clues.
And many will perish before they are through,
But our world will be saved if their art is true.

Bartholomew raised his chin and looked up. Sludge stopped and stared back at him. The flickering torches reflected red flames off his shiny forehead.

"Stupid human. Don't you know the prophecy is for fools?" Sludge took a step forward, lowering Ramses closer to that giant mouth.

"Mmm." Mudlark Maker smacked. His lips sounded like treacherous lava boiling and popping.

"Please don't," Alex pleaded.

"You don't like this, Deliverer? Want me to stop?" Sludge asked.

"Yes."

"I might be persuaded."

"How?" Alex asked.

"Those Knights of Painted Light are thorns in my side. Blocking my dream invaders. I need a shield against them. Only a Deliverer can make such a shield."

"Don't listen to him!" Bartholomew cried. They couldn't give the Shadow Swine any more power. "There has to be another way."

"Is there?" Alex asked Bartholomew in a pale voice. He tilted his head toward Ramses. The pharaoh's regal eyes were wide with terror as he dangled like a fly reeling into a spider's web. "Please, let him go," Alex implored.

Instead of answering, Sludge took two steps forward, lowering Ramses into the monster's mouth. As gargantuan lips were ready to close, he yanked the king up into the air. Ramses cried out in pain, wrenching and writhing as the rope cinched tighter.

"Okay, okay, I'll make your shield. Just stop!" Alex cried.

Bartholomew watched Sludge drop Ramses down one more time. *To make sure Alex knows what could happen if he changes his mind.* Bartholomew looked away, unable to stand seeing his friend's pale face.

"Private, hold the prisoner." Sludge pulled Ramses back onto the platform and shoved the pharaoh into the doughy arms of an obese Shadow Swine, who grabbed the king by the shoulders. It wasn't necessary. All fight was gone from Ramses. His head lolled to one side, and his arms hung limply at his sides.

"Are you okay?" Alex asked, walking to Ramses. Always the hero. Always ready to help.

The pharaoh nodded weakly. He was nearly invisible now. Time was running out, and soon it would be too late to cast the freeing spell.

"But remember, that can change at any moment, Deliverer."

"I understand," Alex said.

When Sludge clenched his clawed hands together, they made squishy sounds. Bartholomew's stomach heaved with disgust.

"A shield. A shield against them all."

Bartholomew shook his head. He couldn't let this happen. He knew what such a weapon could do, not only to Artania but back on Earth as well. People would turn away from art by the millions, all living like Mother did, ready to say, "Filth... I see filth!" from coast to coast. Now was his turn to be the strong one. He had to snap Alex out of defeat. True art had to continue. "Alex, our world will be saved if their art is true! Remember?"

"Quiet!" Sludge rasped before giving Alex a cruel grin. "Now what need you for my shield, Deliverer?"

"Take me to a pool of water. I'll also need some stalactites." Alex's puffy eyes stared off into space, and his voice was distant.

What was he thinking? He couldn't do this.

Sludge ordered his minions to search out a spring.

"No, Alex. Our world will be saved if their art is true. Weapons are not true. Stop!"

"Silence him!"

A trio of soldiers bore down on Bartholomew but halted when the boy held up his scimitar.

"You just try me," he grunted.

"Over here, Captain!" A soldier waved at Sludge from the other end of the cavern.

"It is no matter. He can do nothing. Come, Deliverer, a pool has been found." Leaving Ramses behind, Sludge swaggered down the steps and made his way toward the waving Swiney.

Bartholomew felt hope drowning. His mind gasped for an answer, searching for a lifeline in this muddy sea. Could Alex handle the truth? It was now or never. He swallowed what little spit was left in his dry mouth. "Why did you stop painting, Alex? Huh? Were you scared?" he asked.

Alex turned to glare at Bartholomew. "I have to save him. Don't you see? If I save him—"

"It won't make your mother well," Bartholomew said.

"What do you know, Richie?"

"Our world will be safe if their art is true… if their art is true! Remember? Stop lying to yourself." Bartholomew tried to leap over the Shadow Swine blocking his way, but the wall was too thick.

Sludge led his friend away.

"Be true, Alex!" Bartholomew cried.

Alex kept walking.

There was nothing more that he could do. It was up to Alex, his celestial twin.

Chapter 50

Alex clenched and unclenched his fists as he followed a triumphant Sludge strutting across the cavern.

They halted in front of a circular group of knee-high stalagmites. In their center, fresh water bubbled from a bowl-shaped depression. Alex knelt by it and stared into the inky depths. Bloodshot eyes looked back at him from one corner while Sludge's grinning mouth filled the center.

Pretending to be in a trance, Alex dipped his fingers in the water and swirled it. He didn't even want Bartholomew to know his plans at this point.

"Be true, Alex!" Bartholomew's voice echoed throughout the cavern.

"What are you waiting for? Ramses to be thrown into Mudlark Maker's mouth?" Sludge raised one muddy lip in a sneer. "Or perhaps you need more persuasion. Do you want me to invade your mother's dreams, too?"

Mother? Alex glanced back at his reflection in the pool. At first, he only saw his own face. Then the water rippled, and the smiling face of Mom appeared.

She was so beautiful. So full of love. Just like that day before her attack when she'd been baking raspberry muffins. "Welcome home, kiddo! Want to try one?" She held out a plate of rosy steaming muffins.

Alex bit into the soft dough. Yum! But his mind had been in other places. He'd gobbled it down, dreaming of his new creation.

"Where are you?" Mom asked.

"Painting. A creature with seven legs and arms. What do you think?"

She tousled his hair. At least he'd let her do that much. "Create whatever is in your heart."

"But it is different."

"I wouldn't have it any other way."

He'd painted until late into the night. Never stopping to see how Mom was, but she didn't complain. She'd always encouraged him to paint whatever was in his heart. Telling him to be true to who he was. Be true.

"Our world will be saved if their art is true!" Bartholomew shouted again.

Alex reached into his pocket and felt the brown button. Now he understood why it had led him here, and what true art was. When Bartholomew sketched Mom in class, it had been true. His paintings from deep inside of him—true as well.

When Mom got sick, he'd stopped going to the special place within. Well, not any more. It ends here. He broke off a few soda straw stalagmites and swirled them in the water.

"Soon all the power will be mine. Mine. Mine!" Sludge cackled behind him. "Sickhert and I will rule all dreams."

Dream on, slime bucket.

The swirling stalactites became paintbrushes as the water turned into a palette of colored streams. Alex dipped a brush into the softest of browns and made two dots on the ground beside him. Then for the peach. And the golden yellow. Her blouse had been aqua. Don't forget white. Oh, how her teeth had shone.

Sludge was so busy flaring his piggy nostrils while bragging and boasting that he wasn't paying very close attention to Alex. *Good.*

His long claws tapped together like clicking cockroaches over a stony floor. Alex smiled. *Keep drumming, Sludge. I have the exact bug spray to stop your clatter.*

"What is this?" Sludge's slimy jaw dropped open. By the time he turned, it was too late. In place of the giant shield he'd ordered was the painting of a woman.

"True art," Alex replied dabbing a bit of yellow on her wedding band.

A tiny bit of light emanated from the gold ring. Mom's fingers glistened. Alex reached out to touch her hand. and it glimmered, growing brighter until the entire cavern was basking in a warm glow.

Alex embraced his mother. A single beam formed in the center of their chests. Alex took a deep breath. *See it. Believe.* A fiery rose bloomed between them, and thousands of golden rays shot forth.

To Alex, the multiple lightning bolts were living beauty, but to the Shadow Swine, they were death. The muddy creatures scattered to escape, hopping, dodging, and darting. A light beam hit one, and he melted into a puddle of mud. Another scurried for the shadows, but his feet turned to slush as he ran.

Throughout the cavern, silvery rays reached strong arms to strike the fleeing creatures. With a hissing zap, Swiney after Swiney collapsed into splotches of brown jelly.

Those near Sludge were the last to go. With an apologetic look at their leader, they vaulted over the sticky remains of their comrades.

"Come back! Where are you going, fools?" Captain Sludge bellowed.

Even the Swiney's rage couldn't darken the glow of Alex's chest. With every swelling breath, Mom's love filled him more and more, encasing him in light. Like a gibbous moon emerging from a cloud, it helped him realize she'd forgiven him long ago. Now, finally he could forgive himself. Alex turned to Sludge. "If I were you, I would go, too," he said in a soft voice.

The barrel-chested captain roared and threw punch after desperate punch. Expecting the worst, Alex cringed, but it wasn't necessary. Each blow bounced back with slingshot force. Nothing could get through his shield of light.

The sound of padding paws made him turn. Bartholomew and Ramses were galloping to him astride Lion. Bartholomew pulled back on the feline's straw colored mane and halted in front of the two. "I would do as Alex says. You cannot survive in the presence of true art."

Sludge looked down at his melting jackboots. Steam was rising from both of his feet. "Bah!" he bellowed as he spurted toward the nearest tunnel. "You haven't seen the last of me. You just wait, Deliverer!" he warned when he reached the entrance.

With a final sigh, Alex released his mother's hand. The glimmering rays retreated into her ring. The cavern dimmed until the only light left was the sparkling shine in her eyes. Her image smiled up at him.

"You found true art," Bartholomew murmured.

"I know. I'd almost forgotten."

"You could never forget, Alex."

"Maybe. But this is not its true place." Alex picked up a paintbrush and dipped it in the pool of water. Gently, he let the bristles caress the portrait then watched the colors flow together and disappear. He stood for long moments staring at the bare ground.

"We have to go," Bartholomew said quietly.

Alex dipped his arms into the pool. The water was clear now. He raised cupped hands to his lips and drank. It was the sweetest he'd ever tasted. He didn't need to quench his thirst. He'd already done that. He let the water escape his fingers.

"I thought you might want this." Bartholomew handed him his skateboard and turned Lion toward the stalagmite forest. With a lurch, he galloped again across the cavern like a wild stallion.

Alex placed his board on the ground. He glanced back at the pool one last time. "Hey, wait for me!" he called, kicking off after them.

Chapter 51

Thoth was holding an hourglass in one hand and the papyrus in the other when they arrived at the bottom of the exit ladder in the stalagmite forest. The sand had nearly all run out. "Deliverers, seconds short now remain. To save Ramses from Mudlark's deathly pain." He held out the fabric for the boys to grab.

They each took an end and stretched it. Ramses was almost invisible now, Artanian power nearly gone from his body. Heeding Thoth's words, he drifted to the front of the papyrus. His hands were as clear as glass as he placed them on his cartouche.

Once again Bartholomew stared into Alex's eyes, but this time was different. In place of a fearful frown was a cocky smile. *We did it, Alex. You and I. We saved them.*

Thoth chanted the words. All the while Bartholomew held Alex's gaze. The cartouche glowed, and Bartholomew's smile grew. Alex grinned back and shook his head. Bartholomew could almost hear his friend's thoughts: *Goofy B-Three.*

A thundering crack echoed throughout the cavern and into the tunnels.

"Pharaoh, pharaoh, name of Ramses, Step forward for you are now free!" Thoth crowed.

Ramses held up his now solid hand. A cheer rose from their throats but was cut short when the walls shook. Bartholomew put out a hand to steady himself.

"Make haste. The doorway closes!" Ramses cried.

"Hey, where are the sculptures?" Bartholomew said, looking around.

"Lion, Soldiers?" Alex called.

Bartholomew joined in. "Wolf, Bear, Rams. Hurry!"

There was no answer in the rumbling darkness. Thoth placed a hand on their shoulders. "Creations made you down below. Formed to fight the evil foe. Must return to whence they came. And become the ground of Sickhert's domain," the ibis god said.

"Thank you," Bartholomew mouthed to his creations before following his friends up the ladder.

They rushed back through lava tube tunnels to the zigzagging stairway. They'd have to climb quickly if they were going to make it before the doorway closed. It wouldn't be easy; the long flight of stairs was already shaking. At the same time, moss nearly covered the stones, and trickling water pooled on every third tread. It was going to be slippery.

Thoth led the way. He was in human form now, and even though his legs were no longer a bird's, he still paused at every step like a stream-hopping ibis. Behind him, Ramses kept patting his body as if not believing he was whole again. Alex came next, followed by Bartholomew who took up the rear. Chewing on his lower lip, he swung his leg over a puddle stretching as far as he could. Still his toes just barely reached the step above.

When a teetering Bartholomew stopped to catch his balance, the ground rumbled, a stronger shake this time. He stared at the walls. Like veins in thin skin, huge cracks appeared on either side of him. They snaked upward, branching out near the limestone ceiling.

The sound was deafening.

"What's happening?" he cried.

"Sickhert's doorway is disappearing!" Ramses shouted, his voice barely audible above the rocks' creaks and moans.

"Go," Thoth cawed.

The stairway crumbled beneath them. Beginning with the bottom step, each riser throbbed and convulsed before breaking off and crashing into the tunnels below. Five were already gone, and more were developing fissures.

Squawking at them to hurry, Thoth quickened his pace. The cracks deepened and made new forks. Bartholomew looked at the dark crevices with a shudder.

"Come on!" Alex broke into a sprint.

Bartholomew scrambled after him, but his foot hit some moss, and he slipped. *Don't fall!* his mind screamed. He clawed desperately for handholds, and sharp rocks cut into his palms and forearms.

"You all right, B-Three?" Alex called over his shoulder.

"Fine," he replied in too loud a voice.

Alex turned and searched Bartholomew's face.

Bartholomew tried not to grimace, but his hand throbbed. He rubbed it.

Alex raised his eyebrows when he saw the cut on Bartholomew's palm.

"It's nothing," he argued, thrusting his arm behind his back. "Just go."

Alex nodded and kept climbing. Another step gave way. The light grew dimmer as dust and debris filled the air. The stairway broke off in huge chunks now, but the four of them were still only halfway up. At least a hundred more twisting steps stretched above.

More dust swirled around Bartholomew. It clung to his hair in sticky strings and filled his lungs. He coughed and cleared his throat trying to think of something besides the stinging pain in his hand.

Thoth, who had turned to make his periodic check, shouted down at him. "Faster, faster must we go. Or fall us far below."

Bartholomew nodded, but it was becoming more difficult to climb an ever-crumbling staircase. Every step was a shuddering struggle to stay upright. Three more stairs fell away in a crashing roar sending quavering aftershocks throughout his body.

The stairway was now suspended in space as if invisible hands held up the few remaining sections. It all looked upside down. So odd. The only part making sense gravity-wise were the rivulets of water still streaming over each tread. A thin waterfall trickled on the last one into the darkness below. Bartholomew thought it was kind of beautiful.

Another step broke off. Bartholomew blinked. His friends were way ahead, scurrying upward. He sprinted to catch them.

Just as he reached their heels, he heard a creaking sound from above. He glanced up. Right over the pharaoh, a huge stalactite swayed like a pendulum in a clock.

"Look out!" Bartholomew cried. He vaulted over the steps and shoved Ramses out of the way.

Smack! The huge stalactite crashed into the staircase above them. Bartholomew stumbled back, holding his arms out for balance. When he was steadier, he squinted but still couldn't see through all the dust. "Ramses? Are you all right?"

In the mist a crowned figure took shape. "Fear not, Deliverer. I live."

Bartholomew let out a sigh, but it didn't last. His jaw clamped shut when he realized where the stalactite was now. Like a monstrous rhino raising its gigantic horn and daring them to pass, it was stuck in the center of the stairway.

They were trapped.

Try your sword!" Alex shouted as he dropped to his knees and pushed on the giant stalactite blocking their one escape route.

Bartholomew pulled his scimitar from its sheath and hacked at the cone shaped rock. He might as well have been hitting it with air. All he did was bend the blade.

"Hit it harder while I push." Alex nudged him when Bartholomew stopped to catch his breath.

"It's impossible." Bartholomew held out the sword. "Why don't you try to see how well it works?"

"Okay, stand back," Alex ordered, lifting the curved blade over his shoulder. He hit it once. Nothing.

"Try over there," Ramses suggested, pointing to a corner.

Alex tried again, but the blade only bent more. "Stupid rock, break!" His face colored to purple as he raised his arms. He swung and that beautiful sword crumbled into a thousand pieces.

Bartholomew groaned and looked to Thoth. "Help us!"

"Caw, Caw, Seek shall I." Thoth disappeared from his place on the top stair into King Tut's tomb.

Alex turned to Ramses.

"If we all push together—"

A violent jolt cut his words short. The stairway lurched to one side. The three of them leaped back. A few pebbles broke off and rolled past them. Bartholomew watched them tumble into the darkness below. "What's going on?" he cried.

Ramses's double crown teetered. He placed one hand on the cloth to steady it.

"The stalactite is too heavy." Alex said. "Hold on. It's going through!"

They barely had a chance to brace themselves before there was a creaking groan like the whole cavern was breaking apart. The stalactite convulsed and shuddered. It cut through the stair and crashed in the tunnel below with a deafening boom.

A dazed Bartholomew clung to the rocky wall. The stalactite took out most of the stairway, and the three of them huddled on five suspended treads. A large gaping hole now was above them and a black abyss below. At least their section was partly attached to the wall, though Bartholomew knew it wouldn't last. "Now what?" he asked as he leaned over the edge, gulping at the long, dark drop.

"One false step could mean our deaths," Ramses said.

The ground shook again, knocking all three of them down. The mossy tread soaked through his pants. Bartholomew crouched and crawled to Alex. "That gap is huge."

"We can't jump. We'd never make it," Alex said.

Ramses shook his head, his rectangular beard still straight after all he'd been through.

Another stair below them gave way. Only four remained. They huddled close together. If only they had a rope. Bartholomew sighed and bit his lip in frustration. No cable. Or was there?

"Thoth! The papyrus!" Bartholomew cried.

Thoth dipped his head through the hole and nodded. He reached around behind him and pulled out the papyrus. Osiris appeared next to him. They each grasped a corner and tossed it down.

"Net do grab, and pull we will, before stairs are all nil," Thoth called.

"Ramses, you go first," Alex said.

Bartholomew gave a half smile. Always thinking of others.

The pharaoh nodded and wrapped the papyrus around his waist.

"Ready?" Osiris called.

"Proceed!" Ramses cried with a quick tilt of his crowned head.

"Hold on tightly," Osiris said as he and Thoth backed up and pulled Ramses higher and higher. He looked a lot like he had when Sludge suspended him over Mudlark Maker's mouth.

"Soon I will be more acrobat than pharaoh!" the king quipped as he swung to and fro above the gaping hole in the stair.

Alex chuckled, obviously relieved that this time the rope around Ramses was pulling him to freedom instead of Sludge dangling him over a monster's mouth. Bartholomew would have laughed, too, if he weren't so worried. He held his breath. Was the knot tight enough? *Hold on, Ramses. Just a few inches more.*

When Ramses reached the top and extended one hand, Thoth pulled him into Osiris's waiting arms, and Bartholomew let out the breath he'd been holding.

"Creator Alex, you are next," Osiris said.

"You okay, buddy?" Alex asked a look of concern on his face.

"I'm fine. Just go. Hurry."

Alex gave him a quick punch in the shoulder before bracing himself against the wall and tying the papyrus around his waist.

"Ready!" Alex shouted through cupped hands. When his feet left the tread, he wiggled them. "No problem." He gave Bartholomew a wink.

Another step gave way. Three left. Still on his knees, Bartholomew inched upward. His nose pressed into the stone, and the smell of damp earth filled his nostrils. His sweaty hands were as slick as the slippery moss beneath him. They were shaking. Odd, he hadn't noticed it before.

Leaning to the side, he rubbed them on the front of his slacks. Long, dirty streaks joined the already stained khakis. What would Mother say when she saw them? He could hear her now. *What germs have you gotten into, Bartholomew?* He was going to be in so much trouble. If he ever got out of here.

Something soft hit him on the head.

"Come on, B-Three!"

Bartholomew blinked, but he didn't waste time with another embarrassed apology. Quickly, he grabbed the papyrus and twisted it around his body. He tied it once. Not tight enough. Again. Too crooked. After a third try, he gave a tentative thumbs up.

Hanging there, he tried not to look but couldn't help it. That treacherous drop went down a mile at least! His eyes widened until they were as large as the cavern below.

"Hurry," he gulped. "Come on! Pull!" He squeezed his eyes shut.

"We got ya," Alex assured him.

Bartholomew rose higher as another stalactite came loose and shot past him, crashing into the stair he'd just been standing on. His ascent stopped, and he looked up to see Alex and Thoth chatting away.

Did they want to torture him?

"Faster, please," Bartholomew requested.

Then he was being yanked belly-first into the tomb, and there were warm arms around him. Thoth and Osiris pulled him to his feet and loosened the papyrus from around his waist.

"No problem," Bartholomew said, giving Alex a wry grin.

Alex didn't tease him. He didn't tell him what a goof he'd been. Instead, he exchanged a solemn glance with him and nodded.

In silence, Bartholomew turned back to the opening in the floor and stared into the dark void of Subterranea.

The ground shuddered one final time as the doorway slid closed.

Chapter 52

Bartholomew was amazed. King Tut's tomb had completely transformed. Now, it looked as it did before the battle. All the wounded and fallen from when Sludge invaded were gone, the shrine was back in place, and not a single weapon littered the floor.

Everything was bright. Oil lamps and torches flickered everywhere. The smell of lotus water and woody incense wafted throughout the tomb. Tinkling music echoed off the walls. Even the furniture twirled with glee.

"I know. Blows you away, doesn't it?" Alex commented.

Bartholomew nodded.

"You are a most welcome sight, young ones." Osiris crossed his crook and flail over his chest and bowed his green head.

"You're telling me," Bartholomew replied, pointing a thumb at the place where the hole had been.

"What went on down there, B-Three?" Alex put his hands on his hips. "Thought you'd put on a show for us?"

"A show? You almost dropped me! Chatting away while I was dangling close death."

"I thought you might be getting bored. Figured you needed a little excitement."

"Excitement? I...uh...what?" Bartholomew stammered to Alex's teasing chuckles and playful jabs in the ribs.

As Osiris led them out of the tomb, Bartholomew tried to think of a witty retort, but he couldn't come up with anything. Instead he gave Alex a gentle shove and fell in line behind Thoth and Ramses until they reached the end of the passageway where the rest of their friends stood waiting.

Rushing forward like fruit tumbling from a basket, the gods and pharaohs welcomed them back, enveloping all three of them in a warm homecoming. Bastet mewed her hello, while an exuberant Anubis wagged his jackal-tail. Khufu and Akhenaton even stopped their bickering long enough to shake Alex and Bartholomew's hands.

Ramses smoothed his beard and adjusted his crown before giving Hatshepsut a long hug. When he didn't let her go after thirty seconds, a few eyebrows rose, and surprised glances were exchanged. Finally, Alex cleared his throat loudly, and Ramses pulled away while Hatshepsut blushed and straightened her linen tunic. Bartholomew covered his mouth and giggled.

"Come. A celebration awaits," Osiris said pointing at the exit with his staff.

When their party stepped into the light, Bartholomew couldn't believe his eyes. The cobblestone streets were filled with painted and sculpted faces clamoring to get a glimpse of the Deliverers.

As soon as they reached the walkway, one kilted soldier in the front raised his bow in the air, threw his head back, and gave a yipping cheer. Creation after creation joined in until the entire Valley of the Kings resonated with whoops of joy. Realizing all those rejoicing Artanians were cheering for them, Bartholomew felt a warm blush rise in his cheeks.

"Hail to the Deliverers!" Two tall Nubian warriors approached the entryway and bowed.

Suddenly Bartholomew found himself on their ebony shoulders, carried over the crowd to the head of the parade. Although they were marching, it felt more like floating on a papyrus skiff down the Nile. To his right Alex sat atop a crocodile-headed creature.

"You did it!" Bartholomew cried.

"No," Alex said from his perch. "We did it." He raised a triumphant fist.

Bartholomew got a lump in his throat. His celestial brother. His comrade. Bartholomew finally proved himself worthy.

He glanced back. Each pharaoh was stepping into a wooden palanquin. Watching these kings take their places on golden thrones was something out of a dream. Next, loincloth-clad Egyptians grabbed the carriage poles at either end and hoisted them onto their shoulders. As they paraded through the cobblestone streets, goddesses flew above and dropped feathers to float down like snowflakes.

Friends smiled and waved as they drifted through the valley. Osiris stood atop Taweret, the hippopotamus goddess's head, his crook and flail held high. Anubis, now in jackal form, wiggled his ears from his place on the shoulders of Egyptians. Isis, Horus, and Thoth flew over the procession, diving playfully at Alex's and Bartholomew's heads. Bartholomew ducked. Alex pointed at his red face and threw his head back in laughter.

The crowd morphed like dancing flames. One moment, a painted papyrus woman winked at Bartholomew behind kohl-lined eyes. The next, she became a sunken relief carved into limestone and blew him a kiss. Wooden coffins etched with miniature oxen shimmered until they were gilded panels of gold. One hieroglyphic stallion reared its head and whinnied before it turned to marble. All around, gilded creatures brayed in joy.

They circled the city streets three times before stopping at the entrance to King Tut's tomb. There, Osiris joined Isis and Anubis at the top of a low wall. Bartholomew and Alex followed and bowed repeatedly for the crowd.

Anubis beat his tail against the wall so hard the vibrations almost made them lose their balance. Osiris chuckled before bending down to tell the jackal-god to be more careful. Anubis's ears drooped. He stared at his paws and scratched at the wall. Then Isis patted his head lovingly and whispered something in his ear.

Anubis got a wide grin on his face and wagged his tail. His body shimmered, and the fur shrank back into his skin as he morphed into man form. Soon he was shaking his hips just like before but without a thumping tail to nearly knock people over.

Bartholomew nodded appreciatively. Nice moves. Anubis could have been on U-tube.

"Citizens of the Land of Antiquities." Osiris held up his hand for silence. "Rejoice! The pharaohs are freed."

"All hail the pharaohs!" the crowd cheered.

"Yes. And for this we have our young Deliverers to thank."

"All hail the Deliverers!"

Osiris waited for the crowd to quiet before continuing. "Bartholomew Borax III, step forth." Bartholomew stumbled up from his place behind Anubis and faced the green-skinned god. "For creating animals of battle and beasts of burden, we are most grateful."

"Grateful," the crowd chanted.

"For your bravery in the face of fear and speaking truth when your celestial twin most needed it, Artania thanks you." He paused as his wife stepped forward. "Isis?"

"Take this Scarab Beetle Amulet as a token of our appreciation," The goddess said, holding out her hand. "It was placed over the hearts of mummies to silence their negative confessions. May it aid you forever to only speak your goodness." She pinned a blue insect broach on Bartholomew's now tattered and stained dress shirt.

Bartholomew fingered the pin and gave Isis a hug.

Osiris squeezed Bartholomew's shoulder then turned back to the audience. "Alexander Devinci, approach," he said in a loud voice. Head held high, Alex strode forward and took his place next to Bartholomew. "For those rolling chariots that most of the gods mastered, we honor you."

Osiris smirked at a blushing Thoth. Bartholomew didn't dare exchange a glance with Alex. Out of the corner of his eye, he could already see him trying to suppress a grin. That image of Thoth rolling around the cavern, ibis head bobbing and arms flailing wildly, would always make them smile. Alex cleared his throat and rubbed his mouth.

"For your miniature soldiers and constant strength, the Land of Antiquities is most grateful."

"Grateful," the crowd repeated as Horus approached.

"I present you with our most sacred symbol, the ankh," the hawk-headed boy said. "Since you saved those most dear to us, it is only fitting that we bestow this symbol of life upon you." He slipped the necklace over Alex's head. "Brother, you were true to yourself. Wear this next to your heart always as a reminder." Horus placed his hand over the ankh on Alex's chest.

Alex nodded. Bartholomew knew he would remember. True art would fly from his fingers as easily as Horus's wings through the air.

"Bring forth the celebration!" Osiris clapped his hands three times.

Several loin-clothed men and women in linen gowns brought out more food than Bartholomew had ever seen. Pairs of muscled workers carried fattened calves suspended between poles. Women, their hair oiled and eyes outlined in black kohl, balanced huge platters of figs, leeks, grapes, and olives on their heads. Breads and cakes sweetened with honey were set before the company. Goblets of water, wine, and milk were placed next to them.

Isis pointed to several large cushions appearing out of nowhere. When she sat down cross-legged, Alex and Bartholomew followed suit.

Tentatively Bartholomew placed one of the figs in his mouth and chewed. "Good! Grainy but sweet," he said with a brown speckled grin.

"Hey, Mr. Clean, mind your manners. You're not supposed to talk with your mouth full," Alex teased, both cheeks full of black olives.

Bartholomew started to stutter out an apology but then remembered the scarab beetle on his chest. He stroked it briefly and winked at Alex. They both laughed. He tossed a handful of bread at his friend, who flicked some water back.

Musicians came out with flutes, harps, and oboes. They played a familiar melody. Bartholomew didn't know if it was from a dream or the dream of a dream, but each note painted gold and white sunlight in his mind.

Next came the dancers with their wide circular collars and hair done up in multiple braids. They did backbends, cartwheels, and handstands as their golden bracelets tinkled in the air. Forming a line, they pulled out hidden tambourines from the folds of their dresses and shook them wildly. With a leaping spin, the women took a bow.

"Cool." Bartholomew applauded and nudged Alex.

For hours, they ate, laughed, and rejoiced. Bartholomew pinched himself, but it really was true. He had friends. He fingered the scarab beetle on his chest and heard a voice inside his ears speak like a recording. "Oh, my heart, do not be opposed to me. Go forth to the happy place. My heart is mine."

He gave a start and glanced around.

"It is from the Book of the Dead." Isis smiled at him. "It is our gift to you. A reminder of the joy you can have when you silence your negative thoughts."

Bartholomew nodded. He stroked the scarab again. He understood his gift and vowed to use it well always.

Chapter 53

Alex was in the middle of telling Anubis a joke when it happened. A hush fell over the crowd. All conversations ceased. The music stopped. Even Anubis's regrown tail came to standstill.

Alex looked up. Off in the distance, the throngs parted like a silent comb through hair, making way for the man. His bronze form was stooped as if the weight of the world rested on his shoulders. He reminded Alex of how tortured Dad had looked in the hospital awaiting news of Mom. The bent man hobbled up the cobblestone path, while the rhythmic scratching of his bronze feet dragging along the road ticked hourglass seconds. Artanian after Artanian bowed reverently as he slowly made his way toward them.

"Who is he?" Bartholomew whispered.

"Beats me," Alex replied with a shrug, unable to take his eyes off the steely figure.

When the bronze man drew closer, Alex noticed the metal face was etched with lines of worry. The statue gave each boy a long gaze that Alex was surprised to find comforting.

"Dear friends," the man said, turning to the silent crowd. "Many years have passed since I asked you to wait. The boys have grown, and now it is their eleventh year. All which was foretold has come to pass."

"The Soothsayer Stone," the crowd chanted in unison.

Butterflies fluttered in Alex's chest, and a proud shiver traveled down his spine.

The bronze continued in a gravelly voice. "But do not forget the prophecy:

Our world was born from the magic of two.
The smiling twins whose creations grew.
They painted walls with ideas anew.
Until the dark day we came to rue.
When one jealous hand used mud to undo.
And the life of many too soon was through.

"It was the birth of the evil Shadow Swine!" Osiris called out in an angry voice.

The crowd hissed and the bronze man continued.

But listen to this prophecy with open ears.
To know what happens every 1,000 years.
The Shadow Swine will make you live in fear.
Bringing death to those whom you hold dear.

"Our hearts will always cherish those lost in battle!" Isis cried.

Alex remembered his tiny soldiers being crushed in Subterranea. The fallen Egyptians. A lost pharaoh. He nodded and listened to the sculpted man.

For they will open the doorway wide.
That none of you will find a place to hide.
And the Creators will stop
As their dreams are drained
Before twelve moons wax and wane.

The bronze placed his steely hands on the shoulders of Alex and Bartholomew. They were warm and comforting.

But hope will lie in the hands of twins
Born near the cusp of the second millennium.
On the eleventh year of their lives.
They will join together like single forged knives.
Their battle will be long with seven evils to undo.
Scattered around will be seven clues.
And many will perish before they are through.
But our world will be saved if their art is true.

"...if their art is true," Alex repeated softly, remembering the painting of Mom.

"The first task has been completed. Your art was true, celestial twins," the man said. "Now it is time to return."

"Excuse me, sir," Bartholomew began. "But who you are?"

"He is the Thinker," Osiris said. "The tortured one who guides us in this troubled time."

"Pleased to meet you, sir," Bartholomew said extending his hand. The Thinker took Bartholomew's hand in his. He turned it over and looked at the palm.

"A unique lifeline. It seems to have no end." Then the Thinker did the same with Alex's hand. "Yours is the same, Twin of the Heavens."

The boys looked down at their palms. Alex had never noticed how alike his and Bartholomew's hands were.

A wind picked up, blowing their hair against their cheeks. The sky brightened. Alex heard the whinnying of horses from above and glanced up.

"Hello, Alexander! Greetings, Bartholomew!"

"Apollo!" the boys cried.

The god pulled on the reins, turning the stallions toward them. When the chariot landed on the road in front of them, he bowed to the Thinker.

"It is time. Your home awaits," the Thinker said.

Alex hung back. All along, the only thing he'd wanted to do was go home, but now that he could, he didn't want to leave. He looked around at his companions and felt a lump rise in his throat. Thoth with his long beak bobbing up and down. Anubis with twitching ears and devilish grin. Bastet mewing sadly. Osiris and Horus standing arm in arm, gazing warmly at him. When he met the kohl-lined eyes of Isis, he had to swallow. She had been like a second mother to him, a healthy strong mother. A mother who reminded him of his true powers. He ran a finger over the ankh tracing its looping "T."

"We are part of the eternal life force when art is true. Remember that, young one," Isis said, opening her brown arms to Alex.

He squeezed Isis tightly. When they pulled away Alex saw that there were two ankh shaped creases on her linen gown. One for him and one for her.

"Because of you two, the pyramids still stand. We are forever grateful," Osiris said, leading them to Apollo's chariot. Bartholomew shook Osiris's hand, grasped the railing, and bit his lower lip. Alex knew his friend was trying to hold back tears.

"You may have completed the first task, but six more remain." The Thinker leaned in and gazed meaningfully into their faces. "Only you can carry them out. We will be calling upon you to use your talents. Be prepared."

Alex nodded solemnly as he took his place next to Apollo.

"Go home and be what you were born to be. Creators!" the Thinker cried.

Apollo cracked his whip, and the stallions leaped forward. Their hooves clattered over the cobblestones before they rose into the air. Alex waved slowly as the Egyptians shrank away.

In the painted sky of Artania, Isis took flight behind them. She shot multiple rays from her sun disk. Each exploded in ankh and scarab beetle shapes. Alex felt like he was in the center of a gigantic fireworks show. Green, blue, red, and orange flashes filled the sky.

"Farewell, young sons of my heart!" Isis called after them in the fading halo of a lavender ankh. She lifted her horned crown. The sun's reflection rippled on the disk, and the sky turned white.

Now the light was all he could see, a pearly canvas wrapping them in brilliance. Alex heard Apollo's laughter and looked back to see he had disappeared. In his place, were spreading bands of color.

They were finally riding that gentle rainbow home.

THE END

Acknowledgements

This book would not have been possible without the support of a number of friends and family. First I'd like to thank my critique group of Bart Gardner, Debra Davis Hinkle, Karen Juran, Carter Pitman, Destry Ramey, Christine Taylor, and Susan Tuttle. For close to a decade, you have helped to mold me into a better writer. A very special thanks goes out to Cathe Olsen, who spent much of her Christmas vacation combing through page after page of my manuscript. Her keen eye for weak spots, flaws in characterization, and flagging plot lines helped make the book what it is today. Cathe, you rock as a friend, editor, and author.

I am so grateful to Dean Bernal for his unflagging support and belief in the project. He encouraged me to see beyond and dream of what Artania could be.

I'd like to acknowledge my students both present and past. You touch my heart and remind me of why I write. Each of you inspires me daily to see the true artist in all of us. Also to my fellow educators and school personnel: your hard work and dedication makes me proud to call myself a teacher. Your extraordinary gifts often go unsung, but know that children are finding the magic inside themselves because of what you do.

Most of all to my son and daughter: Nicholas and Jessica. For years, you patiently waited while I scribbled away at my notepad or bent over the computer keys. You might have had to tap me on the shoulder once or twice to bring me back from Artania, but you always understood when I got a distant look in my eye, I wasn't forgetting you. I was just dreaming of fantastical worlds. But these worlds could never have taken shape without the love we share. It is why this book is dedicated to you.

About the Author

Laurie Woodward is a school teacher and the author of the fantasy books: *The Artania Chronicles.* Her *Artania: The Pharaohs' Cry* is the first children's book in the series. Laurie is also a collaborator on the award-winning Dean and JoJo anti-bullying DVD *Resolutions.* The European published version of Dean and JoJo for which she was the ghost writer was translated by Jochen Lehner who has also translated books for the Dalai Lama and Deepak Chopra, In addition to writing, Ms. Woodward is an award winning peace consultant who helps other educators teach children how to stop bullying, avoid arguments, and maintain healthy friendships. Laurie writes her novels in the coastal towns of California.

Why do I write? I get to be a kid again. And this time the bully loses while the quiet kid wins. Also, I get to have awesome battles with wings and swords, while riding a skateboard.

Why did I write Artania? Several years ago when education changed to stress test score results over everything else, I began to think of art as a living part of children that was being crushed. But I have watched children create and discover the wonder inside. To me, Shadow Swine represent bullies who subdue that most beautiful part of children.

"Our world will be saved when their art is true," the Artanian Prophecy says. Every year I tell my students how every sketch, painting, or sculpture instantaneously becomes a living being in Artania.

Then I stand back as they hurriedly scribble a creature, hold it up, and ask, "Was this just born?"

"It sure was," I reply with a smile. "You just made magic."

And for that cool moment, they believe.

Made in the USA
San Bernardino, CA
30 October 2018